"Close the door."

His voice sounded closer. "No talking and follow my instructions to a tee."

"Look." Eden took a step closer to the door. "I'm sorry, but I don't think I can do this."

"Obviously. You seem to have a problem keeping your mouth shut."

Suddenly, she wasn't scared as much as annoyed. "And you seem to have control issues."

"I believe I'm paying two thousand dollars for that control." The words were spoken so close to her ear that she released a strangled gasp. "I don't know what kind of deal you made," he said, "but the deal I made was for a woman who will do exactly what I say."

Before Eden could make it very clear that she wasn't about to do exactly what he said, he moved away. The Dark Seducer stood by the window, his tall, lean body outlined by the small amount of light that filtered in through the curtains.

"Now take off your dress," he said. "Take it all the way off."

PRAISE FOR THE DEEP IN THE HEART OF TEXAS SERIES

THE LAST COWBOY IN TEXAS

"Sweet, funny." —*Publishers Weekly*

"4 stars! The larger-than-life world of Katie Lane's Deep in the Heart of Texas series offers colorful, rowdy characters and passionate love stories that are easy to enjoy and hard to forget." —*RT Book Reviews*

A MATCH MADE IN TEXAS

"4½ stars! Lane's outlandish sense of humor and unerring knack for creating delightful characters and vibrant settings are on full display...She does a marvelous job blending searing heat and surprising heart."
—*RT Book Reviews*

"Fun-filled and heartwarming...a wildly sexy romance with a beautiful love story [that] old and new fans definitely do not want to miss."
—**BookReviewsandMorebyKathy.com**

FLIRTING WITH TEXAS

"4½ stars! [A] complete success, blending humor, innovative characters, and a wonderfully quirky town with an unlikely and touching love story."
—*RT Book Reviews*

"Every turn of the page is an unexpected journey full of humor as well as emotion."
—**FreshFiction.com**

ACCLAIM FOR THE HUNK FOR THE HOLIDAYS SERIES

UNWRAPPED

"Delightful...Readers will love the appealing McPhersons, and savor Jac and Patrick's sizzling chemistry."
—***Publishers Weekly***

"[A] sweet and spicy holiday romp...Fans will love returning to the middle of the crazy and lovable McPherson clan in this tale of fate and fateful decisions."
—***RT Book Reviews***

RING IN THE HOLIDAYS

"A return visit to the headstrong McPherson family for another year of holiday high jinks...Lane's trademark brand of humor will keep the pages turning."
—***RT Book Reviews***

"*Ring in the Holidays* is all at once extremely sexy, intense, and a compelling story.
—**FreshFiction.com**

HUNK FOR THE HOLIDAYS

"4½ stars! Sharp, witty dialogue, a solid sense of humor, and a dab hand at sizzling sex is going to push Lane far, if this is an example."   —***RT Book Reviews***

"I was interested from the first page to the last...There was enough chemistry between Cassie and James to set the place on fire."
—**Romancing-the-Book.com**

A BILLIONAIRE

after dark

A BILLIONAIRE
after dark

KATIE LANE

FOREVER

NEW YORK   BOSTON

Copyright © 2016 by Cathleen Smith
Excerpt from *Waking Up With a Billionaire* © 2016 by Cathleen Smith

Cover design by Elizabeth Turner
Cover photography by George Kerrigan
Cover copyright © 2016 by Hachette Book Group, Inc.

Forever
Hachette Book Group
1290 Avenue of the Americas
New York, NY 10104
forever-romance.com
twitter.com/foreverromance

First Edition: March 2016

Forever is an imprint of Grand Central Publishing.
The Forever name and logo are trademarks of Hachette Book Group, Inc.

The publisher is not responsible for websites (or their content) that are not owned by the publisher.

The Hachette Speakers Bureau provides a wide range of authors for speaking events. To find out more, go to www.hachettespeakersbureau.com or call (866) 376-6591.

ISBN 978-1-4555-3317-6 (mass market); 978-1-4555-3315-2 (ebook)

Printed in the United States of America

OPM

10 9 8 7 6 5 4 3 2 1

To Jeffe Kennedy, for understanding the passion, the craziness, and the sheer joy of being a writer <twirls>

CHAPTER ONE

If you want to make it in this business, you must immerse yourself in the story."

That was the advice Eden Huckabee's editor had given her. But what Eden was getting ready to do was more than immersing herself. It was like jumping into the San Francisco Bay in a pair of cement shoes. How did she know that the man who waited behind the double doors of the penthouse suite wasn't another Zodiac Killer? Or the real Zodiac Killer since he'd never been apprehended? All Eden had was the word of a prostitute who said that he wasn't.

"He's a really respectful guy," Madison had said, "who must be afraid of women. That's the only reason I can think of for the 'no touching' rule."

No touching. That's what clinched the deal for Eden. She could immerse herself in the story as long as there was no touching.

Taking a deep breath, she tapped on one of the doors. Per instructions, she'd stopped by the concierge's desk for a room key, but she felt it would be rude to just walk in without knocking. The door handle turned, and for a moment, Eden tensed for flight. Her body relaxed when a young man who looked like Harry Styles from the boy band One Direction peeked out. He had long hair and pretty eyes, and still carried baby fat in his cheeks.

This was the man who Madison called the Dark Seducer? No wonder he kept the lights off; he probably didn't want the escorts carding him. Eden bit the inside of her cheek to keep from laughing. It appeared that all she needed to worry about now was being asked to perform a cheer in a pleated parochial school skirt. Pleated skirts made her butt look the size of a front-loader washer, and she had never been what you would call coordinated.

While she was trying not to laugh, the young man was giving her a thorough once-over. His gaze wandered over her damp hair, rain-drenched coat, and wet high heels. It was raining cats and dogs, and since she had forgotten to bring cash to tip the valet, she'd been forced to park a good block and a half away. San Francisco had a lot of things, but parking wasn't one of them.

"So are you a hooker?" The young man finally spoke. "Because you don't look hot enough to be a hooker."

All the cuteness drained right out of him, and Eden had the strong urge to pinch his baby-fat cheeks until his eyes watered. "I believe that hot is in the eye of the beholder. And we're called escorts, not hookers."

"What's the difference?"

Eden had wondered the same thing, but after meeting Madison, she'd learned that there was a big difference between being a hooker and being an escort. Hookers had pimps. Escorts had services. Hookers worked nightly. Escorts worked rarely. Hookers barely made enough to keep them in drugs. Escorts made a boatload of cash—not to mention the jewelry, vacations, and homes they received as bonuses. Hookers weren't picky about their clients. Escorts were very picky.

Which didn't explain why Madison had chosen this smart-mouthed yahoo.

"Are you going to let me in?" she asked. "Or am I not hot enough?"

He shrugged and opened the door.

The suite was over-the-top lavish. The marble floors of the entryway gleamed in the light of the overhead chandelier. There was an opulent contemporary dining room table on the right. And in the living area, white couches and chairs surrounded a fire pit coffee table with blue quartz in the center that flickered with gas flames.

Being wet and cold, Eden wanted to move closer to the fire. Instead she stood there, dripping on the marble floor and staring in awe at the spectacular view of downtown and the Bay Bridge. Obviously the kid made money. No doubt one of the growing numbers of Internet baby billionaires who struggled to spend their wads of cash. It wouldn't be a bad angle for a story. But one story at a time. This story was about Madison. It was Madison's perspective Eden needed to channel. What ran through her head when she walked into a hotel room? What did she see? Feel? And ultimately, how did she deal with selling her body for—

Eden's mind came to a screeching halt when hands settled on her shoulders. She jumped and then turned to point a finger like a mother with a naughty toddler. "No touching, young man."

Looking duly chastised, he held up his hands. "Okay. Okay. I was just going to take your coat."

"Oh. Sorry." She slipped off the coat and handed it to him. Beneath she wore a black sequined cocktail dress that she'd worn to the office Christmas party. She thought it was sexy, but Baby Cheeks seemed thoroughly disappointed. His eyes lost their gleam of anticipation, and his shoulders slumped in the ill-fitting burgundy jacket. A burgundy jacket with a gold nametag pinned above the breast pocket.

Jeremy Ross.

Eden's eyes widened. "You work at the hotel?"

"Yeah," he said. "I wanted to work at Starbucks, but they won't let you show a tattoo on your neck. Not that I have one, but I want to get one. I'm thinking that one of those Chinese dragons on my chest with its tail wrapping around my throat would be so wicked—"

A cell phone rang, and he pushed aside his jacket and took the phone off his belt clip. When he spoke, he used a lot more respect than he had with Eden. "Yes, sir. Okay, I'm leaving now." He hung up. "I gotta go. The concierge said that if you need anything, just call." He was almost to the door when she stopped him.

"Wait! Where is my . . . date?"

He shrugged. "I don't have a clue. I just dropped by the complimentary fruit basket that goes with the suite." He nodded at the basket of fruit on the bar. "Maybe the guy stiffed you." He gave her the once-over. "If so, what could I get for twenty-one dollars?"

Eden arched an eyebrow. "How about a swift kick in the seat of your pants?"

He rolled his eyes. "I don't see how you make a living

as a hooker. You've got way too much attitude." He turned and walked out the door.

When he was gone, Eden stood there for a few minutes not knowing what to do. Part of her was relieved that she wouldn't have a hand in sexually corrupting a minor, and the other part had gone back to being scared. So much so that she thought about helping herself to a couple of minis from the bar. But Eden wasn't a drinker. Or a smoker. Or a midnight toker. Something that really annoyed her grandparents. Pops and Mimi believed that a glass of wine or the occasional hit of marijuana kept you from being an uptight asshole.

Which probably explained Eden's personality.

Trying to stay focused on the goal, she glanced around the suite and started her story: *The blue flames of the fire reflected in the floor-to-ceiling windows that offered a spectacular, rain-drenched view of the city. A view that had been bought for a price. But Madison had learned early on that anything could be bought for a price... including your soul.*

Or was that too dramatic? Eden's boss and the editor of the small newspaper she worked for always got on her for being too dramatic.

"You should write romance novels," Stella would say. "Because with that kind of mushy prose, you'll never make it as a serious writer."

But Eden would make it. She might write a little dramatically, but she had something that other people didn't have. Her father called it true grit. Her mother called it enlightened aura. And her brothers called it pain-in-the-ass stubbornness. Eden called it goal setting. And she had never left a goal unaccomplished.

Never.

And right now her goal was to become the next Woodward or Bernstein. She wanted to do investigative reporting like her father had done before he started teaching college journalism. So far, Eden had been given only human-interest stories. Charity walks, doggy costume contests, and a night at the opera. But now she had a story that she could sink her teeth into. A story about the underbelly of prostitution. It was the first real news story Stella had given her, and Eden was determined to knock her editor's socks off with it. Even if it meant she had to go above and beyond. And this was certainly going above and beyond.

Taking her phone from her purse, she made a few notes describing the furniture, fireplace, and view. But the living room wasn't what she needed to describe as much as the bedroom. She glanced at the double doors to her left, and after only a moment's hesitation, she walked over and opened one.

Light from the living area sliced through the dark, across plush, white carpet and the puffy satin duvet on the bed. Was this the room where she would be expected to strip? Not that she was actually going to strip down to her skin. She wasn't about to go that far for a story. All she needed was a taste of what it felt like to be in Madison's shoes. Just a glimpse of the debauchery of the escort world. Once she had that glimpse, she intended to contract a bad stomach virus and get the heck out of there.

But for now, she might as well get a feel for her part. Channeling Mimi's favorite actress, Mae West, Eden placed a hand on her hip and strutted seductively into the dark room. "So what do you want, big boy?" She ran a finger along the cool, slick fabric of the duvet. "You want a slow burn or a fast trip around the world?"

There was a rustle before a smooth Southern voice spoke. "Personally, I've always liked things slow and hot. But I am a little curious as to what going around the world consists of."

Eden dropped her phone, and it thumped to the carpet, but not half as loudly as her heart thumping against her rib cage. "I-I'm sorry," she stammered as she turned toward the voice. "I didn't realize someone was in here."

"Then who were you talking to?"

She tried to collect herself, but it wasn't easy when her knees felt like overcooked spaghetti. "I was just…" Unable to think up a lie, she told the truth. "Practicing."

There was a long pause before he spoke. "Close the door."

She tried to clear the fear that clogged her throat. "There's no touching, right?"

"I thought I explained the rules to your service." His voice sounded closer. "No talking and follow my instructions to a tee." The door slammed closed, causing Eden to almost jump out of her heels.

Being in the dark with a complete stranger had her reevaluating her goals. And becoming a good investigative reporter took a backseat to self-preservation.

"Look." She took a step closer to the door. "I'm sorry, but I don't think I can do this."

"Obviously. You seem to have a problem keeping your mouth shut."

Suddenly, she wasn't scared as much as annoyed. "And you seem to have control issues."

"I believe I'm paying two thousand dollars for that control."

"Two thousand?" Eden couldn't hide her shock. She knew that Madison made a lot of money as an escort, but she hadn't thought it was that much. "Are you kidding me?" Realizing that she didn't sound very professional, she backpedaled. "I mean, Madison told me that I'd make much less."

"She lied." The words were spoken so close to her ear that she released a strangled gasp. She backed away and bumped into the bed, sitting down with a hard bounce. The mattress dipped as his hands pressed on either side of her hips. "There will be touching."

"B-but that wasn't part of the deal."

"I don't know what kind of deal you made," he said, "but the deal I made was for a woman who will do exactly what I say."

"Exactly?" she squeaked.

He leaned closer, his breath falling against her lips like steam on a bathroom mirror. "Exactly."

Before Eden could make it very clear that she wasn't about to do exactly what he said, he moved away. Only a few seconds later, a light clicked on. Not a light that lit up the room, but a soft, recessed light that shone only on the bed. The Dark Seducer stood by the window, his tall, lean body outlined by the small amount of light that filtered in through the curtains.

"But you're right," he said. "I won't be doing the touching. And you won't be touching me. Now take off your dress."

With his words, Eden's determination to succeed

returned. All she had to do was slip off her dress and endure just a brief sampling of the humiliation that Madison went through. Of course thinking you could do something and actually doing it were two different things. Her hands shook so badly she had to fist them for a few seconds before she reached for the straps of her dress. She tried to calm her nerves with a little mental justification: *This is no different from going to a nudist beach with your grandparents.* Except she hadn't been to a nudist beach with Pops and Mimi since she was three. *The human body is beautiful and should be shared.* Except her body wasn't beautiful and she had never been good at sharing. *This is only a few minutes of your life.* Except as the dress slipped to her waist, time seemed to stand still.

"Take it all the way off," he said.

She swallowed, then got to her feet, allowing the dress to drop to the floor. Beneath, she wore a bra and panties that had been chosen for coverage more than sex appeal. The black, fully padded bra was more similar to a bulletproof vest than a piece of lingerie, and her multicolored-heart boy shorts could've easily been worn for a pickup game of volleyball. Still she felt exposed and vulnerable standing under the light like a piece of fried chicken beneath a deli warming lamp. She tried to assess all the emotions racing through her so she could write them down later. Humiliation. Fear. Excitement. Excitement? Yes, it was there nibbling at the edges of her humiliation and fear.

"Now the bra and panties," he said, "slowly."

This was Eden's cue to exit—to grab her dress and

phone and get the hell out of there. But the shadowy man who stood so rigidly in the corner had her curiosity getting the best of her. "Why do you do this?" she asked.

"Excuse me?"

"Why do you hire women?"

There was a pause, and she thought he wasn't going to answer. Then his voice came out of the darkness, low, deep, and Southern-soaked. "Why else? Because I'm sexually deviant."

His blatant response should've reinforced her belief that he was a wealthy man who enjoyed victimizing women, but somehow it did the opposite. It made her see him as a human being with flaws. And Eden had always had a weakness for flaws. Probably because she had so many herself.

"Watching a woman pleasure herself while you sit in the dark really isn't all that deviant." She took a step closer. "I'm sure a lot of men would want to do the same thing if they had the money."

His laughter wasn't filled with humor as much as derision. "Somehow I doubt that."

"Okay, so maybe they would want to do more than watch." They also wouldn't worry about being seen. She squinted. Was he ugly? Disfigured? A pitiful Elephant Man shunned by society? Again she felt sympathy for the man. "If you're worried that women won't find you attractive, you shouldn't be. Unlike men, women aren't hung up on physical looks. We prefer a good personality. And with all the dating sites, you should have no trouble whatsoever finding a companion."

"The problem isn't finding a companion."

It took only a moment for the truth to dawn on her. "Oh. I'm sorry. But look on the bright side. They have medicine for that now. One little pill and things are looking up. And you shouldn't be afraid to tell a doctor. Lots of people suffer from it. Even me."

"What?"

Eden's face filled with heat. She had never shared that information with anyone and didn't know why she did so now. But since it was out, she continued in hopes that, if she shared her truths, he'd share more of his.

"I don't know if it's called impotency with women, but it runs along the same lines. I've never experienced an orgasm." Her hands gestured as she talked, something she did when she was nervous or trying to get a point across. "Weird but true. And I don't think it's a physical problem as much as a mental one. I just have other things besides orgasms to concentrate on right now—although I have faked a few. Men seem to get very depressed if you don't make them think they're good in bed."

There was a long stretch of silence and then the light clicked off. Eden barely had time to tense before her dress was slipped over her head and within seconds, she was completely clothed.

"What are you doing?" she asked.

"It's time for you to leave." With a hand on the small of her back, he pushed her toward the door.

"But—" Before Eden could finish, she was standing outside the closed bedroom door, listening to the click of the lock.

Obviously, faked orgasms had been the wrong subject for an escort to bring up.

CHAPTER TWO

$\mathscr{I}$ realize you've always been a daydreamer, Nash, but lately you've become more of a sleepwalker. Now wake the hell up and pay attention!"

Nash Lothario Beaumont looked away from the view of the bay just in time to deflect the lingerie catalog that came sailing at his head. Once the catalog was lying at his feet, he lifted an eyebrow at his older brother, who sat behind the large desk. "You want to head to the gym and go a couple rounds, Deacon?"

Since all three of the Beaumont brothers loved to box, Deacon smiled. "I would like nothing more than to take you out in the first. But right now we've got to figure out why our bras aren't selling."

As much as Nash wanted to stay at the window and continue to ignore business, he walked to the chair across from his brother's desk and sat down. "You do realize that if anyone back home in Louisiana could hear you, they would revoke your redneck country boy card."

Grayson, who was sprawled out on the couch, looked up from his sketchpad. "I think those were revoked the moment we inherited a lingerie company. Do you realize that duck season came and went and neither one of you seemed to notice?"

"I noticed," Deacon said. "But I've been too busy saving a company from bankruptcy to go on a hunting trip."

"Which hasn't stopped you from taking Olivia on numerous vacations."

Deacon scowled. "One was our honeymoon, and the rest were business."

"What business did you have in Cancún?" Nash teased before looking at Grayson. "And I don't know what you're talking about, baby brother. You aren't a hunter. You'd rather draw a bird than shoot it."

"I've gone hunting." When Nash sent him a skeptical look, Grayson backpedaled. "Okay, so maybe I haven't hunted as much as you two, but I've bagged my share. And I've never drawn a duck in my life."

"He's right, Nash. Grayson prefers his subjects to be human, female, and naked." Deacon tossed down the sales report and leaned back in his chair. "Which brings up something else I've been wanting to discuss." He pointed a finger at Grayson. "Leave the supermodels alone."

"Me? What about Nash?" Grayson asked. "I only want to paint them, and I never choose a time that interferes with their work. Nash, on the other hand, wants to do a lot more than paint. The kiss he gave Natalia in front of millions of television viewers is a perfect example."

Nash hadn't kissed Natalia. The aggressive Russian had kissed him. But since it went with the playboy persona he had perpetuated, he didn't enlighten his brothers. "You're just mad because sales for my Lothario Collection went up twenty-five percent after the kiss aired."

"Enough," Deacon said. "Both of you are banned from photo shoots from now on." He looked at Nash. "But I'll expect you at the fashion shows. Customers seem to love your smiling face." He glanced at the sales reports, and his brow furrowed. "If not our new line of bras."

"They're selling, Deacon," Nash said. "They just aren't selling as quickly as you would like them to. You need to relax. Christmas sales weren't good, but I'm sure sales will pick up around Valentine's Day."

"We can't relax. Not if we want French Kiss to continue to be the leader in women's lingerie."

Nash wanted to argue with his brother but knew he couldn't. While Nash was good with people, Deacon was good with business. He was the reason that French Kiss hadn't been sold to the highest bidder. He was also the reason that Nash and Grayson found themselves living in San Francisco.

They had wanted to sell their controlling shares of French Kiss right after they'd inherited them from their uncle. But then Deacon had fallen in love with the company...and their uncle's stepdaughter, who also happened to be French Kiss's CEO. And since after their mother died from cancer, Deacon had become more of a father to Nash and Grayson than their own father, they had made the sacrifice of moving to the West Coast. Not that living in San Francisco as a wealthy billionaire was that much of a sacrifice. After a year of getting used to living with money and fame, Nash was starting to enjoy his new lifestyle. He slipped his hand in his pant pocket. And maybe he'd been enjoying it a little too much.

The phone was still there, cool and slick against his palm. It was an older version in a case that matched the dress she had worn. Black. No frills. But attractive. And he had been attracted to her. The moment she sashayed into the room and made her outrageous offer, his senses came alive. It didn't have to do with her looks. She was pretty, but not breathtaking. It had more to do with the way she carried herself—as if she had the world by its tail. She had been afraid of him for only a split second before she regained her confidence.

He almost smiled at the thought of her trying to make him feel better about being impotent. It was sweet. And hot. But not as hot as her confession about being an orgasm virgin. If she hadn't blushed, he might've thought it was a ploy to turn him on. And maybe it was. If so, it had worked. There was a moment when he almost lost control. When he almost stripped off her ugly bra and boy shorts and showed her what she'd been missing. But if he had, it would've ruined the entire point of the exercise.

He couldn't lose control.

Never again.

"What do you think, Nash?"

He blinked from his thoughts to see Deacon waiting for an answer. He could only hope that they were still talking about bra sales.

"What about if we do an online survey?" he said. "Not just for the customers who have bought the new bras, but for all women. We could ask what they look for when shopping for a bra—pretty material, comfort, support, whatever."

"What would be their incentive for taking it?"

Nash shrugged. "For every person who answers the questions, we offer a twenty-percent-off coupon to French Kiss."

Deacon grinned. "I knew there was a reason you were in charge of customer satisfaction. Although I don't know if a twenty-percent-off coupon will hook them. What if we entered them into a contest to win something bigger?"

Grayson set down his sketchpad. "What about a trip to San Francisco and tickets to the fashion show in the fall? Or we could do tickets to the Lover's Ball."

"The Lover's Ball is too close," Nash said. "Valentine's Day is only weeks away."

Deacon groaned. "Don't remind me. Olivia's mother has made our lives hell the last few months with all the details for the ball. I wish Olivia had never put her in charge." He glanced at Nash. "Or that you hadn't come up with the lame idea in the first place."

"Don't blame me. You were the one who wanted me to come up with a charity event sponsored by French Kiss. Since our great-grandpa started the tradition of naming Beaumont boys after famous lovers, it just made sense. And according to ticket sales, it's already a success."

"Let's hope we can get our bras to sell as well," Deacon said dryly. "So let's go with the prize of a trip to San Francisco and tickets to the fashion show—including dinner with Nash Lothario." Before Nash could object, he leaned up and pushed a button on the phone. "Kelly, could you come in here? I need you to take some notes. And see if you can pull Olivia away from the design studio for a few minutes."

No more than fifteen minutes later, the door opened, and Deacon's assistant, Kelly Wang, walked in with a tray of coffee. She wore the standard gray and purple that all French Kiss employees wore, but Kelly always added a dash of her own personality. Today that dash was a pink headband printed with little cartoon cats.

"Mrs. Beaumont is on her way, boss. But she wasn't exactly happy about being taken away from her sewing machine." She handed Deacon a cup of coffee. "Black and strong, just like you like it. Something I hope you remember when you're passing out raises. My wedding plans have gotten completely out of hand."

"You should've stayed with your first idea for a wedding," Deacon said. "A wedding during the seventh-inning stretch of a Giants baseball game wouldn't have cost you more than the tickets and a catcher's mitt."

"If I didn't come from a traditional Chinese family, it might've worked. But my grandmother won't ever talk to me again if I don't wear her Chinese wedding dress. And I can't see myself standing at home plate in a *qipao*." She handed Grayson a cup, then brought Nash his. "Do not throw that away. Lothario Beaumont cups are going for twenty-five dollars on eBay."

Nash sent her a skeptical look. "You've got to be kidding."

She shook her head. "I got a hundred for one of Romeo's."

"Ha!" Grayson punched the air. "I knew I was seventy-five percent better than you, big brother."

"Only because you had doodled a naked model on it," Kelly said. "The art dealer I sold it to was ecstatic to get it for a hundred. Especially when your nude paintings are going for thousands."

"Wait a minute," Deacon said. "You're selling our used coffee cups on eBay?"

Kelly shrugged. "Did I not just tell you that my wedding has gotten completely out of hand? And unless I want to live on the streets, I've been forced to take extreme measures. But don't worry, boss. I'm not selling yours. No one seems to be interested in the married Beaumont's coffee cups. Of course, they might've heard about your wife trying to hijack an airplane and they're scared she'll fly into a jealous rage and murder them in their sleep with her lemon juicer."

"I did not try to hijack a plane." Olivia breezed in the open door wearing a flirty little purple polka-dotted dress along with the signature purple high heels that all female employees wore. Since Nash had always liked a woman in heels, he was all for the company dress code—at least, the female company dress code. Whenever possible, he ignored the male company dress code of gray suits and purple ties.

"That entire hijacking incident was blown completely out of proportion," Olivia continued. "I was just making sure that the plane didn't leave."

Deacon came around the desk and pulled his wife into his arms. "You mean you were just making sure that I didn't leave."

"You are extremely arrogant for a man whose coffee cups won't sell on eBay," she said before she gave him a quick kiss. "Now why did you pull me away from the design studio?"

Deacon placed a hand on her stomach. "You need to be pulled away from the design studio more often. In fact, you should be at home resting."

Olivia covered his hand with hers. "We've been over this before, Deacon. I'm pregnant, not an invalid. And I want to work for as long as I can before the baby gets here."

There were few people on the face of the earth that Deacon would concede to. His wife seemed to be one of them. "Fine, but stop wearing those damned high heels. I'm a nervous wreck that you're going to fall." He released her and then pulled out his chair and waited for her to sit down. "Nash has a good idea about doing a survey for the new bra line to see what people think of it."

A frown marred her forehead. "So sales are still down?" When Deacon nodded, she released a sigh. "I blame myself. I was so busy working on the Legendary Lovers Line that I didn't pay much attention to the new bra line. I just thought that Samuel had it under control. I should've realized that he was depressed and done something to help him."

Deacon sent her a warning look as he leaned on the edge of his desk. "You're not still thinking about matchmaking, are you?"

"I just think that if Samuel had a partner—"

He cut her off. "Samuel's personal life is his own, Livy. And unless he asks for your help, you need to stay out of it. Besides, I don't think it's the design of the bras that's the problem—something I think we'll discover when we get the results of our survey." He clapped his hands. "So let's get started."

With Olivia and Kelly's help, it didn't take long to pull together some questions for the questionnaire. When Deacon was satisfied, he called an end to the meeting and took Olivia to lunch. Grayson headed to a design meeting for the new catalog, leaving Nash to finish up with Kelly.

Since he had gotten little sleep the night before, he stretched out on the leather couch while Kelly sat at Deacon's desk and finished inputting the questions on her laptop.

"Times have certainly changed," she said as her nails clicked on the keyboard. "In my grandmother's time, it was the woman being auctioned off to the highest bidder. Now it's the men."

"I'm not being auctioned off. I'm simply taking the winner to dinner."

"Are you going to include sex in the deal?" Kelly asked. When Nash opened his eyes and sent her a dubious look, she shrugged. "I know, I'm not supposed to talk about sex at work, but since I can't have it, it's the only enjoyment I get."

"So Jason's sticking to his celibacy before marriage pledge?"

She closed her laptop. "The man has the willpower of a Buddhist priest. Jason says he wants our wedding night to be special, but what's so special about ripped clothing and premature ejaculation?" She got up and started collecting coffee cups. "I mean, wouldn't it be better if we weren't so primed and ready?"

One of Nash's biggest attributes was knowing when to keep his mouth shut. He stretched before he got to his feet. "Well, thanks, Kelly. I think we should get it up on the website tomorrow, then follow with a social media blitz."

"The media blitz is all yours. All you need to do is tweet it. Every woman who has a phone or computer is following you. And speaking of phones..." She walked over and bent down. "Whose is this?" She held up the escort's phone, and Nash felt his heart drop to his feet.

"I found it." He reached for the phone, but she turned away and tapped the screen.

"And you didn't check to see if you could figure out who it belongs to?"

Oh, he'd checked. He'd spent most of the night trying to figure out the passcode. He hadn't had any luck. Kelly, on the other hand, figured it out in three tries.

"People don't usually think up complicated passcodes," she explained at his look of surprise.

"Great. Thanks. I'll take it from here." He held out a hand, but she ignored it.

"The best thing to do is call the most recent number. If it isn't the person looking for their phone, it's a friend or family member who can tell you how to get ahold of them." She tapped the phone and then hit speaker.

With each ring, Nash grew more and more uncomfortable. All he needed was Kelly finding out about the escorts he hired. There was absolutely no chance in hell that she would be able to keep her mouth shut. And Nash didn't want his midnight rendezvous being tweeted around the world.

"Obviously, no one's at home." He went to hit the button to end the call, when a man answered.

"Well, it's about time you called your grandparents, Eden. Your grandmother was about to call out the National Guard. And don't give me any excuses about having two jobs. I called The Lemon Drop last night, and the girl who answered said you'd taken last night off. And if you can take off a night from your busy schedule, you can stop by to see your grandparents."

"Excuse me, sir," Kelly said. "I'm sorry to bother you, but I found your granddaughter's cell phone last night."

"Found it? Or stole it? I'm calling the cops—"

"No!" Nash said a little too quickly. "I mean there's no need to involve the police. I'm sure your granddaughter just accidentally dropped it."

"Who the hell are you?" Grandpa asked.

Nash cleared his throat. "I'm the one who found your granddaughter's phone. And if she works at The Lemon Drop, I'll be happy to see she gets it back." Then before the man could ask any more questions, Nash hung up. He turned to find Kelly studying him with a calculated look.

"Okay, so what's going on?" she asked.

He tried to give her a carefree smile. "Nothing's going on. I happen to know where The Lemon Drop is, and I'm going to make sure the woman gets her phone back."

Kelly's eyes narrowed. "If you say so. But that doesn't explain why the coolest Beaumont looks like a little boy who just got caught with his hand in the cookie jar."

CHAPTER THREE

*H*ey, Huckabee." Mike Foster peeked over her cubicle. "The Dragon Lady wants to see you in her office."

Eden saved the article she'd been working on about the upcoming Bay City Marathon before giving Mike her attention. "Now?"

"No." He smirked. "Tomorrow."

Using her toes, she searched for her high heels beneath the desk. "Did she look happy or mad?"

"It's hard to tell. With circulation down, she constantly wears a scowl. So I wouldn't keep her waiting if I was you." He watched as she slipped on her shoes. "So did you get my text about going for sushi tonight?"

"No. I lost my phone last night and haven't had a chance to get a new one." Or not lost it as much as left it. Once Eden had discovered that she'd left her phone in the suite, she'd called the hotel looking for it. It still hadn't shown up. Which meant that a deviant pervert or someone in housekeeping now owned her cell phone. Between getting rejected by the Dark Seducer and losing her phone, last night had been a complete bust.

"Thanks for the invite," she said as she saved her article and got to her feet, "but I'm bartending tonight."

Mike shook his head. "Did anyone ever tell you that all work and no play makes for a pathetic life, Huckabee?"

"Just my entire family," she called over her shoulder as she headed down the hall toward Stella's office. When she got there, she tapped lightly on the open door before walking in. Stella sat behind the desk wearing her usual beige pants and black sweater. She had her chair swiveled toward her computer and was reading the article on the screen. Even from that distance, Eden could see that it was the first story she'd written about Madison. Excitement swelled, and it took everything she had not to slap the air in a high five. This was it. All her hard work and dedication was finally going to pay off. Stella was going to promote her, and Eden was going to reach her goal of becoming a true journalist.

Stella swiveled the chair and looked at Eden through the red-framed reading glasses perched on her nose. "It's shit."

Eden blinked. "What?"

"Your story is shit." Stella grabbed one of the many coffee mugs on her desk and took a sip. Her scowl deepened. "Is it too much to ask for a hot cup of coffee?" She set the mug down with a thump that had coffee splashing on the stack of articles beneath it. She ignored the mess and pointed to the chair across from her. More than a little stunned, it took a moment for Eden to sit down. Once she did, Stella leaned back in her chair and released a long, exasperated sigh.

"When I asked you to do a series of stories on prostitutes, I wanted a dark, bittersweet series about the nefarious side of the streets of San Francisco." She waved a hand at her computer. "I did not want stories about a high-end escort who plays canasta with wealthy old men for a new bauble or a vacation to the Bahamas."

"But Madison doesn't just play canasta," Eden said. "That was just one story she told me. She's told me a lot of others. Including one about a guy who hires escorts to take off their clothes while he talks dirty in the dark. In fact, I actually met the guy—"

Stella's chair squeaked as she sat forward. "A guy who talks dirty in the dark? Just what is nefarious about that? My husband talks dirty in the dark. Now if it was the mayor talking dirty to a high-end hooker, that would be a story. But some Joe Blow hiring an escort to take off her clothes means absolutely nothing to anyone."

It had meant something to Eden. After leaving the hotel, she couldn't seem to get the man out of her head. The hint of Southern drawl in his voice. The scent of musk. The heat that seemed to emanate from his pores like asphalt in the middle of August as he'd slipped her dress on and walked her to the door. Everything about him had stayed with her. And she couldn't understand why a man she hadn't even seen had such an effect on her.

She also couldn't understand how Stella could think her story was shit.

"I guess I wasn't sure what you wanted," she said. "But if you want nefarious, I can give you nefarious. I'm sure Madison has darker stories about—"

Stella held up a hand. "Please, I can't take any more

stories from the Happy Hooker." She picked up one of the tubes of ChapStick that littered her desk and liberally coated her lips with it before continuing. "Look, Eden, I'm going to be honest with you. You're not a writer. At least, you're not a newspaper writer. The only reason I gave you the job is because you bugged the hell out of me. In fact, I've never met a more determined young lady in my life. I just happen to think you're determined to do something you're not well-suited for."

"So what are you saying?" Eden tried to keep the panic from her voice. "Are you firing me?"

Stella didn't hesitate to answer. "Yes. It's time you release the chokehold you have on being a newspaper reporter and try something else." She paused. "Anything else. But if you want, you can finish the stories you're working on."

Eden sat stunned in her chair for a moment. But just a moment. Then her resolved kicked in, and she got to her feet. "I'm sorry that you didn't like my article, Stella, but that doesn't mean I'm going to give up on being a reporter." Her voice gained in volume and strength. "Because I'm not a quitter. And to prove it, before I leave this newspaper, I'm going to get you your story on prostitution." She punched the air. "The best darned story this newspaper has ever seen. Or I'm not Eden Tulip Huckabee!"

Stella took off her glasses and rubbed her eyes. "Somehow, I knew that."

Once Eden left Stella's office, she forced herself to go back to her tiny little cubicle and finish her story on the marathon. As she wrote about the strength and endurance it took to complete the run, she set another goal. She would sign up for the marathon. She would train and get herself in shape because she could do anything she set her mind to. Including write a story about the seedy side of being an escort.

After finishing the marathon story, she reread the first story she'd written about Madison and realized that Stella was right. It wasn't very dark or nefarious. Obviously, Eden had just scraped the surface of the escort world. If she wanted a great story, she needed to delve deeper. She needed to stop worrying about hurting Madison's feelings and ask some hard-core questions. Something she would do that very night when Madison showed up at The Lemon Drop.

The Lemon Drop was a trendy bar that catered to the businesspeople who flocked there after work to grab a drink and decompress. Since working at the newspaper didn't pay the bills, Eden bartended there four nights a week. It was where she had first met Madison.

Madison was one of those women who stood out from the pack. Not just because she was beautiful and gregarious, but also because she had a heart of gold. Eden had witnessed her giving a loan to a regular who was struggling to pay his bills, her couch to a waitress who had been kicked out of her apartment, and a designer coat to an old street bum who was cold.

That night, as Eden watched Madison breeze in the door of The Lemon Drop with a bright smile on her face, she had to wonder if Stella wasn't right. Madison was the walking definition of a happy hooker. There wasn't a time when she seemed depressed or angry or frustrated. But certainly underneath the mink-trimmed coat and

Tiffany diamonds there had to be a dark story. Why else would you become an escort?

Madison jockeyed through the crowd until she reached the bar. All the stools were taken, but it didn't take long for a guy to notice Madison's pouting lips and offer his seat to her. She took it with a husky "You're such a sweetie" before greeting Eden. "Hi! So how did it go with the Dark Seducer?"

Eden finished pouring the grapefruit and vodka into a salt-rimmed glass and placed it on the tray with the other drinks. "Not so great. He kicked me out." She started to ask the guy next to Madison if he wanted a refill on his rum and Coke, but Madison had taken her coat off and the guy's attention got captured by the full-figured body beneath the white sweater dress. Madison was one of those women who could be fifteen pounds overweight and still cause men to salivate. Probably because most of her weight was carried in her boobs and butt.

"You didn't listen to me, did you?" Madison said, seemingly unaware that the guy was drooling. "You talked." The look in her clear blue eyes wasn't mad as much as sympathetic. As if she pitied Eden's inability to shut her mouth...or seduce a man. Which annoyed Eden. Probably because she was right. And Eden couldn't help wondering what would've happened if she'd kept her mouth shut and followed all the Dark Seducer's commands.

"Okay, so maybe I talked too much," she conceded. "But I think him kicking me out had more to do with his disappointment that I wasn't you."

Madison looked surprised. "Why would he be disappointed? He's not my client."

Eden almost dropped the bottle of rum she'd just picked up. "He's not your client? Then why did you fix me up with him?"

"Because none of my clients would work as research for an erotica novel." She giggled. "Unless lots of elderly women read erotica."

Eden hadn't wanted to lie to Madison about being a romance novelist. Even now, she felt guilty about deceiving her. But if she wanted to be a news reporter, she would have to learn to stretch the truth. No one would want to confide in her if they knew she worked for a newspaper.

"So whose client is he?" Eden asked.

"Chloe's. She's the young girl I was telling you about. The one who got mixed up with that asshole Zac."

"The guy who runs your escort service?"

"Yeah. Zac has to be in his mid-thirties and Chloe's not more than twenty, tops. Too young to be in this business." Madison picked up a maraschino cherry from the condiment tray and sucked on it. It was like watching a television ad for lipstick. The guy next to her must've thought so too because he released a groan when she pulled it from between her lush red lips with a pop. "Are cherries fattening?"

"Those are. They're soaked in syrup." Eden leaned closer. "So she's had a hard life?"

"More than hard. She doesn't say much about it, but one of the other escorts told me that she was a runaway." She set the cherry on a cocktail napkin and pouted. "Everything seems to be fattening. Which explains why I can't lose weight."

"You're not fat. You're voluptuous."

"Only because you've never seen me without my Spanx."

Eden laughed, then took the cocktail napkin with the cherry and tossed it in the trash before giving her a clean napkin. As she started mixing Madison's usual martini, an idea struck her. "You should run in the Bay City Marathon with me. I did an article—I mean I read—an article about it, and people who train for the marathon lose tons of weight and completely tone their bodies."

"I don't know. Anything with a 'thon' attached to it sounds hard to me. It's too bad I'm not famous enough to get on *Dancing with the Stars*. I'm a good dancer, and those contestants look great afterwards."

Eden handed her the martini. "We could look just as good if we trained together. In fact, why don't you invite Chloe along? The bigger the group, the more likely we'll succeed. We could start Saturday at Golden Gate Park."

Madison picked up the toothpick with the olive. "I guess I could try it. But I'll definitely need a massage after."

"I'll be happy to give you a massage," the guy next to her said.

Turning, Madison flashed him a smile. "Now aren't you a honey." She waggled her hand with the wedding band on the ring finger. "But I'm afraid Rocky wouldn't like it."

Eden had seen the wedding band prop used before. Madison might be an escort, but she was a picky one. In fact, Eden had yet to see her leave with a guy. Or even flirt with one.

A waitress squeezed between Madison and the guy and

set her tray on the bar. "I guess I got it wrong. The woman didn't want a Salty Dog. She wants a Salty Chihuahua. And I need two margaritas on the rocks and an iced tea with plenty of sugar." She leaned in closer. "And you'll never guess who the sweet tea is for." Before Eden could guess, she hurried on. "One of the panty billionaires."

Eden filled two glasses with ice. "The who?"

"The panty billionaires. You know, the three brothers who inherited the French Kiss lingerie company." She glanced over her shoulder. "He's the middle one. Nash Lothario Beaumont."

"Holy smokes," Madison breathed. "Are you kidding me?" She stood on the rungs of the barstool and tried to see over everyone's heads. "I see him. He's sitting at that table chatting with those two women. Or more like keeping them from eating him alive. God, he's so-o-o cute. It sorta makes you want to run out and buy a pair of his panties—even if the Lothario Collection is a little racy for my taste."

Wanting to see what all the fuss was about, Eden finished pouring the margarita mix and tequila before she stepped up on a plastic crate they used for glasses. Her gaze scanned the tables. "So what does he look—?" Her breath left her lungs in a rush as her eyes landed on the man sitting at the corner table.

Cute? Cute was the last word Eden would use to describe the guy. Gorgeous, breathtaking, and smoking hot all came to mind but still didn't capture his amazing good looks. His thick brown hair was combed back from a high forehead, and a wayward lock hung over the dark slash of one eyebrow. A day's growth of stubble shadowed his angular jaw and square chin and framed a pair of full lips. Lips that were tipped in a smile that took her breath away. She looked at his eyes to see which of the two women he found so amusing and realized that he wasn't looking at either.

He was looking straight at Eden.

Completely embarrassed to be caught staring, she hopped down from the crate. "He doesn't look that hot to me," she lied as she went back to filling the order.

Madison laughed. "Which explains the blush on your cheeks."

After getting caught staring, Eden purposely ignored the panty billionaire for the rest of the night. Which wasn't hard to do. The next few hours went by in a flurry of drink orders. Madison left only an hour after she'd arrived, promising to meet Eden at the park on Saturday morning. Eden was excited about the prospect of killing two goals with one marathon. She could pick Chloe's brain and train at the same time. Chloe sounded like just the type of escort her editor had been talking about: a young, disenchanted girl forced to sell her body on the streets.

Around eleven, the crowd at The Lemon Drop dwindled to the diehard drinkers and poor souls who just didn't want to go home to an empty house. The poor souls she felt sorry for. But the diehard drinkers could get annoying. Especially when she had to cut them off.

"What do you mean, you won't s-serve me another drink?" The guy in the ill-fitting suit leaned over the bar and grabbed Eden's arm. "Are you sayin' I'm drun-nk?"

Before Eden could deal with the drunk, the panty billionaire appeared. And while she'd had no problem ignoring him when he sat across the bar, it was impossible to ignore him now. Especially when he was even more dev-astatingly handsome up close. Beneath the gray Henley, his shoulders looked wide and his chest nicely muscled. Faded jeans hugged his lean legs and hips... and the nice package that snuggled right between.

Her gaze snapped up, hoping he hadn't caught her again. But this time, he wasn't looking at her. He was looking at the drunk's hand wrapped around her wrist. His jaw tightened for only a moment before he flashed a smile that seemed to light up the bar like late-afternoon sun.

He pointed a finger at the drunk. "I thought that was you." He gave the guy a hard whack on the back, causing him to release Eden's arm. "Hell, it's been ages. How are you doing? You still working over at Merrill Lynch?"

The drunk tried to say something, but the panty bil-lionaire didn't give him a chance before he hooked a muscled arm around his neck and pulled him to the door. "You've got to come home with me and say 'hi' to the family. They'll be thrilled to see you."

Before Eden could blink, he had the drunk out the door. It didn't take her long to figure out what had hap-pened. The panty billionaire had just rescued her, and he'd done it so slick that the drunk didn't even have time to cause trouble. Eden stared at the door for only a second more before she turned to the other bartender.

"Can you take over, Jen? I'll be right back." She lifted the gate in the bar and headed for the door. She told her-self that she just wanted to thank him. But deep down, she knew that she also wanted to see all that hotness just one more time. When she got out front, the two men were nowhere in sight so she headed for the parking lot in back. She stopped in her tracks when she rounded the corner of the alleyway and saw that the billionaire had the drunk shoved up against the wall.

"Now here's how this is going to play out," he spoke in a low, deep voice that no longer held one trace of friendliness. "I'm going to call you a cab and you're going to go home and sleep it off. But when you get up tomorrow, you better remember four words. Don't. Touch. Her. Again."

While the drunk stammered his agreement, Eden slipped back around the corner of the building and held a hand to her thumping heart. Because while she hadn't recognized the friendly billionaire's voice, she had recognized this one. She recognized the huskiness. The authority. And the smooth Southern drawl.

For a moment, she just stood there and tried to catch her breath as the truth dawned.

The panty billionaire had a dark secret.

And Eden had a great story.

CHAPTER FOUR

The mansion in prestigious Pacific Heights had once belonged to Nash's uncle. When Michael Beaumont had died, he had willed it to his wife. At one time, Deirdre Beaumont had planned on selling it to help Olivia buy out Nash and his brothers' shares of French Kiss. But fate had changed those plans when Olivia and Deacon fell in love. Once they married, they bought the house from Olivia's mother to start their family in.

Nash understood why his brother wanted to keep the mansion. The house, with its multiple rooms and large garden, was the complete opposite of the fishing shack the Beaumont brothers had grown up in. There were no sad memories lurking in the corners, no hidden skeletons waiting to jump out of the closets. The move to San Francisco had been a new start for Deacon. Too bad that wasn't true for Nash. The past clung to him like the thick fog that rolled in from the sea, heavy and suffocating. And it seemed that wherever he went, the sad memories followed, and every closet door held a skeleton waiting to jump out.

Climbing the row of steps to the front door, Nash pressed the buzzer and waited for the housekeeper to answer. Lucia was from Peru and spoke very little English, but she smiled broadly when she saw Nash and waved him inside.

"I get missus," she said before she hurried up the massive staircase.

Like he always did when he came to the house, Nash wandered into the front sitting room and paid tribute to the portrait of his uncle. He had met Uncle Michael only once, and it hadn't been under the best of circumstances. Nash's father had dragged his sons from Louisiana to San Francisco to beg for money from his only brother. His uncle hadn't given them a dime at the time, but later he willed them a billion-dollar lingerie company. Which Nash figured made up for the slight in spades.

"Thanks again, Uncle Mikey," he whispered with a smile and a wink. The stern man in the painting didn't smile back. Nash understood completely. Leaving behind all those lingerie models was no laughing matter. Especially for a Beaumont.

Rumor had it that the Beaumonts were direct descendants of the legendary lover Casanova. Nash didn't believe it. But he did believe that the Beaumont men had a way with the ladies. Or perhaps just a love for the ladies. Nash certainly couldn't seem to stay away from them—even when he should. Once again his uncontrollable desire had put him in an awkward situation.

Eden.

The name went with an escort, but not with the ponytailed

woman in the T-shirt and jeans whom he had watched bartend the night before. That woman had looked like the girl next door. The one you wanted to ride bikes with. Go fishing with. The one who shared her peanut butter sandwich with you at lunch, who took your side against teachers and parents, and who kept your deepest, darkest secrets.

Which probably explained why so many men clustered around the bar to talk with her. It annoyed Nash. But not as much as the drunk who had grabbed her arm. Just seeing the guy's fingers curled around Eden's wrist had made Nash want to slam his fist into the drunk's face. Repeatedly. He didn't, but only because he didn't want to give French Kiss any bad press.

"Sorry I took so long. I was changing out of my work clothes."

He glanced behind him to see Olivia hurrying into the room. She wasn't exactly dressed for dinner. She wore a baggy sweatshirt, flannel pajama bottoms, and sheepskin slippers, and her hair was pulled back in a ponytail similar to the one Eden had worn. Except Eden's hair wasn't blond. It was black. A rich, velvety black that made a man want to touch. Of course, touching was out of the question.

He sent Olivia a smile he didn't feel. "I didn't mind the wait." He nodded at the portrait. "I was just saying 'hi' to Uncle Michael."

Olivia studied the picture with obvious love in her eyes. Even though Michael was her stepfather, the two had been close. "I always thought Deacon looked more like Michael, but you've got the same intense look in your eyes."

"Intense? Haven't you heard? I'm the easygoing Beaumont."

Her eyebrow lifted. "I thought so at first. But I think there's intensity in you, Nash Beaumont. You just do a good job of hiding it." Taking his arm, she propelled him through the foyer and up the stairs.

Nash followed, but couldn't help asking, "Did you change the location of the dining room?"

"Of course not. We'll eat in a minute. Right now, we need privacy." She pulled him into the bedroom and closed the door.

Being a Beaumont, Nash had been pulled into many a bedroom—by many a woman. Some of the women were even married. But none had been married to his brother. He immediately became uncomfortable.

"Where is Deacon?" he asked.

Olivia leaned against the door. "He's at the basketball game with Jason. And I'm supposed to be at my mother's going over the plans for the Lover's Ball. But I begged off with a headache because I really needed to see you alone."

"Alone?" His voice hit a high note he hadn't made since puberty. "Why would you need to see me alone?"

She stopped pacing as she chewed on her bottom lip. Something she did when she was nervous. "Because of the crush. And maybe not a crush as much as sexual desire."

Holy shit. Uncomfortable just escalated to frantic. He knew his sister-in-law liked him, but he didn't think that she desired him. The only desire Nash had at the moment was to get the hell out of there. But Olivia stood between him and the door.

"I know what you're thinking," she continued. "You're thinking, why me? Well, since you moved here, I've felt like we've become very close. And I thought if anyone would understand and not judge me, it would be you."

Considering his past, Nash tried not to judge. If anyone knew that the flesh was weak and temptation hard to resist, he did. But just because you were tempted didn't mean you had to give in to temptation. And Nash was proving this point by hiring escorts and staying in control of the situation. But he didn't feel in control now.

"Look, Olivia," he said, "sometimes when a man and woman spend a lot of time together, emotions get muddled—especially sexual emotions. And what you really think you feel, you don't feel at all. It's just a passing…thing."

She looked confused. "So you don't think it will last."

He certainly hoped not. Nash might be the better boxer, but Deacon had a mean right hook. "Of course not."

"But what if I want it to last?" She sent him a sly look while Nash's mouth dropped. "I mean, it's been so long since Samuel has shown any interest in someone that I think it's a good thing."

"Samuel? You're talking about Samuel?"

"Of course, who did you think I was talking about?"

Nash's shoulders relaxed, and he really wanted to pull her into his arms and give her a big kiss. Instead, he walked over and flopped down in the chair across from the bed. "Samuel. Of course Samuel. So start from the beginning, Olivia. What's going on with Samuel? He has a crush on someone?"

She sat on the bed and leaned back against the pillows, stroking her stomach in a gentle back-and-forth motion as she spoke. "That's the only explanation I can come up with for his weird behavior. Samuel is always organized and efficient. But since Doug started working at French Kiss,

Samuel has become unorganized and distracted. Which might explain why the new bra line isn't doing well."

Nash couldn't help being a little surprised. Everyone at French Kiss was convinced that Samuel was gay, but Nash had always had his doubts. Obviously, he'd been wrong. "So who is this Doug?" he asked.

"The UPS guy."

Nash dealt with so many people in any given day that it was hard to keep track of them. But he vaguely remembered a guy in shorts hustling through the halls delivering packages. "So I'm assuming that this Doug is gay?"

"I was hoping that you could answer that question."

He stared at her. "I'm not gay, Olivia."

She laughed. "I realize that, Nash. But he doesn't. So I was thinking that you could do a little flirting—"

Nash held up his hands. "Oh no, I'm not flirting with some guy to see if he's gay."

"But you wouldn't have to flirt much." She sat up. "Just enough to gauge his reaction. One of your smiles should be enough to have him falling all over you. People can't resist your charm."

Nash didn't know why an image of Eden popped into his head. Maybe because she wasn't so taken with his charm. Not that he had been all that charming in the hotel suite. But he gave her a smile at the bar, and she'd completely ignored him. Something that still annoyed him.

"And what happens if this Doug turns out to be gay?" he asked.

Smiling, Olivia leaned closer. "Then you do a little matchmaking."

"Me?"

She glanced at the closed door. "Deacon would kill me if I interfered in Samuel's life. Which is exactly why I had to set up this private meeting with you."

Nash shook his head. "I'm sorry, Olivia, but I'm going to have to pass. I agree with Deacon. Samuel's sex life isn't any of my business."

The look she sent him was all wide-eyed and pleading. "Please, Nash. In a way, it's part of your job description. If Samuel is distracted, he won't make good product. And if we don't produce a good product, how can our customers be satisfied?"

Nash wanted to argue with the insane logic, but her big puppy-dog eyes stopped him. That, and the fact that it was hard to say no to a pregnant woman. "Did anyone ever tell you that you're a mean negotiator, Livy?"

"What did you expect? I'm Michael Beaumont's step-daughter." She smiled hopefully. "So will you do it?"

Knowing when he was beat, he gave in. "Fine, I'll see what I can find out." He pointed a finger at her. "But I'm not playing matchmaker. Once I figure out if he's Samuel's type, I'm out. You can take over from there."

She jumped up and threw her arms around his neck before giving him a big kiss on the cheek. "Thanks, Nash. I knew I could count on you. Now, let's go down and see what we can find for dinner. I'm starving."

The refrigerator in the kitchen was well stocked, and since Olivia didn't cook, Nash was the one who pulled together some chicken fajitas for their dinner. He didn't mind. He liked cooking. After his mother died, he had taken over the job. Grandpa had been too old. Grayson too young. Deacon had been too busy providing for the family. And their father had been too busy finding solace in the arms of every woman in town.

Don Juan, or Donny John as everyone called him, had folded like an old lawn chair when his wife died, leaving Deacon to shoulder the responsibility of raising his two younger brothers. Grayson had been easy. Give the kid some paints, and he'd kept himself busy for hours. But despite his cooking, Nash had been a bit of a troublemaker. He was the kid who refused to do his homework, ignored curfew, and eventually got tossed in jail. If working his ass off to pay the bills wasn't enough for Deacon, he had to spend what savings he had on a lawyer for his pain-in-the-ass little brother. Which probably explained why Nash felt so guilty when Deacon walked into the kitchen and found him eating dinner with Olivia.

Dropping his briefcase and suit jacket on the counter, Deacon tugged loose his tie and looked from Nash to Olivia. "I thought you were going to your mother's."

She hurried over and kissed him. "I was tired so I came home instead. So what happened to you spending a relaxing night at the game?"

"Kelly got the survey up, and I was so interested in the answers that I forgot about the time until Jason called and asked where the hell I was." He looked at Nash. "So what are you doing here?"

Nash shrugged. "I stopped by hoping for some leftovers." He tried to change the subject. "So we already got a response on the survey?"

"Hundreds." Deacon took a chair at the table and massaged his temples. "It seems that nowadays it only takes seconds to get a response from the world."

"So what did they say?" Nash asked.

"That they loved our bras. In fact, there wasn't one negative response." He ran a hand through his hair and released a sigh. "Which doesn't make any sense. If they love them, why aren't they buying them?"

"Enough business talk," Olivia said as she set a plate of fajitas in front of him. "Once you walk through those doors, Mr. Beaumont, you're mine."

Deacon grinned and pulled her onto his lap. There was a time when it took a lot to wring a smile out of Nash's serious older brother. But since marrying Olivia, he smiled often. And if anyone deserved happiness, it was Deacon.

Nash got up. "I think that's my cue to leave. Thanks for dinner, Livy. Talk to you tomorrow, Deke."

"Tell Grayson we need his decision on the model for the cover of the swimsuit catalog ASAP," Deacon said. "I realize he wants her to be perfect, but we need to get that catalog out by March."

Nash lifted a hand. "Will do."

That's exactly what Nash should've done. He should've gone straight home and talked to Grayson about swimsuit models. Instead, he drove to The Lemon Drop. It was stupid, but he couldn't seem to help himself. Like a damned stalker, he parked his half-ton truck out front and waited. Not for one hour, but for over two. A little after midnight, the last of the patrons came out, and the security gate was pulled down and locked by one of the bouncers. A few minutes later, a group of bartenders, waitresses, and bouncers came around from the back. Most headed for the parking garage next door, but a few walked in different directions.

Nash only had eyes for the dark-haired woman who

headed up the street alone. For a second, he wanted to jump out of the car and ask her what the hell she thought she was doing. This wasn't his small town back in Louisiana where you could walk anywhere at any time of day or night and not worry about being accosted. This was a big city with big criminals. The woman, obviously, needed a keeper.

He waited until she was halfway down the block before he started his truck and followed her. She walked at a fast clip and, at one point, pulled her phone from the purse slung over her shoulder and made a phone call. Obviously, she had gotten a new phone, which made him feel guilty for not getting hers back to her. The guilt lasted for only a second when a thought popped into his head. Who was she calling? Was it a client? A client who would touch her like Nash hadn't? A man who would give her the orgasm Nash wanted to give her?

There it was.

The truth.

Nash wanted to be the one to touch her, to pleasure her, to give her an orgasm that would rock her world. It went against everything he had been trying to accomplish, but he couldn't deny the desire. Nor could he stop himself from picking up the burner phone from his cup holder and dialing the only number on it. When the man answered, he made his request.

"Saturday night. The same girl as last time."

"Chloe?"

Nash slowed the truck in front of an apartment building and made note of the address. "No. I want Eden... only Eden."

CHAPTER FIVE

$\mathscr{E}$den spent the next few days Googling the hell out of Nash Beaumont. And there was plenty to Google. All three of the Beaumont brothers had become overnight celebrities when they inherited the French Kiss lingerie company. It wasn't the fact three brothers had inherited a women's panty company that intrigued people as much as the fact that the brothers weren't your typical tycoons.

The Beaumont brothers had grown up in a small town in Louisiana. And from the looks of the run-down shack they'd lived in, they'd been dirt poor. Which made for the perfect "rags to riches" story: Three ordinary Southern boys, who spent their weekdays working at blue-collar jobs and their weekends in camouflage shooting ducks and slamming beers, finally caught a break when their uncle willed them a billion-dollar lingerie company.

Except there was nothing ordinary about the brothers. Not their unbelievable good looks. Their unusual bluish-purple eyes. Or their middle names. Names that had to be a publicity stunt. Because who in their right mind would name their children after famous lovers? Valentino and Romeo weren't so bad, but Lothario had been an unscrupulous seducer of women.

Although after looking at the pictures of Nash, the name was justified. In almost every photo, he was with a beautiful woman. Or two. Or three. Or a hundred. A hundred sexy lingerie models with perfect bodies. No wonder he had kicked Eden out of his hotel room. As one of the panty billionaires, he knew exactly what a woman's body should look like. It made sense that he would take one look at her average body and think he'd gotten the booby prize of all booby prizes.

Of course, that brought up another question. Why would a man who had access to hundreds of lingerie models have to hire women? It made no sense. And yet, the voice Eden had heard in the alleyway behind The Lemon Drop sounded exactly like the voice she'd heard in the hotel suite. Of course, she couldn't write a story based on voice recognition without getting the newspaper sued. She needed substantial proof. She just wasn't sure how to get it. She did, however, know where to start.

Chloe would have more information on the Dark Seducer. It was even possible that the escort knew who he was. All Eden had to do was get it out of her. Which was something she planned on doing when she met Chloe and Madison at Golden Gate Park on Saturday morning.

Eden woke early and made herself a power shake of spinach, fruit, and protein powder that she'd gotten off a website dedicated to marathon runners. If she was going to run the Bay City Marathon, she was going to do it right. After holding her nose and downing the green, sludgy shake, she threw up. Then she rinsed out her mouth, dressed in her new work-out clothes, and headed to the park. Since she was early, she took the time to stretch her leg muscles. Which turned out to be tighter than she thought. She couldn't even touch her toes without bending her knees, which would give her limber yoga mother a stroke if she could see her. Thinking about her mother reminded her that she needed to call her grandparents and give them her new cell number. She had texted it to her mother, but her grandparents weren't text savvy.

Mimi and Pops lived only miles away from Eden. It was one of the reasons Eden's parents hadn't been too upset about her move to the big city. Not that Eden's grandparents were the type to keep a close eye on their granddaughter. Having lived in San Francisco in the sixties, they believed in freedom, including free love and free drugs for all. They also believed that Eden should be experiencing life instead of worrying about her career. Something her grandmother started in on as soon as Eden identified herself.

"If you tell me you're at that conservative newspaper you work for on a Saturday," Mimi said, "I'm going to give up my pacifist ways and paddle your butt, Eden Tulip Huckabee."

Eden couldn't help smiling. "You'll be happy to hear that I'm at Golden Gate Park, Mimi."

"The park? Now that's a perfect place to be on a beautiful Saturday morning. Your grandfather and I attended more than one love-in at Golden Gate Park." Mimi paused as if remembering. "Back then, life was all about love, peace, and rock and roll. Who are you with?"

"I'm waiting for some friends."

"I'm glad to hear it. It's time that you made some friends in the city. You certainly didn't have very many growing up—something that worried your mother silly. Of course, not as much as your anal personality."

"I'm not anal, Mimi," Eden said as she put a foot on a park bench and stretched to the side. "I just like to have a plan and know where I'm going."

"Yes, I know. Which is exactly why you lost your last lover. You had too many plans. Men like spontaneity in a woman."

Was there anything worse than talking sex with your grandmother? "Boyfriend, Mimi. Daniel and I were not lovers."

"Then that was the problem. At your age, you should be experiencing life—all aspects of life. Now there's this very nice young man who lives next door who looks like he knows his way around a bedroom. I'll introduce you next time you come over."

Eden sighed. "Great. So how is Pops?"

"Besides being a little more forgetful, he's fine. If you hold on, I'll take him the phone. As usual, he's out on the balcony." No doubt naked as the day he was born. Eden's grandfather cared nothing about city ordinances on public nudity.

"Eden?" her grandfather asked.

"Hi, Pops."

"So I guess that young man got your phone back to you."

Eden straightened, her foot sliding off the bench and thumping to the ground. "What young man?"

"A woman and a man called here yesterday." He paused. "Or maybe it was the day before. Anyway, they found your phone and were looking to return it."

"Who, Pops? Who found my phone? The hotel?" She cringed when she realized her slip, but luckily Pops didn't catch it.

"They didn't leave their names. The woman who spoke first just said that she had found your phone, then the man hopped on and told me not to call the police and he'd get the phone back to you at The Lemon Drop."

Eden gripped her phone. It could've been someone at the hotel who had called. A maid and the head of house-keeping. But if that was the case, then why hadn't they dropped off her phone that night? She froze. But someone had shown up that night. Someone who was the boss of a big lingerie company.

"Hey, Eden!"

She glanced up to see Madison walking across the grass in hot pink leggings, tie-dyed leg warmers, and a tight T-shirt with a designer logo on the front.

"Listen, Pops," Eden said. "I've got to go. But I'll call you later." She hung up the phone just as Madison arrived, holding up a white bakery bag.

"I stopped to get éclairs first. I thought it would give us energy. Chloe is going to be late. I guess Zac is on the warpath over something. He's such a jerk. If there was another escort service in the city, I'd drop him in a New York second." She sat down on the bench and pulled two éclairs out of the bag.

After throwing up her green power breakfast, Eden should've been hungry. But her mind was too preoccupied with what she'd learned from her pops. It seemed that the panty billionaire had found her phone, which would explain why he had been at The Lemon Drop. It did not explain why he hadn't given her the phone. Of course, he couldn't have given it to her without her knowing who he was. So then why had he called her grandparents? Why hadn't he just trashed it? And who was the woman? Surprisingly, she felt more annoyed that he was with a woman than she was about him taking her phone.

She tried to act nonchalant as she continued to stretch. "So have you ever seen the Dark Seducer, Madison?"

"No. And Chloe only met him once. I guess he's a new client." Madison took a bite of éclair and closed her eyes in ecstasy. "This is delicious. You really need to try one."

"I had a power shake this morning."

"I bet that was tasty," Madison said as she watched a group of joggers run past. "Why is it that everything that's good for you either tastes bad or is painful? And you can't tell me those runners aren't in pain. Just look at their sweaty, scrunched-up faces."

Eden looked at the runners and had to admit that they didn't look happy. In fact, they looked miserable. But she wasn't about to let Madison get discouraged. "No pain, no gain."

"If you say so." Madison polished off the éclair and sucked the chocolate off her fingers. "But I can't stay past ten. I have a date with Freddie."

"Canasta?"

"No, that's Harry. Freddie just likes to sit and talk about his late wife. It's so sad. He and his wife had been married for sixty-five years before she died. Sixty-five years. Isn't that amazing. How long have your parents been married?"

Eden suddenly felt like she always did when the subject of her parents' marriage came up—embarrassed and thoroughly annoyed. "My parents never got married."

Madison's eyes widened. "Really? Wow, I did not see

that coming. Was your mother a teen mom and your father just a high school mistake? Or did your mom fall in love with someone else before you were born?" She placed a hand on her ample chest. "I hope your father didn't die before he could marry your mother."

"Actually, my parents are still together. They just don't believe in marriage." She tried to keep the annoyance out of her voice, but failed miserably.

"I'm sorry," Madison said. "I didn't mean to upset you."

"Why would I be upset? It's not like they don't love each other. And if they want to ignore all societal norms and make up their own rules, who am I to stop them?"

Madison studied her for a moment before she smiled sympathetically. "Well, you know, I bet not getting married has its perks. Like you will never have to worry about losing your wedding band. Or have to return duplicate wedding gifts. Or stand in line to get a new social security card." She shook her head. "I hate standing in a line for anything."

Eden's anger fizzled out, and she laughed. "Are you always so positive?"

"No. Sometimes I can be quite grumpy." She held out the éclair. "Now eat this before I do. And while you're eating, tell me about your family. You've got my curiosity up."

At The Lemon Drop, she and Madison had only been able to talk in between Eden bartending. But for the next hour, they talked nonstop. Or Eden talked nonstop. Once the marriage thing was out, she started babbling like a brook. She told Madison about her mother the yoga instructor and Buddhist and her father being a war correspondent and then a journalism professor. She talked about her twin brothers, whose main goals were catching the perfect wave and skateboarding in the X Games. And she talked about her nudist grandparents who lived in San Francisco and kept dropping batches of magic brownies at Eden's apartment.

"Like marijuana magic brownies?" Madison asked.

"Those would be the ones. I think they believe it will loosen their tight-assed granddaughter up."

Madison laughed. "Well, you are a little tight, Eden. And with a laid-back family like yours, I don't know how it happened. Or maybe I do. I'm not much like my family either."

"Since your mom was the president of the PTA and your father is a preacher, I guess not."

A look of regret entered Madison's eyes, but it was gone so quickly that Eden wondered if she'd imagined it. "Yeah," she said before her eyes lit up. "Look, there's Chloe."

Chloe was nothing like Madison. Madison was average height, blond, and full figured, and Chloe was tall, brunette, and model thin. Madison was probably in her mid-thirties, and Chloe didn't look older than Eden's brothers. Madison was the happy hooker, and Chloe was more the angry dominatrix. She had a diamond stud in her nose, and a tribal tattoo peeked from between her black running pants and the short T-shirt with skulls. But she was just as beautiful as Madison. Maybe even more so. With her rich brown hair and dark eyes, she looked a little like Audrey Hepburn gone Goth.

Madison made the introductions. "Chloe, this is my

good friend Eden. She's the one that helped you out the other night by taking the Dark Seducer."

Chloe didn't look grateful. "So are we going to run or not?"

Eden wanted to point out that they could've been running a lot sooner if Chloe had been on time. But since the girl had information she wanted, she held her tongue and followed her to the running trail.

According to the marathon website, pace was everything. You needed to learn your body's limits and adjust your pace accordingly. It turned out to be harder than Eden thought. Especially when trying to get information out of an athletic girl who looked like she could win a marathon. Chloe had perfect pace. Too bad it was so fast. After only a half a mile, Eden was huffing like a freight train and Madison called it quits.

"That's it for me, girls," she said as she slowed. "My boobs can't take the abuse. Walking is more my speed."

If she hadn't needed answers, Eden would've slowed to a walk too. Instead, she hurried to catch up with Chloe. "So I wanted to thank you for letting me take over for you the other night. The man was quite...interesting." When Chloe completely ignored her, she continued. "So how long have you known the Dark Seducer? The Dark Seducer sounds so silly. Does he have a first name?"

Chloe shot her a mean glance. "What's it to you?"

"Nothing. I was just wondering. I mean, he is kind of intriguing." Eden massaged a cramp in her side as she ran. "So he calls you and sets up the times? Have you ever seen him?"

Chloe stopped running and turned to her. "Look, I

made a mistake by giving you the guy. And if you think that you're going to horn in on Zac's business, then you've got another think coming."

Eden held up her hands. "I don't want to horn in on Zac's business."

"Really? Then why did the Dark Seducer ask for you tonight?"

"Tonight? He wants to see me tonight?"

"As if you didn't know." Chloe leaned closer. "You might be able to pull that wide-eyed, innocent shit with Mary Fuckin' Poppins back there, but you can't pull it with me. You're not some dumb bimbo bartender who wants to write a romance novel, are you?"

"Hey." Madison came walking up. "What's going on? I hope you're not getting crabby with Eden, Chloe. I want her to like you as much as I do."

Chloe rolled her eyes. "Look, Maddie, thanks for inviting me along. But I'd rather run with friends." She glanced at Eden. "And you need to be careful with this one. She's not who you think she is."

After she ran off, Madison looked at Eden. "Are you okay? She didn't hit you, did she? She has been known to throw a punch."

Eden watched Chloe disappear around a bend. No, Chloe hadn't thrown a punch, but she had thrown her for a loop. Nash Beaumont wanted to see her again? It made absolutely no sense. Especially when he was the one who had kicked her out. But regardless of whether it made sense or not, if Eden wanted a story, there was only one thing she could do.

She had to meet with the Dark Seducer one more time.

CHAPTER SIX

She wasn't going to show.

Nash was surprised by how annoyed he felt. And he had no reason to feel annoyed. He should've expected it. Especially after the way he'd treated her the last time she'd been here. She probably wanted nothing to do with the rude pervert who liked to talk dirty to women in the dark. What were the words he'd given her for his behavior? *Sexual deviant.* It wasn't exactly the truth. He wasn't sexually screwed up as much as mentally. These late-night exercises were his way of fixing the broken part of him. Not that he was fixable. And yet, somehow, he felt as if this escort could fix him.

Just her name brought up an image of a beautiful garden in full sunshine. Enough sunshine to seep into all the hidden cracks and crevices and cancel out all the darkness.

Getting up from the chair, Nash moved to the window and drew back the heavy curtains. It wasn't raining tonight, and the half-moon hung like a Chinese lantern in the sky between the skyscrapers that surrounded the hotel. He tipped the Breitling watch Deacon had gotten him for Christmas toward it and read the time before letting the curtain drop. He paced in the dark for a few minutes. Feeling hot, he unbuttoned his shirt and took it off, then stubbed his toe on a table leg when he went to lay it over the back of the chair.

"Shit!" He hobbled to the window and opened the curtain to check his watch.

She wasn't coming.

But instead of ending the farce, Nash sat down in the chair and picked up his phone from the table. He intended to listen to some blues to match his mood. But while shuffling through his playlist, he saw a Bruce Springsteen song and tapped the play arrow.

His mother had loved Springsteen, and Nash had grown up listening to poetic songs about small towns, city jungles, and unrequited love. But "Thunder Road," above all other songs, made him think of his mom. Even now he could picture her stepping out on the porch in the midst of a hot, Louisiana summer, her dress fluttering in the thick, humid breeze that swelled up from the bayou, her pretty brown hair clinging to the sweat at her brow. Sweat not only from the heat but also from hours spent sewing clothes for other people, cleaning house, and raising three boys. And yet, she had never stopped smiling. No matter how hard she worked. Or how many jobs his father lost. Or how many bills three boys could accumulate. Or how destructive cancer could be. Althea Beaumont had smiled through it all.

It was a trait that Nash had acquired. There was only one night he'd forgotten to smile, the night his father had woken him from a sound sleep to say his final goodbyes to his mother. He'd been so upset by the shell of the woman on the bed that he'd stood there mute...until she smiled.

"I love you, Nash Potatoes."

Her smile and the pet name were all it took for him to completely lose it. Not with tears. He wished he had lost it with tears. No, instead, he threw a major tantrum. He kicked over the chair his father had brought into the room and started punching his dad, using every cuss word he could think of. And he didn't stop until Donny John had wrapped him in a bear hug and carried him out.

Not wanting to think about the painful past, he cut off the song in mid-lyric and chose a Maroon 5 song. But the upbeat tune didn't stop his brain from going down the dark path of memories. And soon images filled his mind. Not of his mother, but of Melissa. Sweet, innocent Melissa—

"Hello? Are you here?"

The softly spoken words cut into his thoughts, and he opened his eyes to find light spearing through the darkness from the opened door. Relief caused his shoulders to relax.

He lowered the volume of the song. "What happened to the slow burn and trip around the world?"

There was a slight hesitation. "I figured you knew what was on the menu."

He got to his feet, but kept his distance. "Maybe you should refresh my memory."

Her swallow was audible. "I would still prefer it if you didn't touch me."

She might not want him to, but he wanted to. He wanted it more than he had ever wanted anything in his life. She pulled at him like the tide to the moon. But she was right. Touching wasn't an option. At least not for him.

"I'll make you a deal." He moved a step closer and caught the same earthy scent he'd smelled before. Not floral, but herbal. The kind of fresh scent you catch on a dewy summer morning. He took a deep breath and held it for a moment before slowly releasing. "I won't touch, if you do exactly what I say."

There was a long pause. "O-okay."

He was surprised by how one simple word could make his cock go from semi-interested to fully consumed. It pressed against the fly of his jeans like a divining rod searching for water as an ache grew in Nash's belly. An ache that chanted two words...

I want. I want. I want.

But Nash had wanted before. And too much want could lead to lack of control. And lack of control could lead to another kind of ache. The kind that settled in your heart and refused to let go. So he ignored the throbbing of his cock and walked back over to the chair in the corner. Once he was seated, he lifted his phone. He had hooked the light over the bed to an app on his phone. Deacon and Grayson liked to tease him about being a tech nerd, but sometimes it came in handy. With just a few taps, the light clicked on.

Eden stood just inside the pool of soft light. Her eyes squinted, and her hands clutched her purse as if it were a life preserver and she a drown victim. She wore the same black dress she'd worn the other night. Nash didn't know colors as well as Grayson, but he knew that black was the wrong color for Eden. With her black hair and gold eyes, she needed vivid color. Red would look good. Or bright yellow. Or pink. Any color but black. Although he did like her black heels and the way they made her legs look as long as a slim-grip fishing rod.

How would it feel to have them wrapped around his waist? Straddling his hips? Hooked over his shoulders? He clenched his jaw and tried to push the thoughts from his mind.

"The dress," he said, his voice raspy with desire.

She lowered her hands and set the purse on the bed before slipping down a strap of her dress. The swell of one breast appeared before she pulled it back up. "Look," she said. "I'm kinda new at this. I mean I haven't been escort...ing for very long."

He wasn't surprised. Her behavior the first night had pretty well clinched the fact that she wasn't experienced. Which intrigued him. Or maybe just turned him on. Was he her first? He liked the thought of it. Almost as much as he liked the thought of being the first man to give her an orgasm. But he couldn't think about that. If he did, he would lose all control.

She swallowed again. "So I was wondering if we could talk for a little while?" she asked. "Maybe get to know each other?"

"You don't need to know me."

"I know I don't need to, but it would make me feel more comfortable." She stared at the corner where he sat. "Like where are you from? I noticed you had an accent. Southern?"

"Atlanta," he lied.

She did a little curtsey like she was performing on a stage. "Well, I'm a California girl born and raised. I grew up in a small town just south of here."

Somehow he knew it was the truth. She wasn't the type to keep secrets. That was his type. "And why did you move here?" he asked.

"I wanted to experience life in the big city." She waved

her hands to encompass the room. She was a hand talker, something he'd noticed the first night. At the bar, she'd been too busy pouring drinks, but now her hands gestured like two birds trying to take flight. "I really want to move to New York City. But this is where I got a job first as a new—umm, new escort."

It made sense. She was pretty, but not breathtakingly beautiful. And in order to make it as an escort in New York, you would have to be breathtakingly beautiful. Or have a certain talent. So far, she hadn't demonstrated any talent. And yet, he was still hard as a stone. In fact, he was more turned on than he had been in a long time. Hidden in the dark, he could've unzipped his jeans and taken care of the situation. She would never know. But that would defeat the purpose. This wasn't about his pleasure. It was about hers. And he couldn't give her pleasure if she was talking. Or if she was nervous. And how could she not be nervous when she was new at this and he had a light shining on her like she was the opening act of a play?

He clicked off the light.

"What are you doing?" she asked.

"We're talking." He leaned back in the chair. Although he was anything but relaxed. "How did you become an escort?"

There was a slight hesitation before she answered. "My friend got me into it."

"Some friend."

Another pause. "Actually, she is a pretty good friend. She's one of those people who sees the glass as always being full—like to the brim."

"And you're not?"

"I wouldn't say that. I see the glass as half-full, and it's my job to get the water to the top."

He laughed. "You sound like my oldest brother. He views everything as his job."

She joined in with his laughter. It was a hearty laugh, almost too loud for a woman. But he liked it. He liked its sincerity and lack of inhibition. "You figured me out," she said. "I am the oldest. I have two younger brothers. Both pains in the butt."

"I think that's the job of younger brothers."

"Is your younger brother a pain?"

The smile wilted on his face. "I didn't say I had a younger brother."

"Oh," she said. "I guess I just assumed you had another brother when you were talking about your oldest brother."

The tension left his shoulders. But the scare was a strong reminder that he had no business sharing information with the woman. "No more talking," he said. "Take off your dress."

"In the dark? But how will you see?"

He got up from the chair. "I'll use my imagination."

There was a long pause, and he wondered if she would leave. Physical force played no part in the equation, but he couldn't help getting up and positioning himself between her and the door. There was a whisper of material.

"It's off," she said.

It was strange, but having the lights off seemed to make everything more intense. He could hear her breathing. Smell her sweet, earthy scent. And visualize exactly what she looked like in nothing but her bra and boy shorts. His penis came to full attention once again, and he found it difficult to speak around the desire that clogged his throat.

"Now your bra." He moved closer to the bed. "Hand it to me." Something soft brushed his bare stomach, and he reached for it, his fingers curling around the bra. After a year at French Kiss, he knew his bras. It was slightly padded, and the material wasn't top grade. As for the size, he would guess 34B. He lifted the cup to his nose, and her herbal scent filled his nostrils.

"Now the panties," he said, his voice muffled in the cotton. This time, she took longer. So long that he moved a step closer, his leg brushing the mattress.

"Promise you won't turn on the light? Not that I'm deformed or anything. I just don't exactly have a perfect body." She was talking with her hands again. He could feel the shift of air.

"From here, it looks pretty perfect to me."

Another pause before a whisper of material and her hand brushed a line of fire across his bare stomach. He drew in a sharp breath and tried to calm the heat that ate its way through him as she apologized in a husky voice.

"I'm sorry. I didn't realize that you were . . . so close."

Oh, he was close, all right. It would only take one stroke from her fist for him to shoot the moon. He gritted his teeth. "Lie down."

"I'm not having sex with—"

"No, dammit! We are *not* having sex!" He didn't know if he was yelling at her or himself. Thinking he had frightened her, he started to apologize, when she came right back at him.

"Well, how the heck do I know that? I'm naked!" He

could feel the shift of air as her hands waved. "You're obviously naked. And sex is usually what happens when two people are alone in a bedroom naked."

He released a frustrated sigh. "Granted. But it's not going to happen with us."

"Why?"

He could've lied, but concealed by darkness, he chose not to. "Because then I wouldn't be a fucked-up pervert. I'd just be a loser who has to pay for sex. Now please lie down."

"Fine."

The thump of butt to mattress made his anger leave, but none of his desire. Especially when he heard the wisp of skin against the satin of the duvet. He could picture her now. Seductively stretched out on the bed like he'd wanted the other night. But now she was naked. Completely naked. And all his.

He should've returned to the chair. He was too close. But maybe this would be the final test. If he could resist when a naked woman was only inches away, it would prove that he had control over his body.

And hers.

"Scoot over," he said. "I'm not going to touch you. I'm just going to lie next to you." He waited to hear her shifting before he lowered himself to the bed. The satin still held her heat. But rather than further ignite him, it calmed him enough that he was able to roll to his side and face her.

"Now I want you to close your eyes and touch yourself. And everywhere you touch, I want you to tell me what you feel . . . everything that you feel."

CHAPTER SEVEN

$\mathcal{I}$t wasn't his words that had Eden lying so rigid on the bed as much as his presence only inches away, like a tiger waiting to pounce. She knew he wanted to touch her—to gobble her up—and yet he held himself in check. Why? That was what she wanted to find out. And why she hadn't turned on the flashlight she brought with her the moment she stepped into the door. Shining a light on him would've concluded that the Dark Seducer was Nash Beaumont. But illuminating his handsome features wouldn't have told the entire story.

That's what Eden wanted. She wanted the entire story behind why a billionaire would pay not to touch women. And she knew to get that story she would need to play his game. Except playing his game was dangerous. Because as scared as she was of being eaten by a tiger, she was also sexually excited by the prospect. More sexually excited than she'd been in her life. Her entire body tingled, from her tight nipples to the spot between her legs. Not just from the heat of his body, but also from his breathing. He wasn't panting like a pervert. It was more a deep, controlled inhalation and exhalation that said he was turned on...and trying not to be.

While he was controlling his breathing, hers had stopped. Her breath hung in her chest as she waited for his first command. It came on an exhalation. More air than sound.

"Touch your breast."

She could've pretended to do it, but somehow she knew he would know. So she did what he asked. She awkwardly rested her hand over her left breast. It felt strange touching herself when a man watched. And no matter how dark, she didn't doubt for a second that he watched, his unusual-colored eyes cutting through the blackness to laser out her deepest secrets. A few seconds later, he proved her right.

"Don't just touch it." His breath fell warm against her ear. "Caress it. Test its weight." He paused, giving her time to do what he asked. "Tell me how it feels."

She awkwardly cupped and squeezed her breast, then tried to come up with words. It wasn't easy. Her mind wasn't on what she was doing as much as the man next to her. "I don't know. It's just a breast."

His breathing stopped, and she had to wonder if she was about to get kicked out again. Instead, he spoke in barely a whisper. "Then let me tell you what it feels like. It's like cradling the most precious of gifts...heavy and abundant as much as it is soft and delicate. When you hold a woman's breast, you hold her heart in your hand, the beat thumping solid and strong against your palm. Can you feel the beat?"

Touching her breast hadn't done anything for Eden, but his words did. Suddenly, she wasn't the one cradling her breast. He was. He was just using her body as the instrument of his desire. Her hand started to move. A gentle squeeze. A slight lifting. A brush of fingertips over the soft skin underneath. She could feel her heart beating, its tempo strong and rapid as heat coiled in her stomach and spread out like warm tentacles to every part of her body.

"Brush your thumb over the nipple," he continued. "Slowly. Gently." She did and sucked in her breath as the coil of heat tightened. "That's it." He shifted closer, his breath fluttering the strand of hair covering her ear. "Feel the sweet bud. Pluck it. Tease it. Is it tight enough? Or can you make it tighter?"

She could make it tighter, and she did, her breathing becoming as labored and rapid as her heartbeat. She released a moan and wiggled against the slick satin of the duvet in an attempt to find release from the grip of sensual sensation.

"Where do you burn?" he asked.

"Everywhere," she breathed.

"Everywhere? Show me. Touch the spots that burn."

Feeling completely disconnected, she followed his commands like a puppet with strings. Strings that were attached to the steady controlled breathing at her ear. She continued to brush her thumb over her nipple and squeeze her breast as her hand slipped to the other breast and nipple.

"Here," she said. "In my breasts."

"Where else?"

She released one breast and slid her hand down her rib cage and over her stomach to the spot beneath the strip of pubic hair. "Down here."

His breathing accelerated, but he quickly regulated it. "Slip inside the warm lips. Are they slick? Wet?" She was breathing too rapidly to answer, and he didn't make her. Instead, he continued. "Touch the very point that burns. Touch it and tell me how it feels."

She swallowed and tried to speak around her desire. "It feels amazing. Like all the heat in my body has collected and is throbbing beneath my fingers."

There was a long pause, and his voice hitched when he spoke. "Stro-stroke it," he said. "Stroke the fire."

She did. She stroked and teased the fire until it burned hot and bright. Until her legs quivered. And her body tensed.

"Reach for it, baby," he whispered.

She tried. She really tried. But like every other time, the fulfillment her body craved remained just out of her reach. There her tense body hung on the side of the cliff, unable to reach the summit.

"I c-can't," she said as her hand fell away in frustration. "I can't get there."

A sound like a low growl rumbled in her ear just before hot, skilled fingers covered the spot between her legs. With just a few strokes, the coil of heat exploded. It was like she reached the summit and then jumped off the cliff in a free fall that had her hips lifting and a part scream/part moan coming from her mouth. When she finally glided back to earth, Eden realized what had happened. She had just had an orgasm. And Nash Beaumont had given it to her.

She turned her head, and her nose brushed his. "You touched me." It was a really stupid thing to say, but somehow it managed to encompass exactly how she felt. He had touched. In more ways than one.

They lay there for a few moments with their noses touching and his breathing falling all hot and ragged against her lips. This time, he didn't seem to be making any effort to control it. She couldn't help feeling a little cocky about being responsible, and suddenly, she wanted to make him lose even more control. She wanted to make him soar over the cliff of desire like she had. But before she could lean in and kiss him, he spoke through clenched teeth.

"Let me go."

At first, she was confused. Let him go? He was the one who had invited her there. The one who issued all the orders. The one who had given her an orgasm. A wonderful, earth-shattering, mood-enhancing orgasm that made her smile despite the crazy position she found herself in. Her smile faded when she felt his hand twitch. A hand that was still between her legs. Correction, a hand she was still holding between her legs. Not just with a nail-digging grip, but also with the tight clench of her thighs.

Her face heated with embarrassment, and she was thankful for the darkness. "Sorry." She released him. And as soon as she did, he rolled from the bed as if she had cooties. Which made the giddiness melt right out of her.

It turned to annoyance when a door slammed and a rectangular shaft of light shone through the darkness. She sat up and stared at the bathroom door for a moment before she reached for the lamp. She wasn't surprised that it didn't work. Nor did the other one. With no other choice, she searched in the dark for her clothes. Even after she was fully dressed, Nash still hadn't come out. She located her purse and checked her cell phone, waiting a good fifteen minutes before she grew concerned. Was he sick? Injured? Maybe she had unknowingly kneed him during her orgasm. Or maybe he was just upset that he hadn't been able to reach orgasm too.

She knocked on the bathroom door. "Umm...excuse me. But are you okay?"

There was a long stretch of silence followed by a harsh

laugh. "No, I'm not okay. I'm as far from okay as you can get." It sounded like he'd turned to the door so his next words would be heard loud and clear. "Your money is on the dresser. I'm sure you know your way out."

She stared at the doorknob. That was it? He was just going to give her a great orgasm, pay her a couple thousand dollars, and kick her out without even a goodbye? Of course, when she thought of it like that, he was the one getting the short end of the stick. Why that would bother her, she didn't know. But it did bother her. It made her feel like she hadn't contributed anything. And Eden was the type of person who always contributed her fair share.

"Look." She leaned closer to the crack in the door. "You shouldn't feel bad. Like I said before, it happens to the best of us." She paused. Or it had happened to the best of us. Now she wasn't in the no-orgasm club anymore. Which made her feel even worse for him. "Is it the touching part that turns you off? Because if it's the touching part, maybe you just need to be touched. Not by me, of course. But maybe by another escort."

As soon as the words were out of her mouth, Eden wanted to take them back. She didn't know why, but she couldn't stand the thought of another escort touching him. Or any woman for that matter. Which was completely insane. He wasn't hers to fix. He was just a story.

A sad story.

A very, very sad story.

Although he didn't sound that sad when his voice came booming through the door. "Get the fuck out!"

No longer feeling so sorry for him, she glared at the door and yelled back. "Well, you don't have to be so grumpy!" Turning on a heel, she pulled the small flashlight from her purse and clicked it on. She thought about faking him out by slamming the bedroom door and waiting for him to come out. But then what kind of story would she have? Somehow she couldn't see Stella liking a story about the panty billionaire giving one of her reporters an orgasm. No, Eden needed a story about his dark side. Which meant that she needed to dig deeper. It was unlikely that she'd be invited back. But she could delve a little more into his past and figure out what had caused his problem. What made Nash Beaumont tick?

On the way to the door, she noticed the dresser and turned the flashlight toward it. She wasn't surprised to see her phone and a stack of money. Money that would go a long way if she did end up getting fired from the newspaper. It would also make her an escort for real.

Ignoring the stack of money, Eden grabbed her phone before heading for the door. Tonight she had used the valet service, and once outside, she handed her stub to the young man standing by the valet booth. He turned out to be the same young man who had delivered the fruit basket to Nash's suite the first night.

Jeremy flashed her a sly grin. "Twice in one week. You must have some hidden talent."

Eden lifted a brow. "Obviously, you don't have an older sister to teach you when to keep your mouth shut."

He laughed. "A little sister, and it's my job to tell her when to shut her trap." He made a little bow. "I'll be right back with your car, ma'am." A few minutes later, he pulled up in the old Volvo Eden had inherited from her grandfather when he had to stop driving because of his cataracts. The rusted door squeaked as the kid hopped out, looking terribly confused.

"I thought you'd be able to afford better than this piece of crap." He held the door while she climbed in. "You shouldn't have turned me down. Obviously, beggars can't be choosers."

She patted his chubby cheek before getting in. "You need to remember that people don't tip for insolence."

"After seeing your car, I couldn't take money from you anyway." He slammed the squeaky door. "Hell, it's more beat-up than mine."

Eden ignored the statement, but couldn't help smiling as she pulled away. As much as her little brothers were pests, she realized that she missed them. Maybe she would invite them for a visit. But only after her story broke, and she got a promotion.

It didn't take her long to get home. That late at night, the traffic was minimal. Parking for her apartment was in the back of the complex. She squeezed the Volvo into her numbered spot and had just gotten out when a black SUV pulled in behind her. The driver was out and had her pinned against the car with one hand wrapped around her throat before she could even release a squeak.

He wore a black ski mask, and his eyes and mouth looked distorted through the holes of the mask. At first, she had to wonder if Nash had followed her and was much crazier than she'd thought. But then she realized that this man wasn't close to being Nash Beaumont's height, and his breath smelled like stale beer instead of mint and heat. When he spoke, his voice was nothing like smooth Southern honey. It was gravelly and scary.

"There are rules to follow, little girl." His hand tightened on her throat. "And if you want to play the game, you have to follow those rules." Eden tried to lift her knee and smash him in the nuts, but he was pressed too tightly against her. Still, he must've felt her effort because his hand tightened even more until she couldn't breathe at all. She clawed for release, but he ignored her efforts and leaned in close to her ear. "Now learn the rules quickly or you're going to get hurt."

Then he released her, and while she bent at the waist and tried to catch her breath, he grabbed her purse. She couldn't see what he took out of it before tossing it to the ground, but she assumed it was her wallet. She waited for him to drive away, then she picked up her purse and, on legs that felt as wobbly as Jell-O, staggered to the stairwell. Thankfully, it was only two flights to her apartment. Once inside, she locked the door and dead-bolted it before her knees gave out and she slipped to the floor.

It took numerous deep breaths to get her heart rate to slow. Once it was no longer throbbing in her ears, she opened her purse and searched through it. As she had assumed, her wallet was gone. But both cell phones were there. She pulled her new one out, intending to call the cops, and then realized that she couldn't. The only game she'd been playing lately was the escort game. So she had little doubt that the guy was from the escort service. If she called the cops, they would investigate, and Eden's story would be out. She wasn't ready for that to happen. At least not until it came out in print with her name in the byline.

Still, she would go crazy if she didn't share what happened with someone. And since she wasn't about to worry her family, there was only one someone she could call. It took five rings before Madison picked up, and Eden could tell by her voice that she'd been sound asleep.

"Georgie? Are you having trouble sleeping again,

sweetie?" Madison yawned. "So tell me about your time in the movies. I love the story about how you and Marilyn snuck off the set—"

"It's me," Eden said.

"Eden? What's wrong?"

She took a shaky breath. "Something happened tonight. I got mugged by—"

Before Eden could even finish, Madison cut in. "Give me your address, and I'll be right there."

Not more than ten minutes later, a knock sounded on the door. Eden was still sitting on the floor, and it took a few minutes to climb to her wobbly legs and answer. Madison stood in the hallway wearing a fur coat, silk nightgown, and high heels.

"What happened?" She clicked into the room. "Did someone break into your apartment?" She turned, and her eyes zeroed in on Eden's neck. "Oh my God, someone tried to kill you?"

Eden touched her neck and flinched. Obviously, she'd gone into shock, because she hadn't even realized her neck hurt until that moment. "I think if the guy in the ski mask wanted to kill me, he would've. He just wanted to warn me about playing a game. And since the only game I've been playing lately is the escort game, I'm thinking it might've been the guy who runs your escort service. Does Zac drive a black SUV?"

Madison nodded. "But why would Zac want to mug you? The guy makes a fortune."

"I think he was pissed that I met with Na—the Dark Seducer—tonight, and so Zac followed me home from the hotel."

Madison's eyes widened. "You met with the Dark Seducer again? But I thought you only wanted to meet with him once for research."

Eden didn't want to keep lying to Madison, especially when she had raced over to be with her. But Eden worried that, if she told her about the newspaper article, Madison would let Nash's identity slip before the story broke.

"I just needed a few more details," she said. "And I didn't think it would hurt anything since the Dark Seducer had asked for me by name."

For the first time since she had known her, Madison's eyes registered fear. "He called the escort service and asked for you by name?" When Eden nodded, Madison looked even more scared. "Then it was Zac. He can get very upset if he thinks people are trying to horn in on his business."

"But didn't you tell him that I was only taking over for Chloe as part of my research?"

Madison shook her head. "He never would've gone along with it. So I cooked it up with Chloe on the sly, thinking that he would never find out." She hurried over and slammed the door and locked it before turning to Eden. "You've got to promise me that you won't play escort again, Eden. This is not a game. Zac has done some bad things in his life, and next time, he could really hurt you."

It was a promise Eden had no trouble making. Her days as an escort were over. Not only because she didn't want to die, but also because Nash was never going to ask for her again.

And she didn't know why that made her so sad.

CHAPTER EIGHT

"I'm glad to see that you're finally taking the dress code seriously, Nash," Deacon said as he and Nash sat at his desk and went over the comps from the survey.

Not that Nash was paying any attention to the list of numbers on the computer screen. Instead, his mind was fixated on one thing—the feel of Eden's hot, quivering flesh beneath his fingers as she cried out her orgasm. Which explained why he was wearing a suit. Loose pants and a long suit jacket worked much better for hiding a raging hard-on than tight jeans.

"So what do you think?" Deacon asked.

Nash thought he was screwed. He had hoped that giving Eden her first orgasm would calm the desire she'd ignited. But it had only fed his hunger. And now instead of thinking about her occasionally, he thought about her every second.

"Nash? Are you listening to me?"

He blinked the image of pretty hazel eyes away and

looked at his brother. "I think we should've gone with an independent marketing company and skipped the give-away. It's obvious from the results that these women are just brownnosing to win tickets to the fall fashion show."

Deacon sat back and steepled his fingers. "That's exactly what I think. So let's call an independent and set one up."

"I'll get on it."

"No, I'll handle it," Deacon said. "You need to talk with Grayson again. He's still not moving on the swimsuit catalog models. He's got it in his head that he has to find the perfect woman for the cover shot. I want the perfect one too, but on schedule. We have Miles shooting the photos in Fiji on the Monday after the Lover's Ball. That's less than two weeks away."

Nash got up. "I'll go talk to him now. Are you and Olivia going on the shoot?"

"No, we're headed to Paris that week."

"Business, I presume."

Deacon grinned. "Of course."

Grayson's office wasn't really an office. It was more a studio. His brother had removed all the office furniture and filled the windowed space with easels and canvases and the purple velvet divan he stole from the lobby. The divan now had one of the top supermodels in the world draped over it. Naked, of course. Rarely did a woman enter Grayson's domain and keep her clothes on.

As Nash entered the room, he couldn't help but look. Only a blind man wouldn't. But her phenomenal body didn't get a rise out of him. Lately, a sassy escort seemed to be the only one with that power.

"Hel-lo, Na-ish," Natalia said in her thick Russian accent.

He flashed a smile and kept his gaze on her face. "I see that Grayson finally talked you into posing for him."

"How could I resist posing for a true artist? Every woman wants to be worshiped, and Gar-a-a-son does that with each stroke of his brush. Unlike his brother. I thought you were going to call me."

Nash didn't remember telling her that, but he chose not to point that out. "You know I'm not much of a talker, Nat."

Natalia sent him a seductive smile. "We don't have to talk."

Not knowing what to say to that, Nash tried to change the subject. "So how long have you been here?"

"A good two hours." She directed her gaze at Grayson. "Look at him. He's so wrapped up in his art, he doesn't even know you're here."

It was true. Grayson had gone to that place he always went when he painted. He could sketch and talk all day long, but when he picked up a paintbrush, there was no more communication. There was just total concentration, his eyes flickering back and forth between the canvas in front of him and Natalia. And since he could paint all day without taking a break, Nash was forced to end the painting session.

"Do you think you could give us just a few minutes, Natalia?"

"Of course." She quickly slipped into the robe that was draped over the back of the divan. As soon as she was clothed, Grayson came out of his trance.

"What are you doing, Nat? I wasn't—" He finally noticed Nash. "Hey, what brings you here?"

Nash waited for Natalia to exit before he spoke. "Deacon is getting antsy about the swimsuit catalog. And I can't say as I blame him, Gray. The shoot is only weeks away. Please tell me Nat is your choice."

Grayson turned the canvas. "Does this look like the perfect cover model to you?"

The painting wasn't complete, but it was still beautiful. It always amazed Nash just how talented his brother was. Not that he would ever tell him. "I think if we want to sell lingerie, she needs to be wearing some."

Grayson didn't get the joke. Of course, he never got the joke when it came to his art. "If her body doesn't work naked, it won't work clothed." He put the canvas back on the easel and studied it. "Like I told Deacon, it's not about getting the right lingerie as much as getting the right woman to display it. And Natalia is just not right."

"She looks pretty perfect to me. Just choose her, Gray, and be done with it."

Grayson shook his head. "Perfect isn't what I want for the cover of the new catalog. I want...imperfect perfection."

"What the hell is that supposed to mean?"

He cleaned off his paintbrush. "It means that I'm still looking for the right cover model."

"Well, you better hurry up, little brother. If you don't find someone soon, Deacon is going to find her for you."

"I know. I have another group of models coming in tomorrow." He released a long sigh that had Nash laughing.

"What a tough life you have, Gray."

Grayson grinned. "Yeah, it is, isn't it? And speaking of

tough lives, what has you so tense lately? And don't give me any crap about bra sales being down. Deacon is the one who worries about business. You usually don't worry about anything."

"What makes you think I'm tense?"

Grayson studied him. While all the Beaumont brothers had the same color eyes as their mother, Grayson's eyes were also the exact shape with a clearness that made you feel as if they could delve into your deepest secrets. But Nash had worked too hard to keep his pain from his brothers to let any of it show now. So he told a half-truth to throw Grayson off.

"I met a girl. She's a bartender." That much was true. The escort part he would keep to himself.

Grayson tipped his head back and laughed. "It figures. You're surrounded with supermodels day in and day out, and you choose a bartender." He gave Nash the once-over. "So are you trying to impress her by dressing the part of an executive billionaire?"

"No, I'm not trying to impress her." He walked to the windows. The view wasn't as nice as the view from Deacon's office. He couldn't see the Golden Gate Bridge. But he could see an edge of the hotel where he'd given Eden her first orgasm. And if that wasn't trying to impress a woman, he didn't know what was. But little good it did him when he threw her out before she'd even come down from her high. He ran a hand through his hair. Damn, he *was* screwed up.

"So I guess this girl is different," Grayson said.

Nash had to concede the point. Eden was different. She was an anomaly that he couldn't seem to figure out.

For an escort, she didn't take orders well. She was sassy. And she had walked out of the room and forgotten to take the four thousand he'd left on the dresser. Or not forgotten. Escorts didn't forget money. She had just chosen to leave it. Which made no sense whatsoever. She must need money if her side job was bartending.

Unless... she viewed her orgasm as being worth four thousand dollars. In which case, she had turned the tables and made him the hooker.

He turned back to Grayson. "Yeah, she's different, all right."

"By the sad-sack look on your face, I'm going to make a guess and say her difference lies in the fact that she's unaffected by the Beaumont magnetic charm."

Nash snorted. "You're starting to sound like Dad. We both know that the Beaumonts have no more power over women than any other man."

"Maybe Deacon and I don't. But you've always had something, Nash. All you had to do back in Louisiana was smile, and the women flocked to you like ducks to a pond. And now you're telling me that there's a girl on God's green earth that doesn't like you?" One side of Grayson's mouth quirked in a smirk. "I must meet this woman. Where does she bartend?"

Realizing his mistake in telling his little brother anything about Eden, Nash paused and tried to come up with a good lie.

Fortunately, Grayson wasn't one to push things. "Okay," he said, "if you want to keep her a secret, I'll honor that. You want to get some takeout tonight? The LSU basketball game is on."

Nash headed for the door. "That's sounds good, but I've had enough takeout. I'll cook. You want tacos or lasagna?"

"Tacos, and if you go to the store, get some more sardines for Jonathan Livingston. He ate the last can this morning."

Nash shook his head. "We really have lost our redneck cards. We've gone from owning hunting dogs to owning a seagull that craps on our balcony. We should shoot the damned bird and be done with it."

"I wouldn't do that if I were you," Grayson said. "Olivia will skin you alive if you hurt that bird. He was her pet long before we moved into her house."

Once Nash left Grayson's studio, he went back to his office and tried to concentrate on work, but his gaze kept returning to the digital time displayed in the upper right-hand corner of his computer. Every second ticked closer and closer to happy hour at The Lemon Drop. But he wasn't going. He damned well refused to go. He'd done what he set out to do. He'd given her an orgasm. And in return, she'd given him a permanent hard-on. One that was only going to get worse if he saw her again.

A knock on the door startled him out of his thoughts. He turned to find the UPS guy standing there.

"Mrs. Beaumont said you had a package for me," he said.

Since Nash didn't have a package, there was only one reason for Olivia to send the man over. She was tired of waiting for Nash to figure out Doug's sexual preference and was forcing the issue. Nash should've been annoyed, but instead, he was relieved to have a distraction from the damned clock.

"Hey, Doug," he said. "How's it going?"

"Good, sir." Doug stepped into the room. After a full day of work, most people looked wrinkled and mussed. Doug looked like he had just stepped out of his bathroom after a full two hours of grooming. His uniform shirt and shorts were starched, his knee socks perfectly even, and his hair moussed. So Nash couldn't help but wonder if Olivia wasn't right and Doug was a good match for the fastidious Samuel.

"So I guess you're ready to call it a night," Nash said. "Probably looking forward to getting home to the family and kids."

Doug wrote something on his clipboard. "Actually, I'm not married, and I don't have any kids." He glanced around. "So do you have the package ready, sir?"

"I already took it to the post office. So no wife or kids, huh? A girlfriend?"

Doug's eyes swept back to him. "No, sir. And if you don't need to mail anything, I'll just let you get back to your work."

Nash should've let him go but he knew that if he didn't get the information, Olivia would keep sending the guy over for boxes that Nash didn't have. So he decided to quit beating around the bush and get straight to the point.

"Do you like women, Doug?"

Doug's mouth dropped open for a second before he pulled himself together. "Umm...yes, sir. Of course I like women. Some of my closest friends are women."

"I'm not talking about friends," Nash said, but before he could ask if he might be interested in going out with Samuel, Kelly showed up.

"I just got a call from a woman claiming to be a reporter for *Forbes* magazine—" She paused when he saw Doug. "Hey, Doug. You're working late."

Doug didn't take his gaze off Nash. "It's karaoke night at McGee's. I'll be there until eleven." He winked before he walked out.

Well, that answered that question.

Kelly's gaze followed Doug and then returned to Nash. "What was that all about? You know he's gay, right?"

"Let me guess," Nash said dryly. "You've known that all along."

"Of course. And I think you should know that, living in San Francisco, you've got a fifty-fifty chance that a guy's door swings the other way."

"Thanks for the info. Now what's this about a reporter from *Forbes*?"

"Not a reporter as much as another Lothario groupie. Before I gave her an answer, I called the magazine. They've never heard of a Tulip Bernstein. But at least this woman was more original than the flower delivery girl who thought that a dozen roses would get her into your office. Who would send a guy roses?"

Hopefully, not Doug, but after the wink, Nash wouldn't be surprised. He might've questioned Kelly about the imposter reporter if the time on his computer hadn't finally hit five o'clock. Like Cinderella at the stroke of midnight, he knew he had to leave. It was stupid and totally ridiculous, but he couldn't seem to stop himself as he made his excuses to Kelly and hurried out of the office.

He ended up at The Lemon Drop a mere ten minutes later only to discover that Eden wasn't working. Which put him in an extremely foul mood. After sitting at the bar and drinking enough sweet tea to send him to the bathroom three times, he almost got in a fight with a guy who wouldn't leave one of the female patrons alone. Nash would've loved it if the guy had argued. Instead, he left, leaving Nash with a grateful blonde who wanted to buy him another iced tea. But he didn't want another drink. Or the blonde. He wanted a woman with raven hair who talked with her hands and wouldn't stay the hell out of his mind.

Thanking the blonde, he flipped some money on the bar for his drinks and left. He walked to his truck and then cussed a blue streak when he noticed the ticket under the windshield wiper. He jerked it off and read it, then glanced around for the loading zone sign. Sure enough, the sign was located right next to his front bumper. Something he hadn't noticed in his hurry to get inside and see Eden. Stuffing the ticket in his jacket pocket, he started to climb into his truck when he noticed the bumper sticker on the car parked in front of him.

Nudists Undress Quicker.

Instead of making him laugh, the sticker made him think of Eden and what she was doing tonight if she wasn't bartending. The thought of her getting naked with another man was not a laughing matter. Getting in his truck, he grabbed the burner phone from the cup holder. The same guy answered.

"How can I help you, Mr. Jones?"

"Eden." He paused for only a second. "Tonight."

"I'm sorry, sir," the guy said. "Eden doesn't work here

anymore. But I'm sure we can find you another woman that you'll like just as well."

"Not likely." Nash hung up and tossed the phone so hard at the passenger's seat that he cracked the screen. By the time he got home, his mood hadn't improved. It didn't help that when he pulled into the driveway, he suddenly remembered that he was supposed to cook dinner for Grayson. And with nothing in the house, he had no choice but to go to the grocery store.

"Shit." He thumped the steering wheel with his fist before he popped the stick into reverse and started to back up. He slammed on the brakes when he glanced in his rearview mirror and noticed the passing car. The same old, silver Volvo that had been parked in front of his truck at The Lemon Drop. Obviously, the guy that he'd pissed off at the bar had followed him home and was looking to get even. Nash was more than happy to oblige him.

Turning off his truck, he jumped out and jogged across the street. The guy had put on a baseball cap—no doubt as some kind of disguise—and Nash knocked it off as he opened the door and pulled him out. But the light weight of the man had him freezing, as did the startled hazel eyes that stared up at him.

"Eden?" He couldn't explain the relief the one word gave him. She wasn't with some other guy. She was here. Right here. The soft skin of her arms beneath his hands, her herbal scent filling his lungs, and her gold-flecked eyes staring up at him with... anger? The answer to the question came when she hauled off and slapped him hard across the face.

"It was you who sent someone to threaten me the other

night, wasn't it?" She spoke between gritted teeth. "You caught my slip about your little brother and figured out that I knew who you were and wanted to make sure I wouldn't tell anyone."

So Eden knew who he was and probably had known since he was stupid enough to show up at The Lemon Drop. But that news didn't concern him as much as the other news.

His hands tightened on her arms. "Someone threatened you?"

"Don't try to play stupid now. Why else would you be at my grandparents' house?" She grabbed the front of his shirt in her fist and pulled him closer. "And if you think you can gain my silence by using my Mimi and Pops, you can think again, Nash."

It was a mixture of things that caused Nash to short-circuit. The fact that someone had threatened her. The way his name sounded coming from her lips. The feel of her knuckles pressed into the center of his chest. And the brush of her hips against the hard-on he'd been fighting all day. Unable to fight against his desires anymore, he did what he'd wanted to do ever since she strutted into his hotel suite and offered him a slow burn.

Nash kissed her.

CHAPTER NINE

It was hard to think when being consumed by the big, bad wolf. And Nash Beaumont was the big, bad wolf. Not only was he a master of seduction and manipulation, he was a stalker. Something she had figured out after spending the entire day stalking him. And she might be able to overlook him stalking her at work, but he was not going to get away with harming her grandma. No matter how hungry his wolfy lips, or how nippy his wolfy teeth, or how salaciously hot his wolfy tongue felt against hers.

And she was going to pull back from his kiss and tell him just that . . . any second now.

He didn't kiss gently. He devoured her as his hands gripped her butt cheeks, pulling her against the thick, hard ridge beneath his fly. At the feel of his erection, a moan escaped from a place deep down inside her—a mating call that sounded both aggressive and needy. Nash answered the call by moving her out of the opened doorway and pinning her against the back door of the Volvo with his hips.

"I want you." He muttered the words while still kissing her. "Now."

Eden didn't quite understand what the word *now* actually meant until she heard the zing of a zipper, followed by her sweatpants being tugged down.

She ended the kiss and grabbed them before they dropped to her feet. "Are you crazy? We can't have sex in the middle of the street."

Nash stared at her, then glanced around, as if noticing where they were for the first time, before he stepped away and got mean.

"What the hell are you doing to me?" He zipped his pants.

"Me? I wasn't the one who pinned you against a car."

"No. You were just the one who followed me home, asking for it."

"Asking for it? I did not ask for it. And you should talk, Mr. Stalker Man. What were you doing at The Lemon—?" She paused. "Followed you home? You live here?"

About then, a blinding light flashed in her eyes. She squinted and wasn't surprised when her grandfather yelled down from the top balcony of his house. "Eden? Is that you?" The light moved to Nash, who had turned at her grandfather's voice. "Nathan?"

"Not Nathan, Hammond," her grandmother scolded. "How many times do I have to tell you that the nice young boys who live next door are Nash and Grayson?"

Eden looked at Nash. "You live next to my grandparents?"

"Shit" was Nash's only reply before her grandfather continued.

"Well, I don't know how nice that one is. From what I

could tell, he was trying to get into our granddaughter's pants."

Eden was mortified, and she actually thought about hopping in her car and driving off. But before she could, Nash grabbed her hand and spoke between his teeth. "Don't you even think about leaving me to deal with this alone." He slammed her car door so hard that the entire frame shook, and then pulled her across the street and up the steps to her grandparents' front door.

"What are you doing?" she asked.

"Being respectful." In the brightness of the porch light, Nash didn't look happy. But he did look hot. The photos on the web didn't come close to depicting how good-looking he was. He had a raw, rugged beauty that was all hard angles and lean muscles. Some of those muscles flexed beneath his suit jacket as he reached out to ring the doorbell.

While they waited for the door to be answered, he turned to study her like she had been studying him. In her sweats with no makeup, a scraggly ponytail, and the ugly floral scarf she'd tied around her neck to hide the bruises from the attempted strangling, she wasn't at her best. Still, she met his gaze head-on and tried not to get lost in the indigo depths of his eyes. They stared at one another for a second... or possibly an eternity before his gaze lowered to her lips. Was he going to kiss her again? God, she certainly hoped so. That hope fizzled when he spoke.

"I never should've kissed you."

Eden's anger returned. "Well, don't worry. It won't happen—"

The door opened, and Nash's gaze switched over to her grandmother, and his face transformed with a smile that left Eden breathless and stunned. She had been looking at Nash's smiles for days on the web. But those smiles didn't affect her like this one. Up close, she could see the sparkle in his eyes and the crinkles at the corners. Up close, she could see the off-kilter angle of his lips and the slight dimple in his left cheek. Up close, she could see the whiteness of his teeth and the tiny chip in one incisor. Up close, Nash Beaumont's smile was breathtaking. The type of smile that could make a woman forget her name, not to mention every single one of her goals.

"Good evening, Mrs. Huckabee," he said. "Eden and I apologize for not coming to the door sooner."

Mimi seemed as stunned by his smile as Eden was. She stared at him for a few seconds before she ushered them inside. Thankfully, she was dressed. Her skirt and blouse were throwbacks from the hippie era. The skirt was floor-length and floral and the blouse loose and bohemian. For being in her eighties, Mimi was fit and agile—no doubt due to her yoga and vegetarian diet.

"No need to apologize," she said as she led them up the stairs to the main living area. "Good karma isn't something to question as much as enjoy. Come on in to the dining room; Hammond and I were just getting ready to sit down to dinner. I'd like to know how you met my granddaughter."

"We can't stay for dinner, Mimi," Eden said. "We were just…" She couldn't think of a lie to save her soul. Fortunately, Nash wasn't so dimwitted.

"Eden was dropping by my suit jacket. I left it at her work."

"The bar or the new—" Mimi started, but Eden cut her off before she could blow her cover.

"The Lemon Drop. We met at The Lemon Drop."

Mimi nodded as she reached the top of the stairs. "Bars do seem to be the place to hook up these days. In my day, you hooked up at rock concerts."

"We hooked up at a Creedence Clearwater concert," her grandfather said. Unlike her grandmother, he hadn't put on clothes. He came in from the balcony as naked as the day he was born. Thankfully, the large watering pot he carried covered the most embarrassing parts.

"I told you to get dressed, Hammond," Mimi scolded as she hurriedly grabbed a throw blanket from the back of the couch. "You know that Eden doesn't like us flaunting our beliefs."

Pops exchanged the watering pot for the blanket. "And yet she can almost have sex in the middle of the street." Before Eden's face could finish catching fire, the doorbell rang. "That would be your brother Gary," Pops said to Nash. "I saw him painting through the window and hollered at him to join us."

"Grayson, Hammond." Mimi started for the stairs. "Nash and Grayson."

When Mimi went to answer the door and Pops went to get clothes on, Eden turned to Nash and devised an escape plan. "I'll plead a headache, and you can say you want to make sure I get home safely."

He walked over to the Woodstock poster hanging on the wall. It was hard to keep her eyes off his butt and how nice it looked beneath the soft wool of his pants. He wore the expensive suit as well as he wore the Henley and jeans. Except the suit made him look more dangerous. Or maybe just more powerful. It certainly made him bossier.

"I'm afraid it's too late for that," he said as he studied the poster.

"What do you mean it's too late?" she whispered. "You can't seriously think that we're going to have dinner with my grandparents as if we're a normal couple."

He turned and looked at her, the friendly smile long gone. "That's exactly what we're going to do."

Just then her grandmother came around the corner with Grayson Beaumont. Like all the Beaumonts, he was brown haired, violet eyed, and sexy as sin. But unlike his brother, there was a calming aura around Grayson that put Eden at ease from the first moment she met him. Maybe it was the sincerity in his eyes. Or the way he cradled her hand between his paint-smudged fingers. Or the soothing tone of his Southern voice.

"It's a pleasure to meet you, Eden. Your grandparents talk about you all the time. But I didn't realize that you knew my brother."

"They met at the bar where Eden works," Mimi supplied.

Grayson grinned. It was a boyish grin full of charm and a small amount of devilry. "So you're the bartender."

She was surprised that Nash had told his brother about her. And she had to wonder how much information he'd given Grayson. Certainly, he wouldn't share what had gone on in the hotel suite. Unless all the Beaumonts were kinky. It was a disturbing thought.

"Let's sit down and eat before dinner gets cold," her grandmother said as she ushered them toward the dining room. "Your grandfather can take forever to dress, which is surprising since he can undress so quickly." She nodded at the two chairs closest to the wall. "You and Nash can sit on that side, Eden."

Eden walked around the table, but before she could pull out her chair, Nash was there to do it for her. She glanced at him. His smile was back in place and stayed there for the rest of the dinner. A dinner straight from hell. Not only did Eden hate couscous and steamed vegetables, she had to sit there and listen while Mimi told one embarrassing childhood story after the other. Of course, her grandmother didn't think she was embarrassing Eden. She thought all the stories were cute.

"Remember the time you wanted to be the whale trainer for SeaWorld, Eden?" Mimi laughed, completely unaware of Eden's burning face. "She spent the entire summer on the beach with a pair of binoculars looking for that one whale she could train to do tricks. She finally had to settle on training her goldfish. Although Goldy didn't survive the first forced jump through the fiery hoop."

"I was only five years old." Eden tried to defend herself.

Mimi sent her a pointed look. "Seven. At five, you wanted to become a tap dancer and—"

Eden cut her off. "I'm sure the Beaumonts don't want to hear about my youth, Mimi."

"Actually," Nash said, "I do."

Mimi beamed at him. "Eden looked so cute in her little tutu and tap shoes for her first recital. And you should've seen the determination on her face." She smiled as if remembering. "She was going to finish that tap dance if it was the last thing she did. She didn't care that the music had cut off when the backdrop fell over. Or that the other little girls had scattered offstage like frightened baby chicks. Eden just kept right on tapping until she'd completed her routine."

"I wouldn't call it tapping," Eden said. "From the videos that Dad took, I looked like I belonged in the musical *Stomp*. It took me three years of tap before I figured out I didn't have any rhythm."

"Rhythm comes when you learn to release." Mimi closed her eyes and took a deep, even breath and slowly released it. "Release, and the natural rhythm of your body will take over without any thought whatsoever."

The words *release* and *rhythm* had Eden glancing over at Nash. Sure enough, his eyes weren't on Mimi. They were on her. And there was a hard intensity in the bluish-purple depths that left her feeling hot and breathless . . . and ready to release and find the rhythm. The fact that she could feel that way when in the presence of her grandparents showed just how much control the man had over her. Before she could pull her gaze away, her grandmother spoke.

"So do you know how to release, Nash? Because two tightly threaded screws will never fit snugly together."

Eden wanted to crawl under the table or race out to the balcony and jump off. Instead, she sat there with her face flaming as Nash answered.

"I think I can handle keeping Eden released."

Grayson coughed in his napkin. "Excuse me." His eyes twinkled. "A piece of couscous must've gone down wrong." He got up and started helping Mimi clear the table. Eden would've helped too if her grandmother hadn't stopped her.

"No, you and Nash go sit out on the balcony. It's a beautiful night for young lovers."

The "lovers" part did not sit well with Eden, and after stepping out on the balcony and closing the sliding door, she released that anger on Nash. "We should've gone with the headache. Now they've gotten the impression that we're lovers."

"I think your grandfather got that impression when he saw me pinning you against the car."

His words brought a flush to her body that matched her face. She ignored both and walked to the railing. "It wouldn't be so bad if they thought we were just having sex. But now they think it's something more." Her shoulders slumped. "Why do you have to live next door to my grandparents? I thought you lived in some big mansion in Pacific Heights. And what were you doing at my work?"

"I was thirsty." He moved to stand next to her and rested his arms on the railing. He had taken off his suit jacket and rolled the sleeves of his dress shirt to display strong forearms and an expensive watch. "And the mansion in Pacific Heights belongs to my brother Deacon." He glanced at her. "So how long have you known who I am? I'm assuming you figured it out the moment I stepped into The Lemon Drop."

"Actually, no. I didn't figure it out until I followed you outside and heard you threatening the drunk in the alleyway. Your voice changes when you're angry or..." She let the sentence drop, but he finished it for her.

"Horny?"

"I was going to say being seductive."

His bare arm brushed hers as he angled his body toward her. "Am I seductive, Eden?"

"You know you are. And isn't that the point of the

game you play? You want to seduce women and prove that they have no effect on you."

He studied her for a moment before he turned away. "Something like that. So who have you told about me?"

"No one." It was the truth. At least for now. Eventually she planned to tell the entire world. Which for some reason made her feel extremely guilty. Not to mention kind of sleazy.

He released his breath. "Good. I hope you realize the damage that could be done if you did."

"And I certainly wouldn't want to damage the reputation of the panty billionaire."

He laughed. "I was thinking more of the damage to the image your grandparents have of you. I wonder what they'd think if they found out that their sweet, tap-dancing granddaughter has decided to excel at something besides whale training?"

Obviously, Nash didn't know her grandparents very well. They would probably jump for joy to find out she wasn't as uptight as they thought she was. They would be more disappointed when they found out she had thrown their neighbor under the bus just for a good story. But Eden wasn't going to think about that now. Or about how the moonlight gilded Nash's dark hair and eyes with silver.

"Why an escort?" he asked. "You come from a good family who loves you. Why would you choose that profession? And don't tell me you do it for the money. If you needed money, I'm sure you could borrow it from your grandparents."

This time she had no trouble telling the truth. "Maybe

I don't want to take things from my family. Maybe I want to make it on my own." From the corner of her eye, she watched as he nodded.

"Lately, I've felt like I've been on someone else's roller-coaster ride. A roller-coaster ride that never slows down long enough to let me off."

"French Kiss?"

Again he nodded. "I know it's crazy. Most men would kill to be in my position. And I love it most of the time, but there are times when I feel like I've stepped into someone else's life."

"So if you don't want to sell panties, what do you want to do?"

He stared out at the night. "I wanted to start my own company based on a home security app I invented that would alert you if you forgot to lock your doors, close your garage, or turn off the water. But another company beat me to the punch and got it out on the market. And to be truthful, I wasn't that disappointed." He glanced over at her. "So to answer your question…I don't have a clue what I want to do with my life."

It surprised her how lost he looked and how much sympathy the look evoked. He had started out as the Dark Seducer and had moved to the arrogant billionaire. And now he was just a man. A man with as many faults and insecurities as everyone else.

Just then the sliding doors opened, and Mimi stuck her head out. "You and Nash better get yourselves in here before the dessert is all gone." She smiled. "Grayson seems to love my special brownies."

CHAPTER TEN

What the hell happened last night?"

Nash glanced up from the newspaper he'd been reading to see Grayson stagger into the kitchen in a pair of cutoff sweatpants. "Before or after you started giggling like a girl, telling inappropriate redneck jokes, and eating the Huckabees out of house and home? How many glasses of wine did you have?"

Grayson held up his hands. "I swear to God, I only had one. I think the old gal slipped something in it."

"More than likely it was a sugar high from all those brownies you consumed. By the time Eden and I got inside, there weren't any left."

"You hate chocolate, so stop complaining. And it wasn't a sugar high. It was more of a drug high."

Nash shook his head. "Admit it, baby brother. You've becoming a metrosexual city slicker who gets tipsy after one glass of wine."

"Let's talk about metrosexual. Are those nylon running

shorts you're wearing, Bro?" Grayson opened the refrigerator and took out a carton of milk. He opened it, sniffed, and then took a healthy drink. When he finished, he wiped his mouth with the back of his hand and looked at Nash. "So what was with you last night? I might've been giggly, but that fake smile you wore all night wasn't fooling anyone. I guess you were surprised to find out that the bartender you were lusting after was the Huckabees' granddaughter."

Surprised didn't quite cover it. Broadsided was more like it. But not as broadsided as finding out that Eden knew he was the guy who had hired her. Of course, everything had worked out in the long run. She might know who he is, but he also had found out who she is. Which meant that Nash now had something to hold over her head.

Although he wasn't sure that the fear of her grandparents finding out about her being an escort was enough to keep Eden's mouth shut. Nash had learned from experience that girls liked to tell secrets. They especially liked to tell secrets about boys and sex. Which placed Nash in a quandary of what to do to ensure that Eden wouldn't talk.

"I can see where that puts you between a rock and a hard spot," Grayson said as he carried the carton of milk with him to the cupboard where he pulled out a box of Cap'n Crunch cereal. "It's kind of hard to seduce someone's granddaughter."

"I don't want to seduce her." It was an out-and-out lie.

"Well, you might not want to seduce her, but she certainly wants to seduce you."

Nash dropped the newspaper and stared at his brother. "What?"

Grayson finished chewing the big bite of cereal he'd just scooped into his mouth. "You're so used to women falling all over you that you've lost your perspective. Eden might pretend to ignore you, but when you're not looking, her eyes say something completely different. She wants you, dude."

Eden wanted him? After the way she had treated him last night at dinner, he had been convinced that she only put up with him because he'd paid her. Except he hadn't paid her. She'd refused to take the money. And maybe she refused because she desired him as much as he desired her.

Of course, it made no difference now. Now that she knew who he was, there would be no more sexual interludes. He didn't know why the thought depressed him, and why it continued to depress him during his morning run with Grayson. A run they had to cut short when Olivia called and reminded them that they had their fitting for the Lover's Ball costumes that morning.

"I'm not wearing panty hose," Grayson said as he stared in horror at the cream-colored tights draped over the hanger Olivia had just handed him.

"Those are not panty hose," Olivia said. "They are... well, okay, in Romeo's time, I guess they were called hose, but all the men wore them."

"Well, I'm not." He lifted a puffed sleeve of the velvet top. "And I'm not wearing this either."

"It's better than wearing white balloon pants and a bunch of scarves." Deacon held up his costume. And as far as Nash could tell, it did look like balloon pants and a bunch of colored scarves.

"Now, honey," Olivia said, "you don't want to hurt

Mother's feelings, do you? She went to a lot of work to get these costumes put together. I realize that she's taken the job of party coordinator to a new level, but I'd rather see that than her moping around like she did after Michael died."

"I never mope." Olivia's mother swept into the design studio looking like the high-society matriarch she was in her fashionable dress and matching shoes. Deirdre Harrington Beaumont had always been a force to be reckoned with. When she wanted something, she usually got it. And right now, she wanted the Beaumonts to be her dress-up dolls.

"Deacon, Rudolph Valentino wore similar pants and a headdress in the movie *The Sheik* and won the hearts of millions of women. So quit your whining and go try it on." She looked at Grayson. "And that goes for you too, young man. You are Romeo, and Romeo wore tights." She turned to Nash. "I take it that you don't have anything to say about your costume, Nash."

Nash glanced at the black pants and shirt on the hanger he held. Compared to his brothers' costumes, he figured he had gotten off easy. "No, ma'am."

"Well, you might be fine with it, but I'm not. While it wasn't difficult to come up with costumes for your brothers, Lothario had me completely baffled. So I figured solid black would have to do for the seducer of women." She clapped her hands. "Now let's see them on you."

Minutes later, Nash stood in a line next to his brothers while Deirdre walked in front of them like a general with her troops.

"Nash's sleeves are too long," she said to Olivia, who walked next to her taking notes. "You'll need to have one of the seamstresses take them up." Her gaze moved to Grayson. "And Grayson's doublet is too short. It needs to cover his manly display in those tights or he could be arrested for indecent exposure."

Grayson's face flamed bright red, and he waited for Deirdre to move on to Deacon before he whispered to Nash under his breath. "I'll give you ten thousand dollars to switch costumes with me."

"Sorry, little brother, but I wouldn't be caught dead in that getup. Besides, Deirdre isn't going to let you get away with that."

"She won't have to know—"

"What is all the whispering about?" Deirdre glanced over at them. "You sound like a bunch of schoolgirls." She looked around. "And speaking of girls, where is Samuel? I want to go over some of the decorations with him."

"I'll go over the decorations with you, Mom," Olivia said. "I think Samuel has had enough party planning. He seemed upset when he found out that you were taking over his studio for fittings today and disappeared without a word."

Deirdre smiled. It wasn't a happy smile as much as a sly one. "I'm sure he did. But as amazing as you are at lingerie design, Olivia, you're horrible at decor. So if you'll finish up with the costumes, I'll go find Samuel." As soon as she was out the door, Grayson turned to Olivia.

"Help me out, Livy," he pleaded. "I can't spend an entire night in these tights. They itch like hell."

Olivia lifted her shoulders in a small shrug. "I'm sorry, Grayson, but I can't see any way out of it. If it's any consolation, everyone will be wearing masks. So people might not recognize you. And since everyone is coming dressed as lovers, I'm sure there will be other Romeos in tights."

"Great," Grayson grumbled before he turned and headed for the dressing room.

"He'll get over it, Livy," Deacon said. "As for me, I'm starting to like my costume." He placed his hands on the colored scarf tied around his waist and struck a pose similar to a runway model at the end of the catwalk.

Olivia giggled and held the back of her hand to her head. "I'm your slave, Sheik."

He grinned. "I would love to whisk you away to my sultan's tent, but I have a meeting in ten minutes. So I'll see you for lunch. And I expect you to eat more than you did for breakfast. Remember... you're eating for two." He gave her a quick kiss before he followed Grayson to the dressing room.

When he was gone, Olivia wasted no time in cornering Nash. "So did you talk to Doug?"

"Unfortunately, yes. And not only is he gay, but now he thinks I am too." He plucked at the satin shirt. "And if he could see me now, it would only confirm it."

Her eyes sparkled with humor. "I think you look a little like Zorro." She took some pins out of the cushion on her wrist and cuffed Nash's sleeve. "Now all we need to do is figure out how to get Doug and Samuel together. Samuel has been acting more and more depressed with every passing day."

"Are you sure it has to do with Doug, Olivia? Maybe Samuel's just tired of working. Hasn't he been doing it for over thirty years?"

She pinned his shirt sleeve. "He has been doing it for a long time, but designing is his life."

"Then why does he need a companion?"

"Because everyone needs a companion, Nash." She glanced up. "Are you bringing someone to the ball?"

He didn't know why an image of Eden popped into his head. But there was no way he could see Eden again. Not if he wanted to keep any kind of control over his life.

"Now why would I only bring one woman to the ball, Olivia," he said, "when there will be so many beautiful women there looking to hook up?"

She started to say something when her eyes widened. "That's it! We'll invite Doug to the Lover's Ball. It would be a perfect place for Samuel and him to hook up."

"How are you going to manage that with hundreds of people in attendance?"

Olivia eyes squinted in thought before they widened. "We could make them a couple. Like I'm going as a harem girl to match Deacon's sheik. And Mother's date is going as Lancelot to her Guinevere."

"Who is your mother bringing?"

"She hasn't told me, but I'm sure it will be someone who is wealthy and connected."

"Of course." Deirdre swept back into the room. "Why would I want some poor man who can't keep me in Gucci bags?" She glanced around. "Did Samuel come back? I can't find the blasted man anywhere."

Olivia shook her head. "But he'll turn up eventually, Mother. We have a designers' meeting this afternoon. In the meantime, are you sure you don't want me to go over the decorations with you?"

"I really wanted a man's opinion. I don't want the decorations coming off too froufrou." Deirdre's gaze pinned Nash. "What are you doing right now, Nash?"

If his mind hadn't been wrapped up in Eden, he might've been able to come up with a lie. As it was, he could only stare back at Deirdre, which had her grabbing his arm.

"Good. We'll use Samuel's empty office." She pulled him toward the office in the corner of the room.

"But, Mother," Olivia protested, "I wasn't finished with Nash."

"We'll only be a minute, darling."

Once they were inside with the door closed, Nash found his voice. "Ms. Beaumont, I really don't know anything about decor or decorations."

"Of course you don't, dear." She patted his arm before sitting down in Samuel's chair behind his desk. "Have you ever seen such a sterile office in your life?"

Samuel's office was pretty sterile. The top of the desk held only an ancient laptop, and the bookcase held design books that looked as if they had been shelved according to height and width.

"How can a man live like this?" Deirdre continued as she opened one drawer of the desk after the other. "He needs some serious help."

"Umm...I don't know if we should be going through his drawers, Ms. Beaumont."

"We're not," she said as she pulled out a notebook and thumbed through it. "I am. So who is my daughter trying to fix Samuel up with at the ball?"

Nash blinked. Obviously, Deirdre was more cunning than he'd first thought. He probably should've lied, but he had never been good at lying. Hiding his true emotions, yes. Lying, no. Especially to a mother.

"She is convinced that he's interested in Doug the UPS guy."

Deirdre stopped thumbing through the notebook and stared at him for a split second before busting out in laughter. It was a full, tip-your-head-back barroom kind of laugh that Nash wouldn't have thought went with a woman like Deirdre. Of course, he hadn't taken her for a woman who would eavesdrop and go through people's desk drawers either.

He waited for her to stop laughing before he asked, "I'm going to assume that you didn't know that Samuel was gay."

She smiled the sly smile again. "No, I've heard the rumor." She placed the notebook back in the drawer. "So how does she plan to get them together?"

"She's thinking about inviting Doug to the Lover's Ball and have him and Samuel in couples' costumes."

"Brilliant!" Deirdre clapped her hands together. "That's a marvelous idea. I must say that I'm quite proud of Olivia's deviant nature. She was always so wrapped up in French Kiss that I didn't think she'd gotten anything from me. Obviously I was wrong."

Nash cleared his throat. "Obviously."

"Well." She got up from the chair. "I guess that takes care of that."

"So we're not going to talk about decorations?"

She lifted an eyebrow. "Would you like to?"

"No. I just thought…"

Deirdre walked to the door and opened it. "I've discovered that it's best if men leave all the thinking to women."

CHAPTER ELEVEN

Why don't you just give it up, Huckabee?" Mike Foster stood in the doorway of the janitor's closet that Eden had claimed as her office after the new girl Stella hired had taken over Eden's cubicle.

Eden continued to browse the library periodical webpage. "Because I want to be a reporter."

"And I really wanted to be a professional football player." He walked in and almost tripped over the caster mop bucket Eden had pushed into the middle of the floor to make room for the old filing cabinet she was using as her desk. "But I'm not exactly what you would call coordinated."

Eden swiveled her chair around. "So you're agreeing with Stella and telling me that I suck at being a writer."

"No. I loved the piece you did on the Halloween Pooch Parade. Your flowery prose is very good at enticing people. I wanted to run out and get a 'cuddly, furry friend' after reading your article." The smile faded. "But I don't know if that style works with hard-hitting reporting."

"I just need the right story and I can be hard-hitting."

"Stella fired you, Eden." Mike studied the bulletin board she'd hung over the filing cabinet. Eden had filled it with pictures of her family: Her mom doing yoga on a retreat in Belize. Her dad teaching at the university. Her brothers doing stunts on their BMX bikes. Pops and Mimi celebrating their fiftieth on a nudist beach. Eden had used stickers to cover her grandparents' most embarrassing parts, but Mike still did a double take before he continued. "I don't care how you've fixed things up in here. You're still working in a janitor's closet while Stella hired someone else to do your job."

Eden tried to keep her chin up, but it was getting harder and harder to do. The poor lighting in the closet had given her a headache. The filing cabinet was too low for her chair, and her back hurt from leaning forward. And the disinfectant smell had her eyes burning and her stomach churning. But she still wasn't ready to admit defeat. "Once she reads my story on prostitution, she's going to give me my job back."

Mike released his breath. "I don't care how great your story is, Stella's not giving you your job back. Not when the college coed who took over your human interest stories is working for free."

"What?" Eden felt her heart take a dip when Mike nodded.

"I guess she's taking journalism classes at the university and needs the experience. So she offered to work for free."

"So Stella fired me so she could fill my job with free labor?"

"Pretty much. And can you blame her? She's trying to keep this newspaper afloat as more and more people are getting their news from the web. Hell, the way I see it, all of us are going to be out of jobs in a few years. Which is why I'm going back to school to get my teaching degree."

"But I thought you loved reporting."

"I do love it, Eden. I always will, but I love to eat more." He studied her. "I'm not going to convince you to give this up, am I?" When she shook her head, he laughed. "Okay, I tell you what. You write your story, and I'll give it a once-over and see if I can't give you some helpful hints for how to make it more hard-hitting."

"You'd do that for me?"

"Sure." He shoved his hands in the front pockets of his pants and studied the floor for a few seconds before he continued. "So you want to go to dinner tonight? And don't use work as an excuse. I know you're off on Wednesdays."

"Who's going?"

He shrugged. "Just us. I was thinking of a date."

Eden was surprised. She had no idea that Mike was interested in her. But now that she thought about it, he had stopped by her desk a lot and was constantly asking her to go to happy hour after work. She had just been too wrapped up in her stories to notice. Which made her feel guilty. Which, in turn, made her agree to something she really didn't want to do.

"Okay."

His face lit up. "Great. You want to go straight from here?"

"Actually, why don't we meet somewhere? I'd like to get in a run before dinner."

Since setting her goal, she had run only once with Madison and Chloe. And with the marathon only a month away, she didn't need to be going on dates as much as training. But on the other hand, Mike was a nice guy. And she needed to start thinking about nice guys—instead of intense billionaires with weird sexual hang-ups.

It had been two days since she'd seen Nash Beaumont. Two days since the dinner with her grandparents. She had felt bad about his brother getting stoned on her grandparents' magic brownies. And even worse that it cut short their evening together. Once Grayson and Pops had started singing "American Pie" for the third time, Nash had made their excuses and ushered his brother down the stairs. He hadn't looked back. Not once. But when Eden was getting in her car, she felt like he watched her from the dark windows of his condo. Or maybe she just hoped that he was as infatuated with her as she was with him.

And she was infatuated. She wanted to blame it on the story. But her infatuation had gone beyond writing a story. Even when she wasn't doing research, her mind was consumed with Nash. She pictured him working at his office wearing one of his sexy suits. She pictured him at his condo wearing the jeans and Henley T-shirt he'd worn to the bar. But mostly she pictured him on a bed lying next to her wearing nothing at all. Even worse, she pictured him with Chloe lying on a bed wearing nothing at all. That image had kept her up most of the night. Which was crazy. He wasn't her boyfriend. He was her story. Something she needed to remember. And that being the case . . .

"I better get back to my research," she said as she swiveled her chair around. "I'll see you tonight."

Since Eden now knew everything about Nash the owner of French Kiss, she'd decided to find out more about Nash the Southern boy from DuPont, Louisiana. Thinking that small towns would probably report everything in their local newspapers, she started her search there. She found an article about the Beaumonts striking it big when they inherited French Kiss and another about their charity efforts: Deacon's summer camp for kids, Grayson's art auction for cancer, and Nash's generous donation to a teenage suicide hotline. She could understand the summer camp for kids because it was on land that Deacon already owned. And she could understand Grayson's art auction because he was an artist and their mother had died of cancer. But she didn't understand the teenage suicide hotline. Why would Nash choose that as his cause?

She figured out the years he would've been in high school and added those dates to her search. But all she found were numerous mentions of Nash in the sports section for running in a touchdown or winning a wrestling match. Taking off Nash's name, she left the dates and added suicides. Only one article came up. An article about a seventeen-year-old girl who had taken an entire bottle of her mother's sleeping pills. Melissa Anderson went to the same high school as Nash. So Eden put Melissa's name with Nash's and hit search.

A picture popped up of Nash in an ill-fitting tuxedo, standing behind a young girl in a peach formal. They were a perfect couple. Nash tall, dark, and handsome, and

Melissa petite, blond, and pretty. They were both smiling, and for once, Nash's looked like it came from happiness. His smiles now were sexy, charming, and practiced. This one was real and made Eden sad. Or maybe what made her sad was knowing the girl would be dead by the end of the year. What would prompt a beautiful young girl who looked like she had so much going for her to commit suicide? And was her death what had taken the happiness out of Nash's smile?

"You aren't going to make this easy, are you?"

Eden swiveled to find Stella standing in the doorway, peering over the rim of her red-framed glasses at the janitor's closet. When her gaze returned to Eden, she did not look happy. She wasn't mad exactly. She just seemed tired and exasperated.

"Hi, Stella." Eden lifted a hesitant hand in greeting.

Stella took her glasses off and rubbed the bridge of her nose. "I'm assuming you haven't even been looking for another job."

She got up from her chair. "I've got a story, Stella."

Stella placed her glasses back on and stared at her. "What you've got is a stubborn streak a mile wide."

Eden nodded. "I'll concede that point, but I also have a story. Remember how you said that if I could prove that the mayor was talking dirty to escorts, that would be a good story?"

Stella lifted an eyebrow. "You have proof that the mayor is talking dirty to escorts?"

"No. But I have proof that someone even more newsworthy than the mayor is."

"Who?"

Eden hesitated. "I don't want to give you his name until I have all the proof I need," she said. "But I can tell you that this story could double—no, triple—circulation."

It felt like it took an hour for Stella to finally reply. "Two weeks." She held up her index and middle fingers. "You have two weeks to bring me the story. If I don't like it, you're out. I mean completely out. No moving to the women's bathroom or the lobby. You'll pack up your things and move on."

"I give you my word," Eden said.

Stella shook her head. "Why do I doubt that?"

After Stella left, Eden wanted to go back to her research on Nash. Unfortunately, if she wanted to get in a run before she met Mike for dinner, she needed to leave work right away.

She changed into her running clothes in the bathroom, but kept the scarf tied around her neck. The bruises were fading, but still visible. It was only three miles to her apartment, and three miles wasn't anything compared to the 26.3 miles she'd have to run in the marathon. Or it wouldn't have been anything if she had lived in a city that wasn't built on a bunch of steep hills that felt like Mount Everest when you were running up them. But she hung tough and refused to stop running until she reached her apartment. She would've done a Rocky victory bounce if she hadn't felt like throwing up and had major leg cramps. It took everything she had just to climb the stairs.

Once inside her apartment, Eden tossed her backpack on the coffee table and bent at the waist. That seemed to help her nausea, but not her cramping calves. So she placed her hands on the floor and tried one of her mother's yoga poses. She was struggling to form a perfect inverted V with her feet and hands pressed to the floor when there was a tap on the door, followed quickly by the squeak of hinges.

Eden peeked between her spread legs and almost toppled over on her sweat-drenched head. Nash Beaumont stood in the doorway wearing a gray suit similar to the one he'd worn when they had dinner with her grandparents. A white shirt filled the space between the jacket lapels and was open at the throat. A throat he cleared before he spoke.

"It opened when I knocked." His gaze seemed to be pinned to her butt, which sent heat to her face and the spot between her legs. Bending her knees, she tried to come out of the pose gracefully, but instead stumbled and would've fallen onto the coffee table if he hadn't reached out and steadied her.

She stared at him. "You're here." It was a stupid thing to say. Of course he was there. He seemed to fill every square inch of her studio apartment.

He glanced around, and she realized how dismal her apartment must look. The carpeting was stained. The walls needed paint. And the kitchen faucet was dripping in a rhythmic plop of water. Although he didn't seem to be as interested in those things as he was with the mussed covers of her double bed.

"I'm sorry about the mess." She hurried over and straightened the blankets, then grabbed a pillow off the floor and stacked it with the others against the headboard. When she turned, he was staring at her butt again. She blushed. "So I guess my grandparents told you where I lived."

It was funny how fate worked. She had wanted another chance to talk to Nash and here it was. Now all she had to do was figure out how to keep him there long enough to get the answers she needed.

"Could I get you something to drink?" she asked.

He paused for a brief second, and then nodded. "Water is fine." He slipped out of his jacket and hung it over the back of a barstool, then proceeded to cuff his sleeves.

She froze with the refrigerator door open at the sight of his long fingers manipulating the crisp cotton until he revealed a muscled forearm with its sprinkling of dark hair. Suddenly, his fingers stopped moving, and she looked up to find him watching her with hooded eyes that made warm, moist heat pool deep inside her. And not even the cool air from the opened refrigerator helped.

"Did you want something?" he said in the dark, seductive voice that made her knees weak.

At one point, she thought she wanted answers. But now she realized that she wanted much more from Nash Beaumont. Her body said she wanted another orgasm. But the odd feeling in her chest said something else entirely. For the first time, Eden was scared of Nash Beaumont.

And not just scared, but terrified.

CHAPTER TWELVE

Coming here had been a mistake, and Nash didn't realize how much of a mistake until he'd looked into her eyes. In the late sunlight that streamed through the window, they appeared to be the color of sweet tea—deep amber with hints of brown and gold. But unlike sweet tea, they weren't cold. They held a heat that made Nash want to jump over the breakfast bar, rip off her sexy workout clothes, and take her right there on the kitchen floor. He might've done just that if her phone hadn't rung.

She blinked away the heat, then leaned over the counter and grabbed it. Her eyes widened when she saw who was calling, and she quickly turned her back on Nash and answered.

"Oh my God, Mike, I'm so sorry."

Mike? Who the hell is Mike? Nash felt every muscle in his body tense as she continued to talk.

"I completely spaced out." The hand that didn't hold the phone started gesturing. "Stella stopped by, then I went for a run, and then when I got home a..." She glanced at Nash. "...friend stopped by to say 'hi.'" She paused. "No, don't wait any longer. I still need to shower, and by the time I get there, it will be too late. But I promise I'll make it up to you." Nash's hands tightened into fists as she laughed. "Yes, I'm sure you know how to make me pay. Okay, I'll see you tomorrow." She hung up and turned, a bright smile on her face. "Sorry about that. Let me get you that water." She set the phone down on the counter and walked to the refrigerator.

Nash should've let it go, but he couldn't seem to do that. He waited for her to pull out two bottles of water before he asked. "So who's Mike?"

She bumped the refrigerator door closed with her hip. "Just a friend."

"How many times have you been with him?"

She paused in the process of handing him a bottle of water, and her eyebrows lifted. "Does it matter?"

It shouldn't matter, but damned if it did. And what did he expect? She was an escort. He ignored the water and grabbed his jacket from the barstool. "Look, I've got to go."

She set the bottles down on the counter. "This was my first date with Mike."

"Dates? Is that what you call them?"

She picked up a bottle of water and unscrewed the lid. "What do you call them? Midnight rendezvous? A walk on the wild side?"

"Therapy." The word just popped out, but once it was there, he refused to take it back. It was a form of therapy to him. One he thought would work. Now he had to wonder if he hadn't jumped from the frying pan into the fire. Looking into Eden's hazel eyes, he felt like he was burning from the inside out. He waited for her to ask more questions, but instead she did a one-eighty.

"Do you like spaghetti?" She took a drink of water and then screwed the lid back on the bottle. "I've got some leftover from a couple nights ago, and if you don't help me finish it tonight, I'll be stuck eating it tomorrow. Which will probably result in food poisoning."

"Or you could throw it away."

She shook her head. "My mother taught me to not be wasteful."

Some of the tension in Nash's shoulders eased. "Funny, my mother taught me the same thing." He started to put on his jacket. "But I don't think it's a good idea if I stay."

"Would you feel more comfortable if I turn off the lights and take off all my clothes?"

He paused with one arm in the sleeve of his jacket. "So you're a smartass along with being a hand talker."

She sent him a sassy look that had him smiling. "Pretty much. Come on, stay. I promise to keep my distance."

Her keeping her distance wasn't the problem. The problem was him keeping his. And still, he couldn't seem to refuse her. He placed his jacket back on the barstool. "Fine, but only because spaghetti happens to be my favorite."

"Now I wouldn't have guessed that." Eden moved to the refrigerator and pulled out a plastic container. After opening the lid, she took a sniff before dumping the contents into a saucepan and placing it on the stove. "I would've guessed something Southern fried." She turned the gas burner on high. "This shouldn't take long." At that high heat, it wouldn't take long to burn. She sent him a sheepish look. "Would you mind keeping an eye on it while I jump in the shower?"

The visual of Eden standing in a shower with a spray of water running over her naked body almost had Nash grabbing his jacket and heading for the door again. Instead, he reined in his desires and nodded. He waited for her to disappear inside the bathroom before he got up and walked into the kitchen.

The leftover spaghetti was a lost cause. There wasn't enough sauce, and the pasta noodles were overcooked. He dumped the entire pan in the trash and then looked through the cupboards until he found a package of pasta and a can of crushed tomatoes. After putting on a pot of water to boil for the pasta, he put together a marinara sauce using the tomatoes. He spiced it with salt, pepper, and some minced garlic from the jar he found in the refrigerator, then let it simmer as he looked around.

He wasn't surprised by the small size of her apartment—real estate in San Francisco wasn't cheap or available—but he would've thought that an escort could afford something a little nicer. The neighborhood was seedy at best. There was a crack in the window over the sink. The appliances were ancient. And the faucet leaked. Of course, how could she afford to fix those things when she kept forgetting to get her night's wages? The envelope of money was still in his coat pocket. And he wondered why he hadn't given it to her right away. Probably because that would end their relationship. And for some reason, he wasn't ready for that to happen.

He was reading what appeared to be a running schedule thumbtacked to the wall when Eden stepped out of the bathroom. Her damp hair was clipped up on her head in a haphazard way that was sexy as hell, and her face was so squeaky clean that he could see the freckles on the bridge of her nose and the flush of her cheeks. A blue scarf similar to the one she'd been wearing earlier was tied around her neck. Come to think of it, she had been wearing one the night they'd had dinner with her grandparents. Obviously, Eden liked scarves. Although it didn't exactly go with her baggy T-shirt and sweatpants. He recognized the sweats immediately. They were from the coed collection that French Kiss had put out the previous fall. His brow knotted. Romeo's collection.

"You really need to stop spoiling me with all your smiles."

He glanced up to find Eden watching him with a teasing sparkle in her eyes. "You really are a smartass," he said before he walked into the kitchen to stir the marinara. "So why the running schedule?"

"I'm running in the Bay City Marathon." She peeked over his shoulder, and he caught a whiff of herbal shampoo. "What happened to my spaghetti?"

"I tossed it out."

"Control freak."

He bit back a grin as he added salt and the pasta to the boiling water. "So you're a runner."

"Not really, which is why I needed to set some running goals. I figure if I run one extra mile a day, I'll be able to finish the marathon."

He turned to her. "You mean an extra mile a week, right? How many miles do you run now?"

She fidgeted with her scarf. "Three."

It was hard to keep his mouth from dropping open. "Three? And you think you're going to be able to finish a marathon in a little over a month?"

Her chin came up. "I'm very good at completing goals."

She would have to be better than good. She'd have to

be one dedicated athlete. But he refrained from pointing that out. "Why don't you grab some plates? This is ready."

The dinner wasn't one of his best, but Eden seemed to enjoy it. She ate like she talked. With enthusiasm and no inhibitions. While most girls took dainty bites when eating in front of guys, Eden spooled the long pasta onto her fork before placing the big bite in her mouth, sucking up any loose noodles with a pucker that made Nash fidget on his barstool.

"This is amazing," she said. "I never would've guess that you knew how to cook."

"It was either that or eat my brothers' cooking." He looked away from the dab of marinara on her upper lip and tried to concentrate on the conversation. "And both Deacon and Grayson suck at cooking. Deacon doesn't have the patience, and Grayson is easily distracted."

They ate in silence for a few moments before she spoke. "So I guess it was hard after your mother died."

He wasn't surprised that she knew about his mother. The tabloids had loved the three motherless boys angle. But he was surprised by the pain that the mere mention of his mother still evoked. "I survived." He got up and carried his plate into the kitchen. He was rinsing it off when she came up behind him.

"Is that why you're so unhappy, Nash?"

When he turned around, she was standing too close. So close that his body immediately reacted. His heart rate increased. His palms tingled. And his cock hardened. In an effort to hide his physical reaction to her nearness, he spoke callously. "If we're going to talk about happy, let's talk about you. Are you really happy selling your body for money?"

She looked away as if thinking of a reply, and when she

finally looked back, she sounded like she was reciting a passage she had memorized for school. "I don't consider it selling my body. I look at it like my contribution to a Lonely Hearts Club."

He snorted. "Then you're fooling yourself. You do realize that I'm the exception to the rule. Most of the guys who hire escorts are married."

"Doesn't the escort service screen them?"

It was hard to believe that Eden could be that naïve, but it appeared that she was. "The only thing they wanted from me was ten grand to join their exclusive club," he said. "Once they got that, they didn't care who I was or what I want to do to their girls as long as they get their percentage. Which brings up another point. If you didn't take my money, how did they get their cut?" A thought struck him. "Is that why someone threatened you?"

"Probably." She picked up the minced garlic jar and walked to the refrigerator. She opened the door and placed the jar on a shelf. "Although almost choking me to death seems like more than a threat."

He didn't even wait for her to finish closing the door of the refrigerator before he grabbed her arm and turned her to face him. His gaze went to the scarf around her neck, and he hesitated only a second before he untied it. Beneath, purple bruises marred her pale skin, and anger like he hadn't released in a long time bubbled to the surface.

"Fuckin' sonofabitch." He slammed his fist on the refrigerator door.

"Pretty much," Eden said. "A scary sonofabitch."

"Who is he?" Nash was surprised he could get the words out from between his clenched teeth.

"I don't know. He wore a ski mask. At first, I thought it was you."

His gaze traveled to the bruises and then back to her. "You thought I could do something like this?"

"You told me you were screwed up. I thought it was possible that you enjoyed hurting women."

Her words struck him like a solid jab to the solar plexus, and it was a struggle to breathe let alone speak. "No, I don't enjoy hurting women, Eden." He paused. "But that doesn't mean I haven't."

Eden placed her hand on his bare forearm. It was the first time she'd ever touched him voluntarily, and her warm fingers around his wrist felt like hot brands. He flinched, but she refused to release him. "And have women hurt you, Nash? Or maybe just one woman? Is that why you have trouble having an . . . orgasm?"

"I don't have trouble having orgasms." Just the touch of her fingertips on his arm had him rock hard and ready. "I have trouble with control."

"Control? What do you mean? You're the most controlled man I've ever met."

"Because I work at it."

"Why? Why is it so important to retain control?"

He didn't have to stay and answer. Her hold wasn't that tight on his arm. But for some reason, maybe because he wanted to finally put all his screwed-up thoughts into words, he told her the truth. "Because I'm not like other men, Eden. Sex is more than just a physical release. It's an all-consuming need. And until I learn to control it, I could end up hurting someone . . . again."

Eden's fingers caressed his arm in a back-and-forth

sweep, and when she spoke, it was barely a whisper. "But you touched me, Nash." Her gaze locked with his. "And you didn't hurt me. In fact, I want you to touch me again."

A shaft of heat ricocheted through his cock, and he realized that this was what he'd come for. Not to bring her the money, but to touch her again. To feel her heat. To enjoy the burst of passion when she finally reached climax. And as much as he wanted to have enough control to walk away, he didn't. But he did have enough to set boundaries.

Backing her up against the refrigerator, he leaned close and whispered in her ear. "Do you remember the rules?"

Her breath fell hot against his neck as she spoke. "No talking and do everything you say."

"Good." He allowed his lips to brush the curve of her ear. "Now take off your clothes."

Keeping his hands pressed flat against the door of the refrigerator, he moved back a few inches. Their eyes met, and she held his gaze as she reached for the hem of her T-shirt. She pulled it over her head, her elbows brushing the insides of his arms. Desire hit him hard in the gut as he lowered his gaze to her naked breasts. They were paler than the rest of her body. Two perfect scoops of flesh topped with small, tight nipples the color of sweet cherry wine. The desire turned to a deep ache, but he ignored it.

"Now the sweats."

Hooking her thumbs into the waistband, she wiggled them down her hips and then released them to pool at her feet. His gaze traveled to the triangle of white cotton that covered nirvana. He took an uneven breath through his nose before he spoke.

"Leave the panties and place your hands on the refrigerator."

She pressed her palms against the refrigerator just below her hips and looked at him with desire-drugged eyes. He wanted to kiss her. But after what had happened when she'd followed him home, he knew that her lips were the one area he needed to avoid at all costs. Instead, he kissed her forehead, her cheekbones, her chin, and each bruise that marred her long neck. He kissed the small indention at the base of her throat, the hard line of her collarbone, the freckle on her shoulder. Then he moved to her breasts, using his lips to caress the soft swells around each nipple before taking one into his mouth.

He gently sucked, then rolled it between his tongue and the roof of his mouth until Eden moaned. Then he kissed his way over to the other one and gave it equal attention before bending his knees and moving lower. He kept his hands on the refrigerator, sliding them down as he kissed his way over her rib cage to her navel and finally to the edge of her panties. Kneeling in front of her, he gripped the elastic in his teeth and tugged the piece of cotton down her hips. On the way, his mouth brushed against soft hair and moist heat that had his breath halting and Eden's releasing in a gasp.

He looked up to find her watching him from beneath hooded eyelids. Her bottom lip was wet and puffy as if she'd been biting it, and her breasts rose and fell with every uneven breath she took. The sight of her all lust-drugged almost had him losing control, and he had to close his eyes for a second and focus before he could finish removing her panties with his teeth. Once they slid down her legs, he spoke in a voice thick with desire.

"Your legs...spread them."

Her legs trembled as she stepped out of her sweats and panties, displaying a peek of tempting pink beneath the small patch of dark hair. For a few heart-pounding seconds, he just enjoyed the view. Then he dipped his head and took a sip. She tasted like he knew she would— slightly sweet and earthy. And when a sip wasn't enough, he kissed her deep, using his tongue to explore her heat. With a moan, she broke the rules and furrowed her fingers through his hair.

Until then, the hard-on in his pants had been bearable. Now, it became an ache that he couldn't ignore. Knowing that he was seconds away from getting to his feet and burying himself deep inside her, he flicked his tongue across her clitoris and quickly took her over the edge.

"Nash!" She screamed out his name as she came, her hands clenching his head as she thrust her hips forward. His hands fisted against the refrigerator as he fought for control. Thankfully, about the time he was ready to lose it, she released him and slid down the refrigerator to sit on the floor in front of him.

Knowing that being so close to those lush lips was dangerous, Nash got to his feet and scooped her up in his arms. He carried her to the bed and covered her sinfully beautiful body with the quilt.

She looked up at him, her eyes sated but sad. "So you're leaving." When he nodded, her voice became pleading. "But you'll be back?"

Yes, Nash would be back. Not only to feed Eden's addiction, but also to feed his own.

CHAPTER THIRTEEN

Eden didn't go to work the next day. Instead, she stayed in bed for most of the morning and smiled up at the huge crack in her ceiling. She should've run four miles and then gone into work, but training for the marathon and doing research for her newspaper article took a backseat to the giddy, exuberant bubble that surrounded Eden. For the first time since she could remember, she felt content to do absolutely nothing except enjoy the moment.

And think about Nash.

Another piece of the puzzle had fallen into place. Eden now knew why he hired women and then refused to touch them. It was some type of weird therapy that only a guy could come up with. And Eden thought it was totally ridiculous.

Nash wasn't going to hurt a woman if he lost control. She had known him for only a few weeks, and she knew that wasn't in his nature. Not when he had almost come unglued when he saw the bruises on her neck. Now all she had to do was convince him of that.

She sat up and reached for her laptop, intending to research sex addiction. But when she tapped the mouse and the article she'd been writing about Nash popped up on the screen, she realized how easily a good orgasm could get you off track. She had no business convincing Nash of anything. He was her story. A story she needed to write if she wanted to achieve her goal of becoming a newspaper reporter.

The exuberant bubble popped, leaving Eden feeling depressed as she forced herself to spend the rest of the morning working on the article. Consequently, it was crap. Instead of sounding like an investigative news article, the story sounded like a letter of the month from *Penthouse Forum* magazine. Eden couldn't make what happened in the hotel suite sound newsworthy and not like an erotic fantasy. She had just started to delete the entire story when someone knocked on the door. She jumped out of bed and hurriedly got dressed in her skinny jeans and one of her nicer shirts. But when she pulled open the door, a hot billionaire wasn't standing on the other side. It was a crew of men with tool belts.

"Eden Huckabee?" The guy with the beer belly glanced at his clipboard.

Worried that these guys were sent by Zac to threaten her—or worse, Eden closed the door and quickly put on the security chain before cracking it open again. "Who wants to know?"

"I'm Hank from Brisbane Handyman Service." He pointed to the printed name on the pocket of his T-shirt. "And we're here to fix a few things in your apartment."

Eden was more than a little surprised. For the last three months, she'd persistently called her landlord and left messages about things that needed to be fixed in her apartment. Obviously, her persistence had paid off.

"Just a minute." She closed the door and took off the chain before opening it again. "Did you want me to show you what needs to be fixed or do you have the list I gave Mr. Pruitt?"

Hank grinned. "I think we can figure it out, ma'am."

While the crew went to work, Eden decided that what her article needed was more research. She knew why Nash hired escorts, but she still didn't know what had caused him to go to such extremes. Lots of men were addicted to sex. What made Nash think he was so different—so flawed? Whom had he hurt? Had it been Melissa?

Unfortunately, she couldn't concentrate on researching the questions with all the hammering and thumping that was going on. And since she really didn't have that much to steal besides her laptop and two phones, she collected them and her purse and made her excuses.

"I'll be back in a little while."

"Take your time," Hank said as he used putty and a flat-edged tool to patch a hole in her wall. "I'm thinking it might take most of the day. But I'll know better once we get into it. How 'bout I give you my cell number and you call me in a couple hours?"

Eden pulled her cell phone out of her purse to get his number and noticed that she had a text from Madison.

I guess you're not the only one Zac is mad at.

Eden immediately tried to call her, but when there was no answer, she got Hank's number and then headed to Madison's apartment. While Eden lived in a run-down studio, Madison lived in a high-rise apartment building with a great view and enough walls to hold the expensive artwork Madison's clients gave her. But the walls were empty when Eden stepped through the door, and moving boxes littered the floor of the entryway.

"What's going—?" Eden started to ask, but cut off when she finally noticed Madison's split lip. "The asshole hit you!"

Madison tried to smile, but winced and touched her swollen lip. "Actually, his thug friend hit me. Zac just stood by and watched."

Eden had never been good at consoling people, which was just another reason why she didn't have many friends. After standing there for a moment, she awkwardly patted Madison on the back. "Don't you worry, Maddie, everything is going to be all right. We're going to call the police and nail Zac's balls to the wall."

Madison looked at her as if she was crazy. "Sorry, Eden, but I really don't feel like recovering in jail." She glanced at the boxes in the living room. "Although, since I'm being kicked out of my apartment, I guess jail is as good a place as any to live."

"Zac owns this apartment?"

Madison shook her head. "Zac might be responsible for my lip, but I only have myself to blame for being evicted. For the last few months, I haven't had enough money to pay the rent."

"But I don't get it. I thought you made a lot of money."

"I do. Or at least, I did. Recently, I stopped taking money from my clients. Which is the reason I got a visit from Zac. He thinks I'm holding out on him and starting my own escort service . . . with you."

"But that's ridiculous," Eden said.

"That's what I told him, but he wouldn't listen." Madison moved into the living room and sat down in the one spot on the couch that didn't have a box. For once, she didn't look like the Happy Hooker. "To cover what he thought should be his percentage, Zac and his buddies took all my diamonds, fur coats, and most of my paintings."

Eden sat down on the marble coffee table in front of her. "But I don't understand. Why would you stop taking money from your clients?"

Madison shrugged. "I know it's stupid, but after I got to know Freddie, George, and Harry, I just couldn't bring myself to take money from them anymore. They are such sweet old guys."

It wasn't surprising that Madison had made friends with her clients. Madison seemed to make friends with everyone . . . even a selfish writer who had only been using her for a story. Madison had shown up at The Lemon Drop night after night, hooked Eden up with Nash, and hadn't hesitated to race over to Eden's apartment after Zac had choked her. Even now, it was Madison who tried to lift Eden's spirits.

"Don't look so sad, Eden. It's not that bad." Madison made an attempt at a smile. "In my profession, there's always money to be made."

Eden stared at her. "You aren't seriously thinking about going back to work as an escort, are you?"

"Of course. What other job would I do?"

"You could do anything you want to do. Be anything you want to be. What are you interested in?"

Madison thought for a moment. "Men."

Eden tried not to roll her eyes. "Okay, what else?"

"Art."

"Then why don't you get a job at an art gallery? You're great with people."

Madison looked thoughtful. "An art gallery? You really think I could get a job selling art?"

"Of course you could." Eden glanced at the boxes. "But until you get a job, there's a secondhand store right down the street that will give good money for designer clothes, purses, and shoes." When Madison opened her mouth to argue, Eden held up a hand. "Desperate times call for desperate measures."

Madison sighed. "You're right, but I don't think a secondhand store will give me enough to rent an apartment."

It took only a second for Eden to make a decision. "Then you'll move in with me."

Madison's eyes widened and then filled with tears. "You'd let me live with you?"

Eden felt her own eyes grow watery. "Of course. What are friends for?"

Getting Madison to part with her designer clothes wasn't easy. Everything had some sentimental value. Freddie had given her the Hermès scarf and Harry the Versace shoes and George the Gucci purse. Finally, Eden gave her two big boxes and told her she could keep whatever she could fit inside. They were bulging at the seams by the time Madison got through squeezing all her must-haves in, but Eden considered the afternoon a success when they ended up with four boxes of clothes, purses, and shoes that they could sell. The owner of the secondhand store was thrilled to get the designer clothes, especially when some still had the tags on them, and gave Madison good money for them.

"See, all you needed was a plan," Eden said as she climbed into Madison's Mercedes and handed her the stack of cash. The car, which had been a gift from Freddie, would probably have to be sold for something cheaper and more economical. But figuring that Madison had parted with enough for one day, Eden decided to wait to break the news. Which turned out to be a smart move, because as soon as Madison took the money she burst into tears.

"I don't want money," she sobbed. "I want my Versaces."

Not knowing what to do, Eden tried bribery. "How about a chocolate éclair? My treat."

They drove to a nearby pastry shop, and it took two éclairs to make Madison stop crying over the clothes she sold. Although she refused to completely give up on them. "Do you think if I get a job at an art gallery, I can buy some of them back?" She pulled a napkin from the dispenser in the middle of the table and wiped the chocolate from her fingers.

It wasn't likely that any of the designer clothes would still be there or that Madison could afford them on a starting salary, but Eden kept that to herself. "Of course you can. Once you get established at your new job, you can buy your own designer clothes. And didn't you tell me that your father loves to buy you expensive things for your birthday?"

Madison looked down at the crumbs on the table. "Before I move in with you, there's something I have to tell you. I wasn't exactly truthful about what my life has been like. I mean it hasn't been all wine and roses."

Eden covered Madison's hand that rested on the table and squeezed it. "It's okay, Maddie. You don't have to tell me all your secrets just because you're moving in with me."

"I know, but I want to." She released her breath. "I lied to you about my family. My father isn't a wealthy preacher, and my mother was never on the PTA board. My dad left before I was born, and my mom was so dirt poor that she could barely afford to feed her six kids. Which probably explains why she went through so many men—she was looking for anyone to take care of her and her brood. And I guess I followed in her footsteps. I'm willing to prostitute myself for security. Unfortunately, as it turned out, I'm not secure at all."

For a moment, Eden was speechless. Her newspaper story had been right in front of her all this time and she hadn't even known it. If she had been a hard-core reporter, this would've been the time to ask questions—to delve into all the sordid details. But Stella was right. Eden wasn't a hard-core reporter. Because she didn't care about a story as much as she did about her friend.

"I'm sorry," she said.

Madison nodded. "I guess I just didn't want you to think badly about me because I'd had sex with men for my own gain—something you would never do."

Eden could've kept her mouth shut, but it was hard to when Madison looked so forlorn. And when Eden was far from perfect. "I had sex with the Dark Seducer."

Madison stared at her. "You what?"

"I had sex with the Dark Seducer. Not intercourse but oral sex—well, one time it was oral and the other he used his hand—"

"Oh my God," Madison said. "I'm so sorry, Eden.

Chloe promised me that he wouldn't touch you. If I had thought for one second that he would force himself on you, I never would've let you go."

"He didn't force me. I wanted him to touch me."

"You wanted a pervert to touch you?"

"He's not a pervert. He's just a guy who needs help." The truth of her words made Eden realize that, regardless of the story, she was going to help Nash. She had to. She also had to tell someone else her secret. "If I tell you something, will you promise not to tell another living soul? I mean you have to swear it."

The smile that spread across Madison's face was as bright as the afternoon sun. "We really are BFFs, aren't we?"

Eden grinned. "I guess so. Now do you promise?"

Madison nodded, and then lifted a hand. "I swear on my grandmother's grave."

Glancing around at the other patrons in the pastry shop, Eden leaned closer. "The Dark Seducer is one of the panty billionaires."

Madison burst out laughing. "That's a good one, Eden."

"I'm not kidding. Nash Beaumont is the Dark Seducer. That's why he was at The Lemon Drop that night. He had used the phone I left in the hotel room to find me." Madison's mouth formed a perfect O as she stared at Eden. When she didn't speak, Eden prompted her. "Aren't you going to say something?"

Madison closed her mouth and paused for a moment before she spoke. "So do you think he can get us free lingerie?"

CHAPTER FOURTEEN

After Eden and Madison arrived back at the apartment, they unloaded Madison's boxes and carried them up the stairs. Eden was a little worried about where they were going to put Madison's things. It wasn't like her apartment had a lot of storage space...or space, period. But they would make it work. At least until they could find Madison a job.

As soon as Eden entered the apartment, she looked around, wanting to make sure the workmen had fixed the things that needed fixing. It appeared that they had done that and more. She had expected the kitchen window and leaky faucet to be fixed, but she had not expected a brand-new window and faucet. Or the crack in the ceiling to be patched, or a new dead bolt put on the door.

Eden tried to call Mr. Pruitt to thank him, but he didn't answer. So she left a message, and while Madison unpacked, she hurriedly showered and got ready for work. She arrived a good fifteen minutes late to The Lemon

Drop, but luckily the bar wasn't that busy and the manager cut her some slack.

"Just don't make a habit of it." Joe nodded at the door that led to the bar. "And don't make a habit of your boyfriend coming here either. Especially if he's going to have a bad attitude."

"Boyfriend? What boyfriend?" She peeked out the door, and her gaze landed on Nash sitting at the end of the bar. His hair was mussed like he'd been running his fingers through it, and his brow was knotted. It knotted even more when he spotted her. She, on the other hand, felt like a giddy teenager. Her face filled with happy heat, and the smile that spread over her face hurt her cheeks.

He's just your story, she tried to remind herself. But the feelings that bounced around inside her made her realize that he was much more. Still, she tried to calm her emotions as she lifted the gate in the bar and made her way down to where he sat.

"You're late," he said.

"What? Are you my keeper now?" she teased.

"You need one."

"And you're volunteering for the job?"

He studied her for a second before he got up and took an envelope out of his back jean pocket and handed it to her. "I want you to make sure you give the escort service their percentage. I don't want anyone touching you again."

She hated it when her brothers got protective, but Nash's protective tone made her go all melty inside. She opened the envelope and glanced at the contents. She had never seen so many hundred-dollar bills in her life. She closed the envelope and held it out to him.

"I can't take this."

"You can take it, and you will. Then you will pay off the escort service and quit. You're not working for those assholes."

"You really are a control freak," she said. When he didn't crack a smile, she gave in. "Fine. But I'm only taking the percentage of what I owe the escort service."

He looked confused. "Why? You earned it."

"Not when I was the only one who got any enjoyment out of it." She took out a couple thousand, then folded the envelope and tucked it in his shirt pocket. When she lifted her gaze, he was studying her.

"Who said I didn't enjoy it?"

Not knowing what to say to that, she grabbed a cocktail napkin and set it on the bar. "Let me get you another..." She examined the drink in his glass. "Jack straight up?"

He hesitated for a second before sitting back down. "Iced tea with two sugars."

Tea? The man never failed to amaze her. While she filled his glass from the tea dispenser, Cari walked up with her drink orders. She took one look at Nash and got all starry-eyed.

"Hi," she said in a breathy voice. "After you almost got in a fight with that guy the other night, I didn't think you'd be back."

Since Eden hadn't heard about the fight, she glanced at Nash in question, but he ignored her and flashed his trademark smile at Cari. "I apologize. I'm usually more easygoing."

Easygoing? Was the man living in a dream world? He was about as easygoing as a rattlesnake. Although he looked pretty easygoing now. His smile was bright, and his eyes twinkled as he flirted with Cari. And Cari was eating it up with a spoon.

"I just love your undies," she gushed with a bat of eyelashes.

Nash's smile got sexier. "So you wear French Kiss collections?"

"I wouldn't wear anything else." Cari giggled like a schoolgirl as she placed a hand on Nash's arm. Eden waited for him to pull away, but he just continued to smile. Which really ticked Eden off. When she touched him, all she seemed to get were scowls and...orgasms. Okay, so maybe scowls weren't so bad when accompanied with orgasms.

"Well, I appreciate your loyalty," Nash said. "What do you think of the new bra collection?"

"I love them," she gushed. "In fact, I have one on right now."

Eden rolled her eyes and placed the drink order on the tray. "Here you go, Cari. You better get them delivered before the ice melts." *Or before I get sick*.

But Cari ignored her and twirled a strand of hair around her finger as she looked at Nash from lowered lids. "So if you're not doing anything later, I get off at midnight."

There was a moment when Nash actually looked like he was going to accept the offer, but then he turned to Eden and gave her a sexy smile that she had never seen before. "Sorry," he said, "but I have other plans tonight."

Cari looked between them with surprise. "Gosh, Eden, I'm sorry. I didn't realize he was yours."

It was strange, but just the thought of Nash Beaumont being hers made her weak in the knees. Of course, it wasn't true. Nash wasn't the type of man to belong to any woman. Especially an average bartender/sorta writer. But then why was he here? And why had he shown up at her apartment? And why had he given her two amazing orgasms?

Eden was still mulling over the questions when Cari picked up the tray and walked off. Nash's smile immediately faded.

"So it really is me that makes you grumpy," she said as she turned her attention to cutting up limes. Hopefully, she wouldn't slice off a finger. It was hard to concentrate when being watched by his piercing eyes.

"I think it's obvious that you do more to me than make me grumpy," he said. Then before she could get over her shock, he changed the subject. "Why do you wear my brother's collection?"

"What?"

"My brother's clothing collection. You had on a pair of his sweatpants the other night."

"Oh. They were from your brother's collection? Unlike Cari, I don't pay much attention to what I wear. I just buy whatever's on sale." She pulled a jar of maraschino cherries from the fridge. "Although she's lying, you know. She doesn't have on one of your new bras. She wears sports bras to work because they're more comfortable."

His brow knotted. "Are you saying that our bras aren't comfortable?"

"They're comfortable enough when you think that some guy is going to see your bra and you want them to think you wear sexy underwear all the time. But for everyday life, women prefer comfort and a neutral color that isn't going to show through their white shirts. And your bras aren't comfortable or neutral."

His gaze lowered to her breasts, and damned if her nipples didn't immediately tighten. "And you've worn a bra from our new collection?"

"No." She turned away. "They're too expensive. But I own a couple of your bras from past collections."

"Mine?"

"To be honest, I don't have a clue."

He didn't seem pleased by the news. "So you're saying that price, comfort, and color are the major selling points of a bra?"

"I haven't taken a poll or anything, but that's how most of the women I know feel. And why are you so curious? Don't you have that survey on your website that asks how women feel about your bras?"

"You've been on our website?"

She couldn't keep the blush off her face. "I was a little curious after I discovered who you were."

"And did you appease your curiosity?"

"About where you came from and how you ended up with a lingerie company? Yes. But it didn't tell me a thing about the man. Your likes. Your dislikes . . . why you hire escorts."

"I think I told you why I hire escorts." His gaze lasered right through her. "And as for my likes and dislikes—I don't like rainy days, chocolate chip cookies, and liars. I do like fishing, sweet tea, and running. And speaking of running, are you still training for the marathon?"

The liar thing had her taking a few seconds to answer. "Umm, yes. Although I'm a day behind on my daily goals."

He smiled. Not a practiced smile like the one he had given Cari, but a soft smile that crinkled the corners of his eyes. "I'm assuming you were too tired to add your daily mile this morning."

"I didn't even run." She sent him a sardonic look. "But don't get a big head."

"According to my father, I was born with a big head. And you must've been born with one even bigger if you think you can be ready to run a full marathon in a month's time. You need to start with the half marathon, which is still going to be a major feat to accomplish."

"How many miles is a half marathon?"

"A little over thirteen."

Since her shins still hurt from running three, she had to concede that a full marathon might be more than she could handle. "Okay," she said. "I'll go for the half instead."

The nice smile reappeared. "Okay." He got up and placed some money on the bar. "And since I was the one to suggest the half marathon, I think it's only fair that I help you achieve it. I'll be at your apartment at seven tomorrow morning. Be stretched and ready to run."

* * *

It would figure that Nash would arrive at her apartment promptly at seven o'clock when Eden was still getting her running shoes on and Madison was still sawing logs. And the woman could saw logs. Her snoring had kept Eden awake most of the night. Which made her almost as grumpy as Nash. Except Nash didn't look grumpy when she pulled open the door. He looked happier than she'd ever seen him. He wasn't smiling, but his brow wasn't knotted and there was a definite twinkle in his eyes. Almost as if he was happy to see her. But the twinkle fizzled when he heard the snoring. Without a word, he physically moved Eden out of the way and strode into the apartment. He stopped when he saw Madison sprawled out on her stomach with one foot dangling off the bed and the tangled mass of hair over her face fluttering with every snore that came from her open mouth.

Nash turned to Eden, and she quickly explained.

"That's Madison. She works at the escort service— or used to until the same thug who tried to strangle me roughed her up. And to top it off, she lost her apartment, so I said she could stay here until she finds another job." When his gaze went back to Madison, she couldn't help but add, "But not as an escort. So don't get any ideas."

His gaze returned to her. "Jealous, Eden?"

"Of course not." She gestured with her hands, forgetting that she still held a running shoe. "Why would I be jealous? We're just..." She stopped. What were they? She knew what she was doing with him. She wanted to find out what made him tick for her story. But why was he hanging out with her?

He took her running shoe and pointed to the couch.

Once she was sitting, he knelt like Prince Charming with the slipper and put on her shoe, efficiently tying the laces before he pulled her to her feet.

His gaze was steady. "Running partners. And be warned, I don't put up with slackers."

It turned out to be an understatement. Nash didn't jog. He ran. After making her stretch for a good fifteen minutes, he took her on a grueling four-mile run that felt like it was a good twenty. And she couldn't exactly give up when she'd acted like adding an extra mile a day was no big deal. So even though her shins hurt and her thighs ached and her heart felt like it was going to burst out of her chest, she hung tough. When they were finished, he made her stretch again and drink the water he brought before they walked back to her apartment. He opened the door of the complex and held it for her.

"What time do you go into work tonight?"

"Four."

"You're driving, I presume?"

She paused on her way in. "Why would I drive? It's only a few blocks."

He cocked his head and sent her an annoyed look. "Oh, I don't know, maybe because you still have the bruises on your neck from the asshole who tried to strangle you? Did you pay your escort service their percentage?"

"I gave it to Madison to give to Chloe. And I was driving that night, so walking had nothing to do with it."

He released an exasperated sigh. "Fine. Walk to work, but I'll be there to pick you up when you get off."

She tipped her head and sent him a teasing look. "Now

why would you pick me up from work if we're just running partners?"

His brow furrowed for only a second. "To hell with it." He lowered his head as if he was going to kiss her. And she was surprised at how much she wanted him to. While he had kissed her everywhere else, he hadn't touched his lips to hers since the kiss in the street. But before he could, a white van pulled up to the curb and the handyman crew got out, carrying paint cans and rollers. Eden figured they were working on someone else's apartment until Hank saw her and spoke.

"We'll try not to take too long today, Miss Huckabee. We wanted to paint over the crack we patched. And I figured while we're at it, we'd paint the rest of the living area."

"Wow, that would be great," she said. "I'll just let my roommate know so she can plan to stay out of your way. And please thank Mr. Pruitt for making all the improvements." She looked back at Nash and explained. "He's my landlord. I've been pestering him for months to fix things. I guess he finally felt guilty about the condition of the apartments. I hope he's going to do as good of a job for the other tenants. This building has needed work for a long time."

It looked like Nash rolled his eyes, but since it was so uncharacteristic, she figured she was mistaken. "I guess he doesn't have a choice, now does he?" he said before he jogged down the steps and continued his run as if he hadn't just done four miles with her.

Since Eden didn't want the handyman crew surprising Madison, she hurried up the stairs so her friend could at least get a robe on before they arrived. But as it turned out, Madison was already dressed and examining the boxes that were stacked by the door.

"Please tell me you did not go and buy your clothes back from the secondhand store," Eden said.

Madison glanced up. "No. These were delivered this morning by a really cute special courier. Your grandparents wouldn't send this much pot, would they?"

"Let's hope not." Eden moved over to a box and read the label that was addressed to her before peeling back the packing tape. The box was filled with brand-new, plastic-wrapped lingerie.

"Oh. My. Gosh," Madison gushed as she pulled a lavender lace bra from a plastic bag. "He did send us free lingerie." She held the bra to her big boobs. "Or at least he sent you free lingerie."

Eden took the bra and looked at the tag. It was her size. How had Nash figured it out when he had never even touched her breasts—at least not with his hands? While heat filled Eden at just the thought of Nash's mouth on her breasts, Madison continued to open bags and examine each tag for her size. But the bras, panties, nighties, robes, and sweatpants all seemed to be in Eden's size.

"You do realize what this is about, don't you?" Madison said.

Eden shrugged. "Nash stopped by The Lemon Drop last night, and we started talking about bras. I guess he wants me to try the new line of French Kiss lingerie and tell him what I think."

"If that was true, then why didn't he send you a variety

from all the collections?" She lifted a wicked-looking black corset. "These are all from the Lothario Collection...his collection."

"So?"

Madison sent her a knowing smile. "So...I think the panty billionaire is staking his claim."

CHAPTER FIFTEEN

Good morning," Nash said as he passed Kelly's desk on his way to Deacon's office. "I'm assuming Deacon's fit to be tied that I'm late again."

Kelly looked up from her computer screen, and her eyes narrowed. "Actually, he just called and said that he and Olivia are going to be late as well. Which means everyone is having great sex except me."

"I was running, not having great sex."

She cupped her chin in her hand and studied him. "But you've had great sex within the last twenty-four hours. The eyes never lie, and yours are sparkling with sexual satisfaction."

Kelly couldn't have been more wrong. It wasn't sexual satisfaction. Not when his penis felt like he'd overdosed on Viagra. But despite his physical discomfort, he did feel happy. Happier than he'd felt in a long time. And there was only one explanation for it.

"It's called endorphins, Kelly," he said. "Exercise will do that for a person."

She pointed her pen with the purple feather on the end at him. "Don't tell me that sappy look on your face has to do entirely with endorphins. You always go on a morning run, and you've never looked this happy before. Charming. Sexy as all get-out. But never like you want to join Pharrell for a chorus of 'Happy.'"

Okay, so maybe Kelly was right. Maybe his happiness wasn't all to do with endorphins. Maybe it had more to do with his running partner. Not that Eden was much of a runner. For a person who planned on running a marathon—even a half marathon—she didn't know how to stretch, control her pace, or hydrate. And her gait was endearingly awkward. Probably because she talked the entire time they ran. With her hands gesturing, she talked about needing to find a job for Madison, she talked about her mother being a granola-eating tree-hugger, her brothers being expert surfers, bikers, and skateboarders, and her father being a war correspondent before he became a journalism professor. It surprised him that she had such a normal family. He'd thought, with her choice in careers, she would have some dark skeletons in her closet. But maybe she kept them as well hidden as he did.

Nash had slowed his pace to accommodate her obvious lack of running experience. And occasionally asked if she wanted to stop and walk awhile. But she appeared to be the type of woman who could do anything she set her mind to and had kept up.

He still wasn't sure why he had invited her on his runs. Grayson was a much better running partner. He gave Nash a workout without a lot of talking. But Nash realized that he kind of liked the talking. Not to mention the way Eden filled out a pair of running pants. It was sheer torture watching her bend over to stretch her quads. And he had major fantasies of stepping up behind her and pressing the part of him that ached the most against those firm, sweet cheeks. But he didn't. He didn't touch her nice ass, or her sweet breasts, or her plump lips that were chapped from the wind. He didn't touch her at all.

Instead, he allowed the ache for Eden to grow, to consume him and fill every waking moment and every subconscious thought. Because as much as he ached to touch her, he found deep satisfaction in the pain of not touching her. It was punishment. A punishment that he well deserved. For the first time, he felt like he was paying for what he'd done. And in a weird way, it released him from the guilt he'd carried for so many years.

"What has you looking so happy, Nash?" Kelly's fiancé, Jason, walked up. Jason was a lawyer for French Kiss and the first person willing to befriend a bunch of country bumpkins on their arrival. He was honest and as loyal as the day was long, but had a tendency to be a bit of a slob. Today, he had a smudge of what looked like strawberry jelly on his purple tie.

"Nash had sex," Kelly said. "You know what that is, right? When two people get naked and—"

"Yes," Jason cut her off, "I know what it is, Kels." He looked at Nash. "So I've got an extra ticket for the basketball game. You want to go?"

Obviously, it was the wrong thing to say, because Kelly

exploded from her chair. "You're asking Nash to go? And last week you asked Deacon and the week before Grayson. What happened to us going to sporting events together? Or are you afraid that I'll jump your bones in the bleachers after the first half?"

Jason shrugged. "Well, it does seem to be all you can think about."

Nash cringed while Kelly's face turned a deep red. "Well, it's better than being a repressed virgin boy!" She stormed down the hallway. When she was gone, Jason's shoulders wilted.

"I guess I handled that wrong."

Nash bit back a smile. "I think that's putting it mildly."

Jason released his breath. "You probably think it's strange that a guy wouldn't want to have sex with his fiancée." Since Nash couldn't cast stones on what was sexually strange, he kept his mouth shut and let Jason continue. "It's not that I don't want to have sex with her—hell, I'm so horny that I have to take a cold shower every night before I go to bed."

Nash could relate. Since meeting Eden, he'd taken more than his fair share of cold showers. "So why wait?" he asked.

Jason looked down at the floor. "Because I don't have as much experience as Kelly has . . . and I guess I'm afraid that I won't measure up."

Damn. Sex could really screw a guy up. And he and Jason were perfect examples. But while there was no hope for Nash, there still might be some for Jason.

"Look," Nash said, "I get that you're scared. But Kelly isn't marrying any of those other guys. She's marrying you. Which means you've got a major advantage—she already finds you irresistible."

Jason glanced up, and a smile lit his face. "She does?"

"I think her marriage proposal on the Jumbotron at AT&T Stadium was a pretty good indicator." He slapped him on the back. "Which means you're on third base and all you have to do is run home."

* * *

Since Deacon wasn't coming into work until later, Nash headed to his office to see if any results had come back from the independent survey they'd commissioned. The response hadn't been as great as the response from the French Kiss survey, but the results that had come back confirmed what Eden had told Nash. Wanting to get Samuel's opinion, he headed to the design studio.

He found Samuel in his office, but he wasn't alone. Deirdre Beaumont was there, and whatever they were talking about, Samuel didn't look like he was enjoying it. His hair was standing on end as if he'd been running his fingers through it. His tie was crooked. And he had murder in his eyes as Deirdre pointed at the list in her hand.

"The waitstaff uniforms are way too boring," she said. "They need some pizzazz. Maybe some purple sequins along the edge of their skirts. Or feathers. Feathers would be fun. And I want to change the flower arrangements on the tables. I want something a little more dramatic."

"I am not a florist," Samuel muttered between his teeth.

"No, but you're a designer. And a designer should be

able to design anything—even flower arrangements. Or aren't you talented enough for that?"

The look on Samuel's face said he was seconds away from strangling Deirdre right where she stood. Figuring Olivia wouldn't be too happy if Nash stood by and allowed her mother to be killed, he stepped into the office.

"How's the party planning going?"

Deirdre sent Samuel a hard look. "Fine. If I could get certain people to do their job."

"My job is to design lingerie, not costumes and flower arrangements for a ridiculous party," Samuel said.

"So that's why you never attended parties at the house. You think they're ridiculous." She lifted an eyebrow. "And here I thought it was because you hated me."

"You know exactly why I never attended parties at your house, Mrs. Beaumont."

Deirdre's smile evaporated. "I suppose I do." She carefully folded her list and placed it in the front pocket of her purse. "Now if you gentlemen will excuse me, I have a million and one things to get done before next Saturday." She turned to Nash. "I'm happy to say that Grayson has decided to accept his role as Romeo. He called me last night to see if I could find a Juliet outfit for his date."

Nash was surprised by the news. Grayson had been complaining about his costume ever since the fitting. And Nash knew nothing about a date.

"Who is he bringing?" he asked.

"He didn't say. No doubt it will be one of the vapid supermodels you men seem to salivate over." She glanced at Samuel. "Some men, that is." She looked back at Nash. "Are you bringing a date? If so, I'd be more than happy to pick out a costume for her. I'm thinking a French Kiss purple senorita costume would go perfectly with your Lothario."

With her dark hair, Eden would look amazing in a purple senorita costume. Unfortunately, Nash was too terrified to make that kind of commitment. He and Eden were running partners and that was it.

"No," he said. "I'm not bringing anyone."

"Well, I'm sure the women attending will be glad to see that." She gave him a kiss on the cheek. "Try not to let Samuel's grumpy disposition rub off on you."

Once Deirdre was gone, Nash turned to Samuel. He didn't look grumpy as much as the victim of a hurricane. Witnessing Samuel's uncharacteristic dishevelment, Nash had to agree that something was bothering the man. He just wasn't so sure that it had to do with the UPS guy. At the moment, it seemed to be centered on Deirdre Beaumont.

"That woman is going to be the death of me," Samuel said as he flopped down in his chair.

Nash took the chair across from him. "She is a character. I would've loved to see what she was like when she was younger."

"A lot less annoying."

"So how long have you known her?"

"For over twenty years. I was the one who introduced her to Michael."

The information surprised Nash. "So you knew her first?"

Samuel nodded and then stared off into space as if conjuring up memories. "We were both waiting for the trolley. It was raining like it can only rain in San Francisco, and Deirdre had forgotten her umbrella. So being the gentleman my mother taught me to be, I offered to share mine. Little did I know the kind of hell the gentlemanly gesture would put me through."

Suddenly, Nash wondered if Samuel was just talking about party planning. There was a look in his eyes that could only be described as regret and a deep sadness. And Nash knew both emotions well. He had lived with them for much too long not to. Although lately, the emotions had been muted by a stronger one. Happiness. Looking at Samuel, he realized that maybe Olivia was right. Maybe everyone needed a companion—even if it was just a running partner. Or the UPS guy.

"Is everything okay, Samuel?" he asked. "If there's something you'd like to talk about..."

Samuel shook himself out of his daydream and looked at Nash. "I'm fine, Mr. Beaumont. And I'll be even better when this Lover's Ball is over." He straightened his tie and smoothed back his hair before cupping his hands on the desk. "So what brings you to the design studio? And please don't tell me it has to do with flower arrangements or costumes."

Realizing that Samuel wasn't going to discuss personal matters, Nash moved on to business. "I came to talk about the new bra collection. The independent survey that was sent out suggests that women find our bras uncomfortable."

Samuel nodded. "It's difficult to find beautiful fabrics that are comfortable and supportive. Which puts bra designers between a rock and a hard spot. Do we design comfortable, ugly bras or uncomfortable, beautiful ones? I think you can guess what most designers go with."

"But if we want to make money, I don't know that we have a choice. Comfort seems to be winning over fashion these days."

Samuel cringed. "And don't I know it. Have you seen the way young ladies dress? Sweats at the grocery store. Yoga tops and pants at restaurants. Even professional work spaces have been infiltrated with slobbery." He shook his head. "When I first started working, there was no such thing as casual Fridays. Every day, you dressed professionally." Nash tried not to look down at the jeans and Henley he'd tossed on that morning as Samuel continued. "And I, for one, refuse to feed into a culture where it's okay to wear flip-flops to a night at the opera. And your uncle felt the same way. I believe our mission statement is 'high-quality, cutting-edge lingerie for the discriminating, fashionable woman.'"

"Okay, I see where you're coming from. And that philosophy might've worked twenty years ago when people weren't so wrapped up in comfort, but I don't think it's going to work now, Samuel."

"So you're suggesting we throw out the entire collection and start over?"

Nash shook his head. "But I don't see why we can't sell both practical bras and fashionable ones."

"There's no guarantee that they will sell."

"Unfortunately, in life, there are no guarantees," he said. "Sometimes you just have to take a chance."

The words he'd spoken to Samuel stayed with him for the rest of the day. They stayed with him during his lunch meeting with Grayson to discuss the models for the swimsuit catalog—Grayson still hadn't found his perfect cover model—and his afternoon meeting with Deacon to discuss the results of the independent survey and his idea to sell comfortable, affordable bras. And the words were there at the edge of his mind when he stopped by Kelly's desk before he left at the end of the day.

"Could you do me a favor, Kelly?" he said. "I need you to send out an invitation to the Lover's Ball, and then I need you to call Deirdre Beaumont and tell her that I'd like the senorita costume after all."

Since there were no guarantees in life, Nash might as well take a chance.

CHAPTER SIXTEEN

*Y*ou sold the apartment complex?" Eden glanced down at her cell phone that sat on her brand-new bathroom vanity. "But why?"

"Because I got an offer I couldn't refuse." Her landlord Mr. Pruitt's voice came through the speaker. "And I was sick and tired of getting hassled by my tenants."

Since Eden had called him daily with complaints, she knew what tenant he was talking about. "And not once did you return my messages. So I don't think you were too hassled." Eden released the hair from the curling iron poised over her head and sectioned off another strand.

"Like I said before, you need to take it up with your new landlord."

His snotty tone had Eden bristling. "Well, a new landlord certainly explains why my apartment is finally fit to live in." It was an understatement. Her apartment was more than fit to live in. Every day for the last week, the handymen had arrived to paint, put down new wood flooring, replace windows, and install a new shower/tub, toilet, and bathroom vanity.

"Yeah," Mr. Pruitt said, "but did you think of what those improvements are going to cost you? Maybe I didn't fix anything, but at least I kept your rent the same."

Eden lowered her curling iron. She hadn't thought of that. There was no way that she could pay a higher rent. She was eating through her savings as is. Her car had broken down and was in the shop for repairs, which meant she wouldn't have a cent to spare until Stella hired her back. And Eden was starting to have her doubts that she could get the story finished in time. After a week of morning runs and evening chats at The Lemon Drop, she was no closer to finding that one piece of the puzzle that would complete the picture of Nash Beaumont. That one piece that would explain why he kept such a tight rein on his sexual desires. And Eden didn't want to know as much as she needed to know. Nash hadn't touched her again since the refrigerator sex. She would say that it had to do with the fact that they were no longer playing the roles of escort and client. But if that were true, then why did she occasionally catch a look in those violet eyes that said he wanted to rip off her clothes and take her hard and hot?

No, there was definitely another piece to the puzzle. And Eden wasn't giving up until she found it.

"Well, thanks for nothing, Mr. Pruitt," she said. "I can only hope that no one has to suffer through you as a landlord again." She reached out and tapped the button to end the call, then went back to curling her hair. Since she didn't want Stella to get too used to not seeing her in the office, she planned to do her research in the janitor's closet today.

After finishing in the bathroom, Eden headed for the kitchen to make herself a power smoothie. She had finally gotten her stomach used to the green sludge, but she still needed to hold her nose while she drank it. She pulled open the refrigerator to get the ingredients and experienced the same hot flash she always experienced when she touched the appliance. The erotic memories left her flushed and wanting. Today was no different, and she had to stand in the cool air for a moment to get her thoughts back on track. Unfortunately, her new roommate derailed them.

"So has the panty billionaire given you another orgasm?"

The apple Eden had just grabbed slipped from her hand and rolled across the floor as she turned to Madison. She wore one of the sexy nighties Nash had sent Eden, her breasts popping out of the too-small bodice. She yawned widely and stretched her arms over her head before smiling. "Good morning. So I guess you didn't stop by the bakery on your run."

Eden picked the apple up from the floor and carried it to the sink with the veggies she'd pulled from the refrigerator. "Sorry, I didn't think about it. But I'll make you a smoothie. They're really pretty good...once you get used to them."

"No thanks. I have never associated green with breakfast." Madison waited for Eden to finish making her smoothie in the blender before she picked up the conversation. "So he still hasn't touched you?"

"No, and I don't think he's going to." Eden pulled out a glass from the cupboard and poured the smoothie into it.

"I don't get it," Madison said. "I've met a lot of weirdos in my life, but this guy takes the cake. What kind of man keeps himself from having sex just to prove he has control?"

"Maybe that was just an excuse. Maybe he doesn't find me sexually attractive. Maybe he doesn't even like me."

"Then how do you explain all the time he spends with you? And all the gifts—the lingerie and a fancy new car that was just as expensive as my Mercedes." Her lips protruded in a pout. "I don't know why I let you talk me into selling my precious baby."

"Because you needed the money to pay off those credit card debts you failed to tell me about," Eden said. "And Nash did not buy me a car. The guy at the automotive repair shop loaned it to me while he's fixing mine."

Madison stared at her as if she were crazy. "Automotive repair shops do not usually loan people cars—especially brand-new Porsche 911s."

Eden stopped holding her nose and lowered her smoothie. It did seem strange that they would loan her such a nice car. When she had first gotten it, she had been terrified of scratching the pretty red paint, but Nash had told her that the automotive repair shop had insurance. But now that she thought about it . . .

"So you think the car is from Nash?" she said. "But how would he arrange that?"

"Because he's a billionaire, Eden. Money can arrange anything. Georgie once arranged for me to have dinner with Brad Pitt . . . without Angelina Jolie and all their kids." She flapped a hand. "Of course, it was perfectly platonic. But that just proves that money talks, and if a man wants to give you a gift, he will. And speaking of gifts…" She turned and walked around the breakfast bar. "You have three more. One by regular mail and two by separate couriers." She knelt and pulled three boxes out from under the bed—two average-size and one small. Eden recognized the writing on the small one immediately.

"Mimi and Pops," she said. And even before she peeled back the four layers of packing tape, she knew what she'd find. She lifted out the baggie of marijuana, and Madison's eyes widened.

"And here I thought you were kidding?"

Eden released an exasperated sigh. "I wish." She put the baggie back in the box to flush later before opening the next box. She expected more lingerie. Instead, beneath the layer of tissue paper, she found a beautiful gold gown.

Madison sighed as Eden lifted it from the box. "I didn't know French Kiss made princess gowns."

"I didn't either." Eden stared in confusion at the beaded gown that looked like it belonged in a Shakespearian play. She reached for the purple envelope that was left in the box, hoping for some kind of explanation. Inside was an invitation that matched the envelope, but before Eden caught more than a glance of scrolled letters and dark purple kisses, Madison released a squeal and jerked the invitation away from her.

"Oh. My. Gosh! Do you know what this is?" She did a little happy jump that had her big boobs bouncing. "It's an invitation to the Lover's Ball this Saturday night. And that must be the costume you're supposed to wear."

The ball had been on Eden's upcoming events to cover for the newspaper, but since being fired, she hadn't given it much thought until now. She wondered why Nash hadn't mentioned wanting to invite her.

"Now open this box." Madison thrust the other box at her. "I'm dying to know what goes with your costume."

The other box held another costume. This one a deep purple with black lace. As soon as Madison saw it, she released another squeal. "This doesn't go with your costume at all. And if that costume is yours, then this one must be mine." She pulled out the dress and held it up to her. It looked a little small, but Eden wasn't about to point that out when Madison was so happy. She twirled around the room, the dress flaring out around her. "We're going to the ball! And with any luck, I'll find me a prince."

"Oh no," Eden said, "you're not soliciting at the Lover's Ball. You're not an escort anymore, remember?"

Madison stopped twirling. "I'm not talking about going back to being an escort. You're right, that is too risky a business. But I've been thinking...since I'm so good at taking care of rich, old men, what if I marry one? And don't look so surprised. We both know that, with my lack of job experience, I'm not going to get hired. But even though I have no job experience, I do have man experience. I know exactly what makes them happy. And isn't that a wife's job?"

"But what about love?"

Madison laughed. "I stopped waiting for love a long time ago, sweetie."

It was a sad statement, and Madison's laughing acceptance made it all the more so. And Eden became even more determined to help her friend.

"Well, I love you," she said. "And I'm not going to let you sell yourself to the highest bidder. You're much too smart for that." She moved over to her laptop on the breakfast bar and brought up a job website. "How are you with kids? There's an opening at a daycare for a van driver."

Madison put down the costume and moved behind her. "I'm good with kids. I helped raise my siblings. It's just doubtful that the daycare would hire me to drive their van. As you know, I have a bit of a problem keeping under the speed limit, and besides the speeding tickets, there were a few little fender benders when I first learned how to parallel park."

Eden moved on. "Okay, what about working in retail. There's a job opening at a jewelry store in Union Square—"

Madison clapped her hands. "A jewelry store? Like diamonds and sapphires? Oh my gosh. I would love to work at a jewelry store!"

Realizing exactly where Madison's paychecks would go, Eden closed her laptop and turned with a smile. "Let's keep looking," she said brightly. "I'll find you something better than an escort or gold digger, or my name isn't Eden Huckabee."

* * *

Once at work, Eden spent the first two hours searching jobsites and making a list of possible opportunities for

Madison. After Madison brought up her experience with older men, Eden decided to focus on retirement and convalescent homes. Although most of the facilities wanted experienced applicants, she figured there was a chance that they would hire Madison. Especially if Eden coached her on being persistent.

Eden's job search was more fruitful than her search for information on Nash. She found nothing else on him or his girlfriend's suicide. Wondering if she'd missed something, she pulled up the story again and reread it. Then she pulled up the picture she'd saved of them. She was staring at Nash's smiling face and wondering what had happened to dim the smile when Mike walked into the janitor's closet.

"So there you are."

She closed the file and swiveled her chair around. "Let me guess, Stella hasn't missed me at all."

Mike grinned. "No, but I have. Where have you been?"

"Just working on my story."

"I overheard you telling Stella that you've got a new angle for the story. I'm glad you've moved on from the ditzy prostitute."

"Madison isn't ditzy," Eden said. "She just needs some direction."

Mike shook his head. "Great. Now you've become her life coach. Was she the friend that dropped by and kept you from meeting me for dinner?"

"I'm so sorry about that, Mike."

"Sorry enough to have dinner with me tonight?"

It was her night off so there was nothing keeping her from accepting the offer. Nothing but the hope that Nash would stop by her apartment. And with no customers to wait on, she might actually get some answers. Or maybe some more refrigerator sex.

"I can't tonight," she said. "I need to stop by and see my grandparents." It wasn't a lie. After receiving the marijuana in the mail, she needed to have a little talk with her grandparents. Again.

His face fell. "Yeah, sure. Maybe another time." He glanced at the laptop. "So if you're doing a story on prostitution, why were you looking at a picture of Nash Beaumont? Please don't tell me you're crushing on the guy like every other female in the city."

Crushing? It was more like lusting. And trying to hide her blush, she swiveled her chair back around and shrugged. "I just stumbled upon the picture."

"That's good, because the guy is a pervert."

"What?" She whirl back around so fast that she kicked the mop bucket with her foot and sent it sailing toward Mike. Mike grabbed the mop handle before it hit him in the face, but the bucket still cracked his shins.

"Damn, Huckabee," he said as he grimaced in pain. "I get that you don't want to date me. You don't have to use violence to make your point."

"Sorry," she said. "So how do you know about Nash?"

He rubbed his shins. "I planned on doing a story about the Beaumonts when they first came to town. But after I dug up some dirt, Stella vetoed the story. She said it wasn't newsworthy enough to warrant getting into a lawsuit with the Beaumonts."

Eden stared at him in disbelief. She had wasted all this time working on a story that Mike had already written and Stella had already vetoed. Which meant that Stella wasn't going to rehire her. And unless Eden wanted to spend the rest of her life in the janitor's closet, she needed to pack up her things and accept the fact that she wasn't going to be a reporter here...and maybe not anywhere. She waited for depression and heartache to set in, but all she felt was a slight stab of disappointment.

Maybe Stella was right. Maybe she had been chasing the wrong dream. But if reporting wasn't in her blood, what was? It was a good question. One she needed to find the answer to. But she wouldn't find it here in the janitor's closet.

Getting to her feet, she started taking down the pictures on the corkboard. "Stella is a pretty hard sell."

"You can say that again. I thought I had a great scoop when a friend I know from Louisiana told me his sister sat on the jury when Nash's case went to trial."

The thumbtack slipped from Eden's fingers and pinged off her laptop before it hit the floor. She slowly turned around. "Trial?" Her voice squeaked out the word.

Mike's eyes narrowed. "You didn't know? But I thought that's what we were talking about. What other perverted thing did Nash Beaumont do?"

It was hard to answer when her heart felt like it was getting ready to beat out of her chest. Nash had gone to trial? But for what? Certainly it couldn't be for seducing women in the dark.

She tried to smile, but her lips felt brittle. "Nothing. I just didn't realize he'd gone to trial for...it."

Mike shrugged. "He probably shouldn't have. It turned out there wasn't much evidence. But I guess the girl had yet to turn eighteen and had a father who just happened to work for the district attorney's office. Of course, the jury found him not guilty. Which is why Stella was so against publishing the story. But I think the guy did it. I think Nash Beaumont raped her. Why else would she commit suicide?"

CHAPTER SEVENTEEN

*S*omething was wrong.

Not with bra sales. Or finding the right catalog model. Or hooking Samuel up with the UPS guy. Or even Grayson stealing Nash's Lothario costume and switching it out for his puffed-sleeve, embroidered Romeo shirt and tights. What was wrong had to do with an escort who talked with her hands. Ran awkwardly. And was no longer interested in playing his games.

Nash shouldn't blame Eden—what woman would want to hang out with a guy as screwed up as he was? And yet, he did blame her. He blamed her for canceling their morning runs with the lame excuse of a twisted ankle. He blamed her for treating him like he had a contagious disease when he showed up that night at The Lemon Drop to check on her injury. And he blamed her for completely ignoring his invitation to the Lover's Ball and making him feel like someone had punched him in the chest with a set of brass knuckles.

"I should've known that you wouldn't wear the tights." A woman swept up in a medieval dress with draped sleeves. Even with the long, blond, braided wig and jeweled mask, Nash had no trouble recognizing Deirdre Beaumont. She, on the other hand, didn't recognize him at all. Of course, his face was half-covered by a mask. And all the Beaumont brothers had the same unruly hair and stubborn jaw.

She swatted his arm. "Shame on you, Grayson. Romeo didn't wear faded jeans. Although since your doublet still looks too short, I guess I don't blame you. The women are already eyeballing you and Nash like desserts on a tray. We wouldn't want to start a riot." She glanced over her shoulder. "I must say that Olivia was right. All Nash needs is a black fedora and a sword, and he'd look just like Zorro."

Nash followed her gaze through the crowd of costumed people until he spotted Grayson in the solid black outfit and mask. He did look like Zorro, and Nash had every intention of verbally dueling with him before the night was out.

"So where's your date?" Deirdre asked. "After you made such a fuss about her Juliet gown being perfect, I'd like to see it on." Nash would've told her that he wasn't Grayson if someone in the crowd hadn't distracted her. "Finally," she said. "I had started to think the man wasn't coming."

Nash turned to find a man in full armor standing not more than ten feet away, trying to adjust the visor of the helmet. The costume looked extremely uncomfortable, but cool as hell. "Who is that?" Nash asked.

Deirdre patted his arm. "That, my dear Romeo, would be my date, Lancelot."

"Lancelot? I thought Guinevere's husband was King Arthur."

"You obviously don't know the story of Camelot. King Arthur might've been my husband, but Lancelot has always been my one true love." She smiled slyly. "Even if he doesn't realize it yet. Now if you'll excuse me?" She swept away, but surprisingly, not in the direction of Lancelot.

"So what has Mother in such a hurry?" Olivia walked up with Deacon. Nash had to admit that they made a perfect couple. It wasn't the sheik and harem-girl costumes as much as their smiles of contentment whenever they glanced at each other. Nash didn't feel nearly as content as he searched the crowd for a purple senorita costume.

"So I'm going to assume by the scowl on your face that Grayson shanghaied your costume, Nash," Deacon said.

"What?" Olivia leaned closer. "Oh my gosh, it is you, Nash." She glanced over her shoulder. "So Grayson is Lothario? I thought there was something different about you...him." She giggled. "What fun. I would love to be able to change places with someone for one night."

"Really?" Deacon sent her a pointed look. "And just who would you like to change places with?"

Olivia took only a second to think. "You're right. There's not one person in the whole wide world I'd rather be, my sheik." She rose up on the toes of her satin slippers and kissed him. "Now would you mind finding me something to eat? I'm starving, and all the waiters seem to have is champagne."

"As my harem girl, I think you're supposed to be waiting on me."

She sent him a sultry smile. "Which is exactly what I intend to do . . . later tonight in our reserved room of the sultan tent."

Nash had seen the huge tent that was set up in one corner of the ballroom, and had wondered what its purpose was. Obviously, for Deacon and Olivia to play sex slave.

"That might just make this costume worthwhile," Deacon said. In a swirl of robes, he headed for the buffet table.

Once he was gone, Olivia moved closer. "So have you seen Doug? Do you think he'll show up?"

Nash didn't care if Doug showed up. The only person he cared about showing up was Eden. And it was starting to look like that wasn't going to happen.

Misreading his thoughts, Olivia patted his arm. "It's not your fault if Doug doesn't come, Nash. Of course, he might be here, and we just don't know it. Mom insisted on picking his and Samuel's couples' costumes. While she bullied Samuel into accepting the offer, Doug refused. He said that he had the perfect one in mind. I can only hope that it's not as inappropriate as the Huckabees'."

That got Nash's attention. "You invited the Huckabees?"

"Actually, I think Grayson invited them and their granddaughter."

It figured that Grayson would want to make sure Eden came to the ball. No doubt, he was trying to do a little matchmaking. Which meant that maybe Eden had decided to come with her grandparents instead of him. Nash glanced around until he found the Huckabees. They weren't naked, but they were close. Doris wore a long blond wig and a beige-colored leotard with one strategically placed fig leaf. Hammond wore a beige Speedo swimsuit with a matching leaf. Unfortunately, Eden wasn't with them. Just a woman in a gold princess costume. And as much as he had no business asking the Huckabees where Eden was—especially after she'd given him the cold shoulder—that was exactly what he intended to do.

"I think I'll go say 'hi,'" he said to Olivia.

"But what about Doug?"

"Doug?" Deacon walked up with a plate of food. "Who is Doug?"

Nash left Olivia to explain as he weaved his way through the throng of costumed partygoers. But before he reached the Huckabees, he ran into Grayson.

"Hey, Romeo," Grayson greeted him with a smirk a mile wide. "Lookin' good."

"You want your ass kicking now? Or later?" Nash asked.

Grayson laughed. "I don't know what you're pissed about. You look great in that girlie shirt. Of course, the jeans look ridiculous. Deirdre was right; panty hose make the outfit." When Nash went to grab him, he sidestepped out of the way. "Now remember Olivia's mother, big brother. She'd be upset if you ruined her party with a fight. Besides, I thought you wouldn't be too pissed when Eden showed up as Juliet."

"Juliet?"

"Haven't you seen her? She's standing right over there with her grandparents." Grayson nodded in the direction of the Huckabees.

Nash's gaze snapped over to the woman in the princess

costume, and he was surprised that he hadn't recognized Eden before. There was no woman alive who had hair as beautiful. It fell around her shoulders in a waterfall of dark waves that shimmered in the light from the chandeliers like the ocean at midnight. The embroidered sleeves of the gown encased her long arms and then belled at the elbows like the skirt of the dress belled from her high waist. The bodice was so tight that it pushed her breasts up over the low neckline in soft, pale swells of flesh that Nash longed to touch.

"But she was supposed to come as a senorita," he said more to himself than Grayson. "I sent her the costume."

"Obviously, she liked my Juliet costume better." Grayson slapped Nash on the back. "Sorry, Bro, but I thought you weren't going to invite her. And anyone can see that you two make a perfect match."

The perfect match? Nash wasn't a perfect match for anyone. And he couldn't blame Eden for realizing it. So why was she here? Especially after giving him the cold shoulder.

"Finally! I found you!"

The words pulled Nash's attention away from Eden to the big, hairy guy in the leather bra and boy short set. A bra and boy short set that looked a lot like the one in the Lothario Collection. Except the guy must've had to alter the bra to fit his bodybuilder's chest. A leather mask, thigh highs, heels, and a riding crop rounded out the costume. Nash couldn't help feeling amused that he was talking to Grayson.

"I'm sorry," Grayson said, "but I'm afraid that I don't..."

The guy lifted his mask and winked. "It's Doug." He smacked Grayson's butt with the riding crop. "Like the outfit? It's from your collection."

It wasn't often that Nash had the opportunity to get back at his brother so eloquently handed to him. He took it without even a twinge of guilt.

"I'm sure Nash absolutely loves your outfit. Don't ya, Bro?" Before Grayson could get over his confusion, Nash shot him a smile and walked away.

Once he left his brother, he headed straight to Juliet. He was tired of working his brain trying to figure out what was wrong. He wanted answers. And he wanted them now. Unfortunately, first, he had to greet the Huckabees.

"I think your costumes should win the prize," he said as he moved behind Eden. "After all, Adam and Eve were the first lovers."

Eden whirled around, and he found himself drowning in twin pools of gold that shimmered with fear. And if anyone should recognize the emotion in a woman's eyes, it was Nash. He had seen it too many times not to. But he had never thought he would see it in Eden's eyes. Not spunky Eden's. His name came out of her lips as a hushed whisper.

"Nash."

It was a struggle to keep the smile on his face. "I think it's Romeo tonight." He made a courtly bow. "And from the looks of things, you're Juliet." He watched her struggle for a reply before her grandmother cut in.

"Oh, isn't that cute. You didn't tell me that you were Juliet, Eden."

Eden released her breath as if she'd been holding it. "I wasn't sure. I never liked Shakespeare."

Nash should've left. He should've turned and walked away without another word. Instead, he just stood there, frozen in the fearful eyes surrounded by her jeweled mask. "Then we have something in common. I failed it in high school."

"Well, I think your costumes are adorable," Doris said.

"But not very original, if you ask me," Hammond said. "Now, your grandmother and I have original costumes. We're not Adam and Eve. We're a couple from my favorite reality television show...*Naked and Afraid*. Have you seen the show, Nathan? It's where these couples have to survive out in the elements without any food or water or clothes. Nothing but a knapsack and a knife. Although mine doesn't have a knife as much as goodies." He pulled a brownie out of the burlap bag hooked over his shoulder and offered it to Nash. "Brownie?"

Before Nash could politely decline, Eden grabbed the brownie out of her grandfather's hand. "I thought I told you no brownies, Pops!"

"Stop being so uptight, Eden." Hammond snatched the brownie and took a big bite. "This place could use an ice breaker." He nodded at the orchestra set up behind the empty dance floor. "And where's the DJ? If they were playing rock and roll instead of this elevator music, folks would be dancing."

"Maybe they just need the first couple to break the ice." Doris sent a pointed look at Nash. "And what better set of lovers to start the dancing than Romeo and Juliet? Now get out there, you two, and get things started."

At the moment, the only thing Nash wanted to get started was a large bottle of Johnnie Walker. He was about to make his excuses and go in search of one when Eden turned and headed for the dance floor. He should've let her go. But damned if he could.

Nash knew how to dance. Any Southern boy who loved women knew how to waltz to a slow country song. The song the orchestra played wasn't country, but it wasn't difficult to pick up the one-two-three beat. What was difficult was watching Eden flinch when he placed a hand on her waist.

"I guess you prefer my touch in the dark," he said dryly. He watched her throat move as she swallowed.

"I don't know why I let my grandmother talk me into this. I can't dance."

"Then I guess I'll have to teach you." He took her hand in his and slowly guided her through the steps. Once she had them, he took control and swept her around the floor. Doris had been right. As soon as they started dancing, other couples joined them. They were on their fourth lap when Eden finally spoke.

"Why Romeo? Aren't you supposed to be Lothario... the seducer of women?"

"Grayson had a problem with the costume so he switched with me. That, and I think he's trying to do a little matchmaking." He paused for only a beat. "If you're avoiding me, why did you come?" Her gaze locked with his, and he thought she might make up some foolish lie. Instead she was brutally, painfully honest.

"Madison begged me to."

There were other questions he wanted to ask, but it seemed pointless now. He stopped in mid-step and released her. "Then I won't make you suffer my company

any longer." He turned to walk away when her next words froze him in his tracks.

"Was Melissa in your high school Shakespeare class?"

The fear in her eyes and flinch at his touch all made perfect sense now. He slowly turned back around, then hesitated only a second before he grabbed her hand and led her through the dancers to the sultan's tent. Inside was a series of rooms separated by walls of colorful fabric. He searched until he found the one reserved for the Beaumonts and pulled Eden inside.

The room held one long couch with brightly colored pillows and a coffee table with lit candles and a bottle of champagne on ice. He released the curtain from the hook and closed it before turning to Eden.

"So how did you find out?"

"A friend of a friend served on the jury." She moved as far away from him as she could get, her hands nervously smoothing out the velvet of her gown.

"So you know about the trial."

She nodded, then turned her back to him as if she couldn't stand to look at him for one second more. He knew how she felt. He could barely stand to look in the mirror. She released her breath on a quiver of air before she spoke. "Did you rape her?"

It was hard to believe that Eden was the first person to ask him the question. His brothers and father had never believed that Nash could be capable of rape. And his defense attorney hadn't wanted to know. He'd just wanted to win—to twist the facts until he'd convinced a jury that his client wasn't guilty. It was a relief to finally state the truth.

"Yes, I raped her."

Eden's shoulders fell as her breath rushed out. "Oh my God." She clutched her waist as if in pain. It was her pain that had him trying to explain something that had no explanation.

"I didn't even know her." He swallowed. "Melissa was just a girl in algebra who stared at me during class. I knew she had a crush on me. It was pretty obvious. But we never spoke...at least not until the day she asked me to prom." He tried to take a deep breath, but his lungs seemed to have shrunk to the size of peas. All he could get in were shallow breaths that left him feeling light-headed and dizzy.

"She came up to me right after baseball practice. Some of my friends were there, and they got a big kick out of how flustered and nervous she was. Their smug looks pissed me off, and before I could think about it, I had said yes." He jerked off his mask, hoping that would help him breathe as the memories came flooding back. Memories that had been buried for too long. Or maybe not long enough.

"But the night of the prom, she wasn't the same flustered, nervous girl," he said. "She was different...more aggressive. She wore a lot makeup, and her dress was sexy as hell. She'd hired a limo to drive us to the gym where the dance was being held and snuck in two bottles of champagne. After the dance was over, she had the limo driver take us to a hotel."

He scrubbed both hands through his hair. "I should've left then...or as soon as I stepped in the room and saw the rose petals on the bed in the shape of a heart. But I was already drunk by that time and I decided to give her what I thought she wanted. Except once we started having sex, she panicked." Eden turned, and staring into her hurt eyes, he couldn't continue with the story. The only word he could get out was *fuck* before he jerked back the curtain to leave. Her hand on his arm stopped him.

"So you were already having sex when she asked you to stop?"

"Does it matter when?" he said. "No is no."

She took a step closer. "I agree. But don't you think that there were some extenuating circumstances? You were a drunk kid, Nash. And it wasn't like you forced her to go to the hotel room. She knew what was going to happen and even orchestrated it."

"Bullshit!" The anger that he'd been holding in for so long spilled out. "That's exactly what my lawyer convinced the jury of—what he convinced me of. That it wasn't my fault because Melissa had planned it, and penetration had already taken place. Therefore, I shouldn't be punished. But I wasn't some inexperienced kid. I was eighteen, and I'd had sex—a lot of sex." He thumped his chest. "I knew better than to lose control!"

Eden's eyes filled with tears. "But haven't you punished yourself enough?"

The words felt like a swift kick in the stomach, and Nash had a hard time getting in enough air to answer. "No," he said in a choked voice. "I don't think I've punished myself nearly enough. Not when Melissa is dead."

CHAPTER EIGHTEEN

*E*den tried to stop Nash before he walked out, but her feet got tangled in her skirts. Then once she got untangled, she got lost in the tent's maze of silken fabric and ended up in a room with a group of rowdy underwear models who refused to let her leave until she'd done a shot of tequila. By the time she downed the shot and found her way out of the tent, Nash was nowhere to be found. But she did find another Beaumont.

"Hey, Juliet. Whassup?"

Eden glanced over to find Grayson sitting at a table. His mask was off, his hair mussed, and a sappy smile tipped his lips. But she barely registered his condition.

"Have you seen Nash?" she asked.

"Nash." His smile got bigger. "I want you to know that I love that guy. I mean I really love that guy. And I don't want to see him hurt." He pointed a finger. "And you've hurt him. He's been moping around the office the last few days like he's lost his best friend."

Eden knew how he felt. Ever since Mike had told her about Nash's trial, she had been miserable. She hadn't been able to eat or sleep and spent most of her time on the computer trying to find any information she could. But because a juvenile had been involved, the courthouse files were sealed so she found nothing. Nothing at all. Which should've made her believe the worst. Mike had no reason to lie, and Nash's problem touching women pointed to his guilt. But something inside her had refused to believe that Nash was capable of rape. And as far as she was concerned, it hadn't been rape. It had been a bad judgment call made by a drunken teenager— make that two drunken teenagers. Melissa was just as responsible for what happened as Nash was. She had set the entire scene and brought the alcohol in the limousine. It was just sad that one night had ruined two lives so completely.

Grayson took her hand. "You, my beautiful Juliet, have the power to save my brother...if only you will."

Eden wanted to believe that she had the power to save Nash. Not for a story, but because she truly believed that he was worth saving.

"Where is he?" she asked again. "Where's Nash?"

"He left." Grayson waved a hand. "Without a fare-thee-well." He started laughing as if he found that highly amusing.

Eden studied him. "How much have you had to drink tonight, Grayson?"

He squinted his eyes. "Maybe one glass of champagne."

The way he was acting, it was more like one bottle. But maybe that would work in Eden's favor. She sat down in the chair next to him. "Tell me about Nash, Grayson. What was he like growing up?"

Grayson sent her a loopy smile. "The definition of cool. Guys wanted to be him and girls just wanted him. They swarmed around him like bees to honey."

"Like Melissa."

Surprise crossed Grayson face before he nodded. "She was more like obsessed with him, if you ask me. It was freaky the way she watched him at school. She was different for sure, which probably explained why she didn't have any friends...and why Nash agreed to go to prom with her. I think he felt sorry for her and didn't want to hurt her feelings. He didn't date high school girls. He didn't have to. Not when he had college girls and grown women throwing themselves at him." His eyes narrowed on her. "Are you hungry? Because I'm starving." He lifted the knapsack that sat on the table and pulled out a brownie.

Eden's eyes widened, and she grabbed the brownie before he could take a bite. "No!"

He held up his hands. "Dude, you don't have to go ballistic. You can have the last brownie if you want it."

"The last?" She looked in the knapsack to find it empty. "Please tell me you didn't eat all the brownies, Grayson."

He flashed a grin. "I did not eat all the brownies. After your grandfather asked me to watch his purse while he danced, I only helped myself to one...maybe two."

Knowing that there were eight brownies to a batch, Eden became even more frantic. "Then what happened to the other ones?"

Grayson shrugged. "I don't have a clue." He pointed to the dance floor. "But Pops might know."

Eden followed his finger to her grandparents, who were leading all the dancers in the hand jive. Pops and Mimi's fig leaves were wilted, but they looked as fresh and peppy as Adam and Eve before the tempting. But Eden was tempted. Tempted to knock them both upside their heads for not realizing that it wasn't legal to sneak marijuana into people's brownies.

While Grayson stood up and starting doing the hand jive, Eden rubbed her temples and tried to think. Maybe things weren't as bad as she thought. Since Grayson hadn't pressed charges the first time her grandmother had served him magic brownies, she didn't think he'd do it this time. So that meant all she needed to do was make sure the other people who ate the brownies didn't. But first, she had to make sure that Grayson didn't do something stupid.

Getting to her feet, she hooked an arm through his. "Come on, dude. You need to drink some water and chill out." She headed for the sultan's tent, but ran into Madison before she got there. Madison had tried to alter the senorita gown herself, and the result had left her breasts more than a little exposed.

"Oh my gosh," she said, "you should see the chocolate fountain. It is unbelievable—hey, is that Nash's brother? What's wrong with him?"

Grayson zeroed in on Madison's ample cleavage. "*Hola*, senorita, can I draw you naked?"

Madison giggled. "Only if you like fat women."

"You, my sweet, are not fat. You are voluptuous—ly beautiful."

Madison looked at Eden. "Is he drunk?"

"He ate two of my grandparents' brownies."

"Ahh." She looked at Grayson. "So what are we going to do with him?"

"Do you think you could take him to the Beaumonts' reserved room in the sultan tent and keep an eye on him while I go see who else my grandparents have drugged?'

Madison took Grayson's arm. "Come on, sweetie. How would you like some munchies?"

Once they were on their way to the sultan's tent, Eden headed for the dance floor. Her grandparents had moved from the hand jive to the La Bamba, and they were not pleased when she pulled them off the floor.

"What is going on, Eden?" Mimi asked. "Your grand-father paid a pretty penny for the orchestra to play that song."

"Please tell me that he didn't pay them with brownies." Eden shook the knapsack at them. "You can't pass out drugs to people!"

Her grandparents exchanged looks before Pops spoke. "You really need to lighten up, Eden. You're as tight as an overwound clock."

"You are, dear," Mimi said. "We would never pass out harmful drugs to people—a little cannabis isn't harmful. In fact, it is very medicinal."

Eden sighed in exasperation. "Who did you give brownies to?"

"Just a few people that needed a little loosening up," Pops said. "There was the couple who are getting mar-ried. Jasper and…Kelsey."

"Jason and Kelly," Mimi corrected. "But we only gave one to Jason, remember? Kelly was watching her weight so she could fit into her wedding gown."

Pops snapped his fingers. "That's right." He winked at his wife. "Then you and I each had one, Doris."

Eden calculated. "So that's three, and with the two Grayson ate, and the one still in the bag, that makes six. Which means that only two are missing. Who are the other two people?"

"Lancelot!" Pops yelled as if he was a contestant on a game show.

"You're right, Hammond," Mimi said. "It was Lancelot and Queen Guinevere."

"Okay. I want you to see if you can find this Jason and take him to the tent before he gets in trouble. Grayson is already in one of the reserved rooms. I'll see if I can find Lancelot and the queen. Did you get their names?"

"I didn't catch Lancelot's," Mimi said. "But Guinevere is Deirdre Beaumont, Olivia's mother."

Great. Her grandparents had drugged two Beaumonts in one night.

It wasn't as easy as Eden thought to track down Lancelot and Deirdre Beaumont. The ballroom had gotten even more crowded, and she struggled to get through the mass of costumed people, let alone find anyone. She had about given up when she ran into Nash's older brother.

She wouldn't have recognized him if she hadn't overheard him talking to the petite harem girl at his side. His voice had the same Southern flavoring that Nash's did. But his was louder and more commanding.

"Tell me what's going on, Livy. And don't say 'nothing.' You've been watching the crowd like you're waiting for something to happen all evening."

"Really, Deacon," she said, "there's not anything going

on. I just want to talk with Samuel about some new designs, and I can't seem to find him." She craned her neck. "I thought I saw him earlier, but I was mistaken. He's coming as Hugh Hefner, not Lancelot."

Eden stopped so suddenly she tripped over the long skirt of her dress and stumbled right into Deacon. He easily caught her and set her back on her feet.

"Are you okay?" he asked.

"Just clumsy," she said as she brushed at her dress.

"Or perhaps a little too much champagne?" Deacon flashed a smile. It was similar to Nash's, just not as mind-altering. "Deacon Beaumont." He held out a hand. "And this is my wife, Olivia."

Eden shook his hand. "Eden Huckabee."

"Any relation to Doris and Hammond?"

"They're my grandparents."

"You're kidding." Olivia took her hand from Deacon's. "What a pleasure to meet you, Eden. I used to live next door to your grandparents. My brothers-in-law still do." She tipped her head. "Speaking of which... isn't that the dress Grayson had made for his date?" Her eyes widened. "You're Grayson's date?"

"Actually... I was invited by Nash."

Deacon and Olivia exchanged glances before Deacon spoke. "Really? And where is my brother?"

"I think he might've left. I can't find him anywhere."

Deacon's eyes darkened. "He left you?"

"Not exactly. We really didn't come as a couple." Needing a way out of the conversation so she could catch Deirdre Beaumont, she improvised. "I'm sorry to rush off, but could you point me in the direction of the bathroom?"

"No need for that," Olivia said. "I'll be happy to show you." Before Eden could decline the offer, she took her arm and pulled her away.

"Thanks so much for offering to help me," Eden said, "but if you just tell me where it is, I think I can find it on my own."

Olivia kept tugging her through the crowd. "Of course you can. But I needed the excuse to get away from Deacon. I adore the man, but sometimes he can be a little overbearing." She shot a glance at Eden. "So tell me how you and Nash met."

Eden searched through her mind for a half-truth. "We're training for the Bay City Marathon together."

"Really? I didn't realize Nash was running in the marathon."

"I think it was a spur-of-the-moment decision."

Olivia pulled Eden around a group of partygoers. "That doesn't sound like Nash. As much as he tries to make people think he's this laid-back, fun-loving guy, he likes things to be scheduled and planned. Deacon said that Nash used to plan meals a good month in advance."

"I heard that Nash cooked for his brothers after his mother died."

Olivia stopped and turned to Eden, her eyes direct. "Nash told you about his mother?" Before Eden could answer, she was enveloped in a hug. "That's wonderful news. I've been as worried about Nash as I've been about Samuel." She pulled back. "Both of them keep all their emotions bottled up inside. I'm glad Nash has found someone he can open up to."

Eden wished that were the case. But Nash still kept all

his emotions bottled inside. And now Eden understood why. He blamed himself for Melissa's death, and she had to wonder if what happened that night was the real reason behind Melissa's suicide. It was certainly something Eden wanted to investigate further. Not that Nash would believe her even if she found evidence to the contrary. Nothing short of shock therapy would get him out of his mind-set. Her gaze landed on the man standing behind Olivia in the leather boy shorts and bra that looked identical to the ones Nash had sent her.

Olivia followed her gaze and laughed. "There are some characters here tonight." The man turned to say something to the guy next to him and showed off a nasty black eye that had Olivia gasping. "Doug?"

Doug turned to them. "Oh, hi, Mrs. Beaumont."

Olivia moved closer. "What happened to your eye?"

He touched it tentatively. "Just a little misunderstanding with Mr. Beaumont."

"Deacon hit you?"

"No, his brother." He sighed. "I guess he's not gay."

Eden was having a hard time keeping up, but Olivia seemed to know what was going on. "Of course Nash isn't gay. It's Samuel. Samuel is the one who likes you."

"Samuel?" Doug looked confused. "Samuel in the design department? But that guy's not gay."

"Yes, he is." Olivia stood on her tiptoes and scanned the crowd. "And if we can find him, I'll prove it to you. He's supposed to be wearing a Hugh Hefner costume."

"No, he's not," Doug said. "I just talked with the guy, and he's wearing a really uncomfortable-looking suit of armor."

Olivia looked totally confused. "So he did come as Lancelot?"

"Yeah, he and Queen Guinevere were giggling like schoolgirls on the way to the sultan tents."

Olivia laughed. "You must need glasses. Those two don't get along at all. Which means that I better intervene before they kill each other." She pointed a finger at Doug. "Don't go anywhere. I want you and Samuel to get a chance to talk." She turned and headed for the tents, and Eden followed on her heels.

"Why don't you let me find them?" Eden asked. "You should go back to your husband. I'm sure he'll get worried if you don't show up soon."

"Probably. But this shouldn't take long. I just need to make sure that Samuel doesn't kill my—" She paused just outside the opening to the sultan's tent. "Mother?"

A woman stepped out. If she had been a queen, she now looked like the court strumpet. Her wig was askew, the laces of her gown loose, and her lipstick smudged. When she saw Olivia, she did giggle like a schoolgirl. Or like she'd eaten a magic brownie.

"Livy," she announced in a loud voice. "Lancelot just ravished the queen!"

CHAPTER NINETEEN

It was a beautiful day. The brilliant sun beamed, the blue sky stretched on forever, and the tranquil ocean gently rocked the sixty-foot yacht that Nash and Grayson had chartered for the day. And yet, Nash couldn't enjoy any of it. Not when he felt like he'd been rolled through the wringers of Grandma Beaumont's old washing machine... repeatedly.

"I've found a model for the swimsuit catalog."

Nash turned to his little brother, who sat in the other plush leather chair at the back of the yacht. As always when they went fishing, Grayson didn't fish as much as sketch. His fishing rod and bare feet rested on the edge of the boat while his sketchpad rested on his knees. The choppy ocean waves must've given him some inspiration, because his pencil was flying over the paper.

"Your perfect cover model?" Nash asked.

"She's not perfect, but since the shoot is this week, she'll have to do."

"Where did you find her?"

"Last night at the ball. She helped me come down from the Huckabees' brownies."

Nash didn't want to be reminded of the ball. Or how beautiful Eden looked in the Juliet gown. Or the fear in her eyes when she'd looked at him. He squinted up at the sun, hoping to burn the image from his retinas. "Please don't tell me that you're going to start that again," he said.

"I'm not kidding. I was stoned to the bone last night just like I was the night I had dinner at their house. I'm telling you that those old folks are cooking up some magic in those brownies."

Nash tugged his John Deere hat lower on his forehead. "And I think you've spent too much time sketching and not enough time in the real world. The Huckabees are a little unconventional, but they aren't slipping drugs into their brownies."

"Then explain why Eden was so freaked out last night." Grayson stopped drawing and looked at Nash. "Or maybe she wasn't upset about the brownies as much as something else. What happened between you two to make you leave early?"

The end happened. That's what happened. Whatever he and Eden had was over the minute she found out about Melissa. She might act like it didn't matter—like she thought it was just a teenage mistake—but he knew better. A man being accused of rape wasn't something a woman could forget.

"Eden and I aren't a couple, Gray. We've never been a couple."

"Bullshit. You've had more mood swings in the last

month than our pregnant sister-in-law. Admit it, Nash. You like Eden."

Yes, he liked her. More than liked her. But that made no difference now. And to ensure that there would be no more matchmaking attempts from his brother, he threw Eden under the bus.

"It doesn't matter if I like her. She's a prostitute."

Grayson dropped his pencil. "What?"

"You heard me." He reeled in his line. "I hired her one night."

Grayson released his breath. "Shit. I never would've guessed that. But knowing her crazy grandparents, I guess it's not surprising. What is surprising, is you hiring her. Why would you do that, Nash?"

He could've continued the lie—continued to try to make his brothers think that he was a carefree guy who loved life. But he was tired of the ruse. Tired of being someone he wasn't.

Pulling back the fishing pole, he recast. Then once he'd adjusted the line, he told the truth. "Because your big brother is one screwed-up sonofabitch."

There was a long pause before Grayson spoke. "Because of Melissa? But it's been almost ten years now, Nash."

Nash knew exactly how long it had been. Every day was checked off in his brain like a prisoner drawing chalk tally marks on the wall of his cell. Nash felt like a prisoner. A prisoner in a body that had gone too long without the taste of a woman's mouth and the ecstasy of being buried deep inside her. And yet all the days, months, and years of torturous abstinence still weren't enough to assuage the pain he carried in his heart. Not just pain about Melissa's suicide, but pain about every mistake he'd ever made. Including hiring Eden.

He stared at the horizon where light sky met dark ocean, and tried to figure out where the pain had all started. Mom. All roads seemed to lead back to his mother.

"I should've told her that I loved her." He spoke barely above a whisper. "That night when Dad woke me up, I should've told Mom that I loved her. Instead, I acted like a spoiled, rotten little punk—like she was doing something to me by dying. And my anger didn't stop with Mom. I gave Deacon a hard time and ridiculed Dad for being such a womanizer—even when I'm just like him. Or maybe not just like him. At least he's nice to women. I treat women like shit." He snorted with disgust. "And the one nice thing I do for a girl goes to hell in a handcart." He tossed down his fishing rod and pulled off his hat, running his hand through his hair. "I'm fuckin' pathetic."

He didn't expect Grayson to say anything. His little brother had never been much of a talker. And what was there to say? So they just sat there in silence while the wind picked up and the boat rocked in the waves. Finally, Nash felt something brush his arm, and he looked down to see Grayson's sketchpad. He took it and stared at the drawing of the man slouched in a leather seat with a fishing pole in his hands and a John Deere hat pulled low on his head. He looked like an ordinary man just enjoying a day of fishing. There was no sign of the tortured soul within.

"Did you realize that you were the one who taught me

to fish?" Grayson said. "Deke was too busy making sure the bills got paid. And Dad... well, you know Dad. So you were the one who took me out and showed me how to bait a hook, cast, and patiently wait for the first bite. And not only did you teach me to fish, but you packed my lunch every day for school. You made sure my shoelaces were tied, and my coat zipped when the weather was cold. You kicked Vince Hawthorn's ass when he stole my Halloween candy. And you gave me the sex talk before my first date—although, at fourteen, I wasn't sure what to do with that gross of condoms you gave me."

Nash swallowed hard and forced a laugh. "Because you never did look at women as sex objects as much as creative inspiration for your paintings."

"Paintings that wouldn't be half as good if you hadn't talked Deacon into letting me go to art school."

Nash cleared the lump in his throat. "Yeah, well, that was purely selfish. I wanted to get rid of my annoying little brother."

Grayson laughed. "I knew there was a reason." He sobered. "Look, I can't change how you see yourself. We all paint our own self-portraits... whether they're accurate or not." He nodded at the drawing. "But this is how I see you. A good man who has been a great brother. I love you, Nash."

It was hard to answer that, especially when the lump in Nash's throat had gotten as big as an oyster shell. It was a relief when the zing of released fishing line had them both glancing down at his rod. He dropped the sketchpad and made a diving grab before the fishing pole sailed over the edge of the boat. Another zing had

Grayson diving for his rod. Soon they were both fighting with their catch.

But once they had reeled in the yellow and gray perch and had them on ice in the cooler, Nash glanced over at Grayson. "You know what we were talking about earlier? Well, ditto, baby brother."

Grayson grinned. "Are you getting mushy on me?"

"Not likely. And for the record, my fish is bigger than yours."

It was a good day. By the time the chartered boat got back to the marina, Nash had found a reason to smile again. It was too bad that one phone call changed all that.

He and Grayson had just climbed into his truck when his cell phone rang. He pulled it out of his pocket and glanced at the screen. Every muscle inside him tensed like a taut rubber band. He thought about ignoring it, but for some reason, he couldn't bring himself to do it. So he answered, his voice sounding strange even to his own ears.

"What?"

The voice that came through the receiver was definitely Eden's, but breathier...sexier. "Meet me tonight at nine o'clock in the suite."

* * *

As soon as Nash pulled up in front of the hotel, a valet was there to hold open his door as he got out.

"Good evening, sir," the teenage boy said with a cocky grin on his face. Nash understood the grin when the kid palmed him a room key and winked. "I hope you enjoy your night."

Nash frowned at the key before he pulled some money from his pocket. "Park it out front. I won't be long."

"Whatever you say, sir." He hopped in the car and, with a squeal of tires, parked the truck next to the curb.

It pissed Nash off that Eden was stupid enough to involve a cocky teenager in whatever she had planned for tonight. Of course, Nash didn't care what she had planned. His plan was to make it perfectly clear that he didn't want to see her again. Not as a running partner. And certainly not as an escort.

Which didn't explain why his breathing became harsh and irregular once he stepped into the suite. Or why his heart thumped loudly when he opened the door of the bedroom. Or why his cock got as hard as a piece of granite when Eden's voice cut through the darkness.

"Come in and close the door."

He stepped inside and turned to the shadowy figure in the corner—the same corner where he had once stood. "I'm not closing the door. And I'm not staying."

"I guess I should've explained the rules a little better when I called you," she said in the breathy, sexy voice she'd used on the phone. "No talking and do exactly what I say."

His cock twitched with need, but he ignored it. "Cut the crap, Eden. We both know that this isn't going to work."

"Because I know about Melissa?"

"No. Because you're a hooker."

"Ouch. You're pulling out the big guns tonight." She moved out of the shadows and into the light that spilled in from the other room, and Nash's irregular breath got stuck in his lungs.

Talk about pulling out the big guns. Eden was dressed to kill. At least, it was killing him. She wore lingerie from his collection. And not just any lingerie, but his favorite design: a dominatrix-style corset made of stiff red brocade and black leather. Silver studs ran along the top and bottom edges, and two silver zippers ran vertically over the cups of the bra. Hidden hooks held it together in the front, and in the back, he knew there was a crisscross of leather lacing that could be loosened or tightened at will. If Eden's small waist and breathless speech were any indication, the lacing had been pulled tight. Which made Nash's fingers tingle with the strong need to span the cinched area. But no more than they tingled to touch the soft flesh that swelled over the top of the corset. Lacy panties went with the outfit, but Eden had chosen to leave those off, and a tiny patch of dark hair peeked from beneath the studded leather.

Nash closed his eyes and struggled to pull air into his lungs.

"Too much?" she asked. "Then why did you send it to me?"

He opened his eyes. In the high-heeled boots she wore, her gaze was almost level with his. "My mistake," he said.

"Really? Somehow I doubt that. I think you're begging for something, Nash. Something you can't ask for, but desperately need." She lifted one booted foot and kicked the door closed, sealing the room in total darkness.

"Eden—" That was all he got out before a hand settled over his fly. She didn't squeeze hard, just enough to get his attention. Just enough to make his body hum with desire as her breath fell hot against his ear.

"Melissa was the aggressor, wasn't she, Nash? She was the one who asked you to prom, the one who got the hotel room, the one who seduced you."

He tensed. "If you're trying to make me the victim, Eden, you're way off base. I knew what she was doing, and I should've put a stop to it."

"You should've had control, is that it?" Her hand tightened around the hard ridge beneath his fly, and he swallowed back a moan. "Which is exactly why you hire escorts. To prove to yourself that you are in complete control. But I've been thinking about that. And I don't think hiring escorts to do as you say proves anything. The real test would be if you could stay in control when you aren't in charge." She nipped at his earlobe, and a current of energy coursed through him like an electrical shock. "When someone else is calling all the shots."

He gritted his teeth. "I'm not playing this game."

Her lips brushed along a muscle in his neck. "Afraid you'll fail?"

Not afraid. More like terrified. Even now, he had the strong desire to close his hands around her tightly cinched waist and devour her until there was nothing left. But before he could give in to the desire, she released him and moved away. Only seconds later, the light came on over the bed.

Eden sat in the chair he had once occupied. "Go ahead then," she said, "leave. But then you'll never know the truth, now will you?"

He should've turned and walked out. But his feet seemed rooted to the floor. "You're playing with fire, Eden."

"But that's my choice, isn't it? No one is making me do this, Nash. I'm here because I want to be." She paused. "Now take off your clothes...slowly."

Nash stared at Eden's shadowy outline. Was she right? Did he only have control in situations where he was in charge? What would happen if he gave up that control? What would happen if he let Eden call the shots like he'd let Melissa? Would it prove that he was no more in control than he had been that night? It was a terrifying thought, but one he had to know the answer to.

"One night," he said as he jerked open the buttons of his shirt. "Then I never want to see you again. Do you understand?"

There was a pause. "I understand."

The sadness in the reply wiped away some of his anger, and he slowed his movements, slipping off his running shoes before he unbuttoned his jeans and pulled down the zipper. He made no attempt to hide his desire. Pushing down his pants and boxers, he stood with his erection flagrantly displayed, in hopes that seeing his lack of control would force her to put an end to this farce.

She didn't. Instead, she gave him another order, her voice sounding even more breathless than before. "Lie down on the bed."

"This is insane."

"So you're quitting?"

He sat down on the bed and jerked off his pants and boxers, then pulled his socks off. Once he was naked, he reclined back on the pillows. "Now what?"

The light clicked off, and a second later, he felt a hand on his foot. Just the feel of her touch skin to skin almost sent him through the roof. Her fingers were slightly chilled, but spread a line of fire in their wake as they skimmed up his shin. The mattress dipped beneath her weight as her fingers strummed over the tight muscles of his quadriceps until they jumped. Then her other hand joined in, and Nash dug his head into the pillow and gripped the duvet as he tried to hang on to his sanity.

But it was impossible when Eden's hands seemed to be everywhere. One glided over his hip bone and along his side, while the other sizzled up his arm and over his shoulder. They met in the middle of his chest, then spread out to cup each pectoral muscle. She squeezed, and he bit back a moan. But when her nails flicked over his nipples, the moan resurfaced and came out loud and clear.

"So you like that." She continued to tease until his nipples were tight and aching.

"Enough, Eden," he pleaded.

"Not yet," she whispered. "You haven't had nearly enough yet." She continued the torture, but Nash didn't know hell until her hand closed around his cock. He wasn't surprised by how quickly his body reached for climax. It had been too long since he'd been held in a woman's fist. But before he could completely embarrass himself, she released him. Released him from one torture and moved on to the next.

She went from using her hands to using her lips.

Starting at his forehead, she kissed her way along one eyebrow, over his cheekbone, down the side of his neck. Her hot, wet mouth covered one nipple, and Nash's hips came up off the bed. She suckled then nipped, then suckled and nipped again. When he was mindless, she stopped.

With his breathing harsh and rapid, he waited. He didn't have long to wait before her mouth surrounded his cock in moist heat that sapped the last of his will.

He released his death hold on the duvet and tangled his fingers in her hair, pulling her closer as he lifted his hips from the bed and searched for release. Unfortunately, she wasn't through testing his control. She stopped her deep strokes and moved away. He heard a drawer open, and a few rapid heartbeats later, her hand closed around his cock and she rolled a condom on.

"Don't do it, Eden," he said.

"But I have to, Nash. How else am I going to save you?"

"You can't save me."

There was a pause before she straddled him, her sexy boots on either side of his hips. She didn't sit down, but rather knelt over him as she took his cock in hand. "But I have to try, Nash." With only a slight adjustment, she sat down and imbedded him deep inside her.

After all the years, Nash had forgotten the indescribable pleasure of being surrounded by a woman. The heat. The wetness. The tightness that pulled and tugged a man inside out.

"Let go, Nash," she said. And when she started to flex her hips up and down, he had no choice in the matter.

With a growl, he rolled her over and took what he wanted. He wasn't gentle. He couldn't be. The desire he had caged, when unleashed, cared nothing about gentle. It only cared about satisfying the hunger. Not a hunger for just any woman. But a hunger for this woman. A hunger for Eden.

Pinning her hands to the mattress, he thrust into her hard and deep. She met his thrust, her muscles tightening around him and pulling him down into a spiral of sensations. He thrust again. And again. And again. Searching for the one thing he'd denied himself for too long.

Redemption.

Unfortunately, before he could find it in the hot pull of her body, she spoke one word that yanked it out of his reach.

"Stop."

CHAPTER TWENTY

*E*den felt Nash's entire body tense. He just froze there, his arms on either side of her head and his breath falling hard and rapid against her ear. She felt the twitch of his erection deep inside her. She wanted to answer it with a thrust of her hips. Instead, she remained perfectly still. She had never ached for him more than she did at that moment—not just her body but also her soul. But she couldn't give in. Not now. Not when she needed to prove to him once and for all that he wasn't a monster.

"Stop, Nash," she repeated.

The muscles of his chest tightened, and he held himself rigid for a moment longer before he pulled out and fell back on the pillows. His breath released in a rush. "Get out."

"No."

She could almost hear his jaw clench. "I mean it, Eden, get the hell out before I do something I'll regret."

Eden wanted to touch him, but she didn't. She just lay

there next to him, listening to his harsh breathing. "You won't, Nash. What happened on prom night will never happen again. You just proved it."

He sat up, and the lamp on the nightstand came on. It was the first time she'd seen him fully naked, and she couldn't help the hitch in her breathing when her gaze ran over his broad shoulders, the muscles in his back, and the perfect curves of his butt. He turned, and she forgot about the perfection of his body when she saw the hurt in his eyes.

"This proved nothing, Eden," he said in a defeated voice. "Do you know how close I came to ignoring your request? To forgetting everything but being deep inside you? Even now, I'm terrified of losing it. So get out... please."

She shook her head. "I'm not going anywhere. Not until you accept the truth and quit beating yourself up over a mistake you made years ago. And not just yours, but Melissa's too."

His eyes narrowed. "Don't bring her into it. Don't you dare bring her into it."

"Why? Because you know that I'm right. You know that what happened that night was as much her fault as it was yours. It was her choice to get the hotel room. Her choice to have champagne. Her choice to seduce you."

He came up off the bed. "She's dead for Christsakes!"

Eden got to her knees. "And that was her choice too!" She sighed and sat back down. "I don't know why she did it, Nash. But I don't think it solely had to do with what happened that night."

"You're right. She was in love with me. I knew it, and I took advantage of that."

"By going to prom with her? Or by taking what she freely offered?"

Nash stared at her for a moment before he slumped down on the edge of the bed and cradled his head in his hands. She moved next to him. She didn't say anything. There was nothing left to say. She just wrapped her arms around him and pressed her cheek to his shoulder. They remained like that for a long time until Nash finally spoke.

"So why don't you think her suicide had to do with me?"

"Because you didn't even know each other, Nash. You didn't know her, and she didn't know you. The entire night was based on a fantasy she had. A fantasy that wasn't real. The limo. The hotel. The roses on the bed. I think she thought there would be fireworks and singing angels the first time she had sex with you. And when that didn't happen, she was disappointed and upset. And I get it. My first time wasn't exactly what I had expected either, but that doesn't mean I wanted to kill myself. Something more had to be going on with Melissa."

"But I still played a part." His voice held so much pain and sadness that Eden couldn't keep the tears from her eyes. One must've leaked out and dropped to his shoulder, because he glanced down at her. "Are you crying, Eden?"

She sniffed. "Of course not. I just have bad allergies."

He released his breath, and then turned until he was facing her. "What am I going to do with you?" He cradled her chin and used his thumb to wipe the tear from her cheek.

Looking into his beautiful eyes, she easily found the answer. "How about finishing what we started?"

He blinked. "What?'

"Make love to me, Nash," she whispered. She hadn't planned on using the word *love*. It had just come out. But once it was there, it seemed right.

He hesitated. "I don't know that I can."

She turned her head and kissed his palm. "We'll take it slow. Kiss me, Nash...please."

He feathered his thumb across her lips before tipping her chin and lowering his mouth to hers. Staring straight into her eyes, he took a sip. His eyes remained open as he kissed her again. This time deeper. Sweeter. His hands slid into her hair, his fingers cradling her head as the kiss grew lush and wet. His lips fit to hers perfectly as his tongue brushed against her teeth, then the roof of her mouth, before coupling with hers in a heated dance that drew a moan from deep within her.

The moan caused his eyes to close and his fingers to fist in her hair. He changed the angle of the kiss and became more demanding, sucking her tongue into his mouth and then biting her bottom lip until it ached for more.

She didn't know how long they kissed. It could've been minutes or hours. When she finally pulled away to catch her breath, his gaze lowered to the zippers on her corset. Slowly, he unzipped one...and then the other, carefully folding back each cup until her breasts were exposed to his hooded gaze. When he finally glanced up, it was like looking into twin pools of indigo flames.

"Do you know how hard it was not to touch?" His hand lifted and gently cupped one breast, and his eyes slid closed. "Not to hold this...beautiful sweetness?" His thumb brushed her nipple, and heat spiraled through her.

"I wanted you so damned bad. I still want you so damned bad."

Her breath rushed out on a sigh. "Then take me."

He opened his eyes. "I don't think I can hold back, Eden. And if I hurt you..."

Eden knew that a simple "you won't hurt me" wouldn't work as well as action. Getting to her knees, she shoved him back on the bed and then straddled him. "Who says that I won't hurt you? But let me know if you want me to stop." She lowered her head and took his nipple into her mouth and bit down.

A low growl came from his throat before she was rolled onto her back. "Never." He kissed her deeply. "I'll never tell you to stop, Eden. And forgive me"—he brushed a kiss over her nipple—"but if I don't get inside you..." After only a slight adjustment, he thrust deep.

The sudden stretch took her breath away. He paused and looked at her as if waiting for her to stop him. Holding his gaze, she wrapped her boots around him and flexed her hips, taking him even deeper. He closed his eyes and thrust again.

He wasn't gentle. When he couldn't get deep enough with her lying flat on the mattress, he knelt between her legs and stuffed a pillow beneath her hips. Then he continued his hard, steady thrusts that made the headboard creak and the ache inside of Eden grow. Just when she didn't think she could take another second more, he flicked his thumb over her clitoris and sent her flying. As her orgasm hit, she felt her muscles tighten around him. He groaned and pumped harder, carrying her higher as he climaxed. After the last thrust and tingle, he wilted against her.

"Holy cow," she said.

He laughed, his breath brushing her ear. "I agree one hundred percent." He rolled off her and flung an arm over his eyes. "I think I strained a muscle."

"What muscle?"

"Not that muscle. That muscle is more than ready to go again."

"You're kidding." She rolled to her side and looked. Sure enough, his penis was erect.

"It has a lot of catching up to do." She glanced up to see him smiling, but it faded quickly. "Thank you," he said. "Thank you for making me feel normal."

"You are normal."

He shook his head. "I haven't been normal since the trial." He stared up at the ceiling. "Even though the jury found me not guilty, the stigma of rape was still there. I couldn't be alone with a woman or touch her without seeing doubt and fear in her eyes." He swallowed hard. "So I stopped asking women out. Partly because I couldn't stand to see their fear, and partly because I was punishing myself for losing control with Melissa." He looked at her. "Then you showed up. This sassy escort who talks with her hands, runs like a duck, and refuses to quit—even when she found out the truth."

"I run like a duck?"

"Yes, but a cute duck." His eyes grew intent. "Why, Eden? Why did you refuse to give up on me?"

It was a good question. At one time, it had been to achieve her goal and get the story. But since learning about Melissa, she realized that was no longer true. She couldn't write a story about Nash. She couldn't hurt him any more than he already hurt. And she didn't care if Stella hired her back. In fact, she didn't care if she ever became a reporter. At the moment, all she cared about was Nash. The realization should've scared her. Being a journalist had been her dream ever since she could remember. But it didn't. She just felt content. Content to be right where she was.

She rested a hand on his jaw and felt his prickly, dark stubble against her palm. "I've always been good at seeing potential. And you, Nash Beaumont, have a lot of potential." She intended to make him smile, but instead he continued to look serious.

"You make me feel like I could do anything, Eden." He rolled toward her and kissed her, his hand reaching behind to unlace the corset. When he pulled back, his eyes were heated. "But right now, there's only one thing I want to do."

Once he had removed her corset and boots, Nash held nothing back. He touched her like he had refused to touch her before, his hands exploring her body from the top of her head to the tips of her toes. And when he had her quivering with need, he slowly entered her, pulling out then thrusting deep until she moaned and begged for more. He gave her more—another orgasm that rocked her world and left her limp as a piece of seaweed. She didn't remember falling asleep, but when she opened her eyes again, it was to the sun shining in through the open curtains of the suite. With the warm rays came a flood of memories from the night before, wonderful, amazing memories that had her sighing with contentment as she rolled to her back and stretched her hands over her head.

"Wow. I guess hookers really do enjoy sex."

The unfamiliar voice had Eden grabbing the sheet over her naked breasts and sitting up. Jeremy the valet stood in the doorway looking as cocky as ever. "Get out, you little Peeping Tom!" she yelled.

He lifted the tray in his hands. "I'm not a Peeping Tom. The French Kiss guy paid me extra to bring you some breakfast. I guess he doesn't want it spread around the staff that he hires hookers." He shrugged. "But since I already know..."

Damn. Eden never should've trusted the smart-alecky teenager with delivering the room key to Nash. Since she thought teenage boys would care more about French Kiss's hot lingerie models than the brothers who owned the company, she didn't think Jeremy would recognize him. Obviously, she'd been wrong.

"So where is he?" She reached for the robe that was lying on the foot of the bed. Had Nash put it there? The thought was so sweet that it had her smiling even more. It wilted when Jeremy answered.

"I don't have a clue." He carried the tray in and set it on the table by the window. When his back was turned, Eden quickly slipped on the robe, then got out of bed and tied it.

"You mean he's not in the other room?"

Jeremy turned. "No. I was just getting off work when I ran into him in the lobby. After giving me his orders, he left."

"He left?" Eden couldn't keep the hurt and anger from her voice. "Without even saying goodbye?"

Jeremy held up his hands. "Geez, don't shoot the

messenger. Besides, I don't know what you expect. You're a hooker. You should be glad he ordered you breakfast." He took the covers off the plates to display a breakfast that would feed a family of five. "And not just any breakfast, but the works."

Since she had been too nervous about seducing Nash to eat the night before, Eden's stomach growled at the sight of the fluffy vegetable omelet, pancakes, sausage links, bacon, toast, and orange juice. But her brain wasn't as interested in the food as it was about finding out why Nash had left without a word. After last night, she thought things had changed between them. She no longer thought of him as a story, and she'd assumed that he no longer thought of her as an escort.

Obviously, she was wrong.

Instead of paying her off with money, he was paying her off with food. Her spine stiffened. If that was the case, then she had a few things to say to Nash Beaumont. She strode over to the dresser and grabbed her phone out of her purse. But before she could call him, she noticed the text message.

Good morning, beautiful. Problem at work, but should be back before you finish your breakfast. DON'T GET DRESSED. I plan to spend the rest of the day in the Garden of Eden.

All the anger drained right out of her, and she released a giddy giggle.

"Hookers sure have major mood swings," Jeremy said. "Is it the drugs?"

She ignored the comment and texted Nash back. I thought we took care of the control issue last night.

Obviously not...STOP WITH THE ORDERS! She had barely pushed send when she got a reply. What she had meant as a joke, Nash had taken seriously.

Please don't leave, Eden.

The plea made her heart ache. She quickly texted back.

I'm not going anywhere. Naked and waiting.

Only seconds later, she got a reply. Screw work! Be there in a minute.

Eden laughed as she texted. Go to work. I have a huge breakfast to keep me busy.

Fine, but save room for me.

She smiled, but her smile dropped when she glanced up and saw Jeremy sitting at the table eating her breakfast. When he noticed her glare, he shrugged.

"What? You can't eat this entire breakfast by yourself. And after working all night, I'm starving."

She walked over and took the chair across from him. "Don't touch my pancakes. And no more hooker talk."

"Okay," Jeremy said as he cut off a piece of omelet, "but you can't blame a hormonal teen for being interested— even though there's no way I would ever pay two thousand for a lay. I guess that's how you could afford the new Porsche. That is a righteous car."

"That's not mine. It's a loaner." She poured syrup on her pancakes. "And how did you find out how much escorts make?"

"Your pimp told Joey. He's the other night valet."

Eden paused with the fork of pancake inches from her mouth. "My pimp?"

Jeremy stopped devouring the omelet. "The guy's not

your pimp? I thought that's why he pays Joey to call him when you show up."

A chill ran down Eden's spine. "What does this guy look like that pays Joey?"

Jeremy shrugged. "I couldn't tell you. He never gets out of his black SUV."

CHAPTER TWENTY-ONE

The last thing Nash wanted to do that morning was go into work. He wanted to be back in the hotel suite tucked around Eden, watching her sleep. She snored. Not loudly. More like the nasally purr of a contented kitten. It was almost as cute as her hand talking and duck run. Or maybe what was so cute was the way she snuggled in his arms like she trusted him completely. It had been a long time since a woman had completely trusted him. It had also been a long time since he had completely trusted a woman.

And he did trust Eden. Her brutal honesty had given him a glimmer of hope that he could someday forgive himself for the role he played in Melissa's suicide. Even more than that, Eden had made him realize that happiness was still within his grasp and that it was time to stop living in the shadows and start living in the light. The majority of that light surrounded Eden.

He wasn't ready to dissect his feelings toward her yet. For now, he just wanted to enjoy her... and his desire.

Unfortunately, that desire would have to wait. With Deacon and Olivia in Paris and Grayson not answering the phone, Nash was the only one left to handle the crisis at the office.

Once he arrived at French Kiss, he wasted no time heading up to the executive floor to get the details of the situation from Kelly. Unfortunately, Kelly wasn't at her desk. Rather than hunt her down, he called her cell phone. The ringing that came from his receiver seemed to coincide with the ringtone that came from under the desk. It stopped when Kelly answered in a hushed voice.

"Where are you?"

Nash walked around and peeked under the desk to find her crouched beneath. "Right here."

"Oh." She hung up the phone. "What took you so long? I really think they're going to kill each other."

"Is that why you're hiding under the desk?"

"Of course not. I'm hiding from Jason."

Nash really didn't have time for this, but he couldn't help asking. "Why would you be hiding from your fiancé? I thought he was the one hiding from you."

She sighed. "And I should've left things that way. But when those old people were passing out magic brownies, I thought it would be a good way to get Jason to loosen up. I just didn't realize that once he discovered the delights of Kelly Wang, there would be no going back. The man is insatiable. After three times on Saturday night, he went for a record six on Sunday. I know if he sees me, the poor man won't be able to control himself. And I really don't want to get fired for sex on the desk."

Since there was no good reply to that without crossing

way too many sexual discrimination clauses, Nash chose to move on. "All right then, so where are Deirdre and Samuel?"

"In the design studio. But be warned, it's not pretty. She's locked all the designers out."

"Don't you have a key to the door?"

Kelly fished in her pocket and then held out a key. "I don't get paid enough to go into a war zone."

As it turned out, Kelly wasn't too far off the mark. Nash opened the door of the design studio to find what looked like a battlefield. Dress form mannequins were knocked over, and bolts of material, ribbon, tape measures, and other sewing items cluttered the floor. Amid the chaos, Deirdre Beaumont stood like a woman on the warpath. Instead of being perfectly coiffed, she wore mismatched sweats, her hair was wild, and her face was devoid of makeup. But Nash wasn't concerned with her appearance as much as the pair of scissors she held in her hand.

"Are you saying, you sick bastard," she yelled, "that the only way I could get you in bed is by slipping a roofie in your drink?"

Samuel peeked out from the bolt of purple satin he held like a shield. "That's exactly what I'm saying. And exactly what happened. Why else would I have sex with a spoiled gold digger?"

Deirdre lifted the scissors and took aim, and Nash might've stopped her if he hadn't been so shocked by what he'd just learned. Samuel and Deirdre had sex? What happened to Doug? Nash was still trying to figure things out when the scissors when sailing. Fortunately, Samuel had quick reflexes. He ducked behind the bolt of material just as the scissors stuck in the purple satin with surprising precision.

Samuel peeked out and stared at the embedded scissors. "Why, you little minx." He dropped the bolt and headed toward her with fire in his eyes. "I should take you over my knee for that."

"You wouldn't dare." Deirdre backed up.

"Why? Because I'm gay? Wasn't that the rumor you spread about me?"

Deirdre moved around a table. "People wouldn't believe it if you dated women instead of holing up in your office."

"You know why I don't date, Dee Dee," he said as he followed her around the table.

Dee Dee? Nash was slowly but surely putting the pieces together. And if he hadn't been so distracted by Eden, he might've put them together sooner. Everything made sense now. Deidre and Samuel's dislike for each other had been nothing but a ruse to hide their true feelings. And those feelings seemed to run pretty deep.

Deirdre stopped backing up. "How would I know anything about you, Sammy, when you stopped talking to me? When you treated me like I didn't exist."

"And what was I supposed to do? Show my true feelings?" Samuel slammed his fist down on the table. "You were married!"

"Well, I'm not now!"

"You're right." Samuel grabbed her arm and pulled her over to a chair. "Except now you're just a spoiled brat who has become a pain in my ass." He sat down and pulled her over his lap. But before he could do more than lift his hand, Nash figured it was time to intervene.

"Good morning." He smiled brightly as he strolled in. "Are you thinking of adding some S and M designs to the new collection, Samuel?"

Samuel lowered his hand and looked embarrassed while Deirdre continued her rant as she got up from his lap. "This man," she pointed a finger, "is a bully and a pervert, and I demand restitution."

"Of course, it always boils down to money with you," Samuel said snidely.

"Who said anything about money? I want your resignation."

"What?" Samuel came out of the chair.

"You heard me." She raised her chin. "As a major stockholder, I have the right to ask for your resignation."

Nash held up his hands. "Now, Deirdre, I don't think we need to ask for Samuel's resignation. I'm sure he didn't mean to do . . . whatever he did."

"He drugged me and then dragged me to the sultan's tent and took advantage of me."

"I took advantage of you?" Samuel said. "If I remember correctly, you were the one who helped me get out of that damned uncomfortable suit of armor you forced me to wear."

"Only after you slipped something in my drink."

"You didn't even have a drink!"

"Then you put something in that brownie. There is no other explanation for what happened." She glanced at Nash. "I think that a verbal resignation will work just fine. Wouldn't you say, Nash?"

Nash struggled to play catch-up. Samuel wasn't gay. He and Deirdre had a past. And obviously, Mrs. Huckabee's brownies really were magic. While Nash tried to absorb all the information, Samuel gave in to Deirdre's demands.

"Fine. You want my resignation, Mrs. Beaumont, you've got it!" He headed for the door, slamming it behind him. When he was gone, Nash expected Deidre to gloat or have some snide remark. Instead, she sat down in the chair and burst into tears.

"Why did you have to interrupt when you did?" she sobbed. "I had him right where I wanted him."

Not knowing what else to do, Nash searched around until he found a box of tissues and brought it to Deirdre. Once she had the tears blotted from her cheeks, he asked the obvious question. "So how long have you been in love with Samuel?"

Her head came up. "What in the world would make you think that? I hate the man." Instead of replying, Nash waited her out. She caved only seconds later. "Okay, so maybe I don't hate him. Which is shocking since he is such an annoying man, and has been ever since I met him. But love?" She twisted the tissue in her hands. "Why would I be in love with a man who wasn't even willing to fight for me? When Michael showed interest in me, Samuel just gave up." She looked at Nash. "If he cared for me, why would he do that?"

"Maybe he thought that you and Olivia would be happier with a billionaire than with a young designer who had yet to prove himself."

She nodded. "I've often wondered if it was a test to see

if I was actually the spoiled gold digger he thought I was."
She laughed cynically. "I guess I failed."

Nash leaned back on one of the design tables and
crossed his arms. "Which is why you started the rumor
about him being gay?"

She studied the tissue in her hands. "I thought he would
prove the rumors wrong soon enough. But he hasn't gone
out with one woman in all these years." She swallowed.
"How do you explain that?"

"I think you know the answer."

"But then why didn't he make a move after Michael
died? Why did he ignore me?"

A few days earlier, Nash couldn't have answered the
question. But he could now. It seemed that he and Samuel were two peas in a pod. Samuel had ignored Deirdre
because of his fear of rejection, and Nash had ignored all
women rather than deal with them shrinking from his
touch and thinking him a rapist. And looking back, he
had to wonder if some of the fear he saw in women's eyes
had just been a reflection of his own insecurities.

"I think that Samuel was worried that you wouldn't
return his affection," he said. "And I think that if you
were to show him your true feelings, he'd be willing to
show you his."

"So you think I should go after him?"

"Yes." He grinned. "But not with a pair of scissors."

* * *

After Deirdre left the design studio in search of Samuel,
Nash headed to the executive floor to tell Kelly that the

crisis was over and he wouldn't be back for the rest of the day. But on the way past Jason's office, he decided to stop in and subtly remind the guy that he needed to control his libido at the workplace. But when he tapped on the door and stepped into Jason's office, the company lawyer didn't look like an insatiable sex fiend. He looked like he had been ridden hard and put away wet.

"Thank God," Jason said as he fell back in the chair and covered his face with a hand. "I thought you were Kelly, and she's the last person I want to see." He cringed. "I didn't mean that. I want to see her. I just need a break from being the best lover she's ever had."

Nash bit back a smile. "So I'm going to assume that you had the wedding night early?"

"Yes, and I don't know if I can keep up the pace. How do you do it? Women must expect a lot from a guy like you. How do you keep them happy in the bedroom?"

Nash could've come up with some male-ego pile of crap, but that's not what Jason needed. He needed the truth. "I haven't always made women happy. In fact, I've made more than my fair share of mistakes. But I don't think being good in bed has anything to do with how many times you have sex in one night. My father, who happens to be an expert on women, always says that quality is more important than quantity."

Jason perked up. "Really?"

Nash nodded. "I think you and Kelly were both too uptight about the sex part of your relationship. Now that it's out of the way, why don't you just relax and enjoy each other's company? I'd start by inviting her to the basketball game."

For a moment, Jason studied him. "You know, you're not who I thought you were. I thought you were one of those guys who loved women and left them. I didn't take you for a sensitive guy who believes in long-term relationships."

On the drive back to the hotel, Nash thought about what Jason had said. Nash had never thought of himself as a sensitive guy who believed in long-term relationships either. He had always thought of himself as a cynical guy who believed in nothing. But now he realized that the image he'd carried around for so long wasn't who he was at all. He was sensitive. So sensitive that he'd been devastated when his mother died. Devastated when Melissa accused him of rape. Devastated when she had committed suicide. Each event chipped away at him until there had almost been nothing left of the person he was. But there was something left of Nash. He was sorry that his mother and Melissa had died, but he was alive. And it was time he start acting like it. It was time to start living.

"You look like you're having a good day, sir," the hotel valet said as he held the door while Nash got out.

Nash laughed as he tossed him the keys. "The best."

But some of his enthusiasm fizzled when he walked into the bedroom of the suite and found a rumpled bed and breakfast dishes but no Eden. He was about to panic when she came hurrying out of the bathroom— unfortunately, completely dressed. Although it shouldn't take him long to get her out of the jeans and T-shirt. The fantasy was interrupted when he realized she was talking on the phone and sounded panicked.

"What do you mean you can't do anything until she's

been missing for forty-eight hours? In forty-eight hours, she could be dead!" She sat down on the bed and, holding the phone with her shoulder, pulled on her socks and boots, completely oblivious to the fact that Nash stood in the doorway. "I told you about the guy from the escort service—no, I told you I don't have the escort service's name, but you're the police, for God's sake. Don't you know the prostitution rings in town? Fine! I'll call you back when I get it."

She hung up and tossed the phone to the bed, then glanced at the doorway. The look of relief on her face made something crack wide open inside of Nash. It opened even wider when she ran to him and flung herself in his arms.

"Oh, Nash, I'm so glad you're here!"

He pulled her close, enjoying the feel of her body pressed against his as much as her obvious delight in seeing him. "So I guess you missed me as much as I missed you."

She pulled back. "No—I mean, yes, I missed you, but that's not why I'm so glad to see you. I think Madison's in trouble, and I need your help."

CHAPTER TWENTY-TWO

*E*den was terrified. Not because Zac had been paying a valet to keep a watch on her—that had merely scared her—but because Madison wasn't answering her phone. Nor was she at their apartment.

"I told you that something isn't right," Eden said to Nash as he followed her into the apartment. "Madison never gets out of bed before noon." She pulled her phone from her purse. "I'm calling the police again, and this time, I'm going to force them to do something."

"Wait, Eden." Nash placed his hand on hers. It was surprising how just the touch of his warm skin made her feel better. "The police aren't going to do anything unless we have hard evidence. And all we have so far is the fact that Zac was having you watched. That doesn't mean that he is responsible for Madison's disappearance."

"But it makes perfect sense that he would come here to threaten me after Joey the valet told him that I was with you at the hotel. There's no way he can know that you weren't paying me, especially when I was driving the Porsche, and he'll want his cut. And he'll probably hold Madison until I give it to him."

"That's all just a theory," Nash said. "Since we couldn't get ahold of Joey, we don't even know if he called Zac to tell him you were there. When was the last time you saw Madison?"

"Yesterday, around seven. She was here when I left for the hotel."

"Was the bed made?"

Eden glanced at the bed with its mussed covers. "Yes, which means that she must've slept here—at least for a little while."

Nash nodded. "Does she have any friends in the building? Someone who might've invited her for coffee this morning or needed her help?"

With the way Madison made friends, it was possible. Eden tried to push down her fear and think. "The other day, she did mention helping some guy with his groceries. I think she said his name was Rudy, but I don't know which apartment he lives in." She turned to the door. "But I can find out. I'll just knock on everyone's—"

"Slow down, Eden," Nash said, and when she turned, he had his cell phone out and was dialing. "Let me just make a phone call." He lifted the phone to his ear, then after a few seconds, spoke. "Hi, Dan. This is Nash Beaumont. No, I'm not worried about the remodel—it looks like the handyman crew you hired is doing a great job. I called because I need an apartment number. I don't have the last name, but the first is Rudy."

Eden tried to figure out how Nash would know someone

who kept track of the people in her apartment. And why that man would've hired the handyman crew. "How—?" she started, but he held up a finger and stopped her.

"Thanks, Dan. I'll talk with you next week." Once he hung up, he looked at Eden. "That was Dan Fillmore. He's the new manager of your apartment building."

"But how do you know my new landlord?"

"He's not your new landlord. He's only the property manager. I'm your new landlord." While her mouth dropped, he walked over and held open the door. "But before you start with twenty questions, I think we need to table this discussion until after we find Madison."

Unfortunately, Eden had never been good at tabling things. As they took the stairs down to the next floor, her mind worked overtime...as did her mouth. "So you bought the building? But why would you do that? I could understand if it was a good investment. But it seems like a money pit to me, especially with all the remodeling you've done to my apartment. Unless you're planning on raising the rent. Are you planning on raising the rent?"

"No. I'm not going to raise the rent."

"So you just bought some random apartments and started remodeling them because you wanted to?"

He stopped at a door. "It was not random, Eden. And it has nothing to do with making money. You had a leaky faucet, so I called the landlord to get it fixed. When the guy told me to take a hike, I got pissed and bought the building."

"You bought an entire apartment because you got pissed?"

"No, I bought an entire apartment building because you had a leaky faucet."

"And the Porsche?"

"You needed a car." He knocked on the door. While they waited for it to be answered, Eden tried to detangle her brain. It probably meant nothing. Billionaires bought things all the time on just a whim. Except it hadn't been just a whim. It had been because of her leaky faucet and broken Volvo. And there was only one reason he would concern himself with her broken things.

A smile blossomed on her face to match the smile blossoming in her heart. "You like me, Nash Beaumont. And you liked me long before last night."

He turned and studied her for a long moment. "It would appear that way."

Her smile got even bigger. "Good. Because I like you too."

Before she could gauge his reaction to that information, the door opened. A man who looked about the same age as Eden's grandfather stood there in zippered coveralls and house slippers, holding a little dog that yapped at Nash and Eden in an earsplitting bark.

"Hush now, Scamper," the man said, "or I'll close you in the bedroom." The dog must've understood because he shut up.

"You must be Rudy Garcia." Nash held out his hand. "I'm Nash Beaumont, your new landlord."

Rudy refused the handshake, and his eyes narrowed. "Are you the one who got me the new toilet and fixed my window?"

"Yes, sir," Nash said. Eden was surprised. She had

thought that she was the only one Nash had helped. Her heart swelled, and she smiled at him as he continued. "And if there are other things that need fixing, I hope you'll let Hank know. He should be stopping by every couple weeks to check."

Rudy scowled. "So I guess this means that you're raising the rent."

"No, sir. The rent will stay the same."

After only a second's pause, Rudy held out his hand. "In that case, it's a pleasure to meet you." After shaking Nash's hand, he glanced at Eden. "Aren't you the girl who lives with that full-figured girl in 3C?"

"Yes, sir. I'm Eden Huckabee," Eden said. "Have you seen Madison today? She wasn't there when I got home this morning, and I'm starting to get worried."

Rudy nodded. "I saw her leaving with some guy when I took Scamper out for his morning constitution."

"Was he driving a black SUV?"

"That would be the one."

Before Eden could panic and race back to her apartment to call 911, Nash took her hand and gave it a reassuring squeeze. "Would you say she was being abducted, Mr. Garcia?"

"No. It looked to me like she got in the car of her own free will."

"Thank you for your time." Nash headed for the stairs, pulling Eden behind him.

"So what are we going to do now?" Eden asked on the way back to her apartment.

"We're going to call the police."

"But like you said before, what good will it do?"

"We won't have them looking for a missing person. We'll have them looking for a prostitution ring."

"But I don't even have Zac's last name or his address... or even the name of the escort service."

Nash waited until they were inside her apartment before he spoke. "But I do. I have the name and the phone number."

Eden's eyes widened. "You can't give them that information, Nash. They'll want to know how you got it, and if word gets out about you hiring escorts, your name will be plastered all over the newspapers."

Nash pulled out his phone. "I think Madison's life is worth more than a little bad press." But before he could make the call, Eden looped her arms around his neck and kissed him.

"Thank you," she said.

"I wouldn't thank me yet. I'm not sure my phone call will do any good."

"I wasn't just thanking you for making the phone call. I was thanking you for being such a good person—whether it's taking an unpopular girl to prom, or making sure a woman gets her leaky faucet fixed, or jeopardizing your career to save a prostitute."

"I'm not that good—"

She grabbed his shirt and tugged him closer. "Can you just learn to take a compliment, Nash Beaumont?"

"Yes, ma'am," he said in his sexy Southern drawl, then he dipped his head and kissed her. But before she could melt against him like butter on warm toast, Nash's cell phone rang. He gave her one last quick kiss before glancing at the screen to see who was calling.

"It's Grayson." He answered the phone. "Please tell me that you're on your way to Fiji for the shoot, Gray. Deacon will kill you if you don't get that bathing suit catalog ready by the end of this month." He paused. "Good. So I'm assuming you talked your perfect model into joining you." His brow knotted. "What kind of problems?"

Before Eden could eavesdrop more on Nash's conversation, her phone rang, and she hurried over to answer it. There was no way to describe the feeling of relief she felt when she saw the name on the screen, and she started talking as soon as she answered.

"Madison? Where are you? Are you all right? Did that bastard hurt you?"

"I'm fine, Eden," Madison said. "But Chloe isn't. Zac got pretty pissed when she tried to protect you"

Eden was struggling to follow. "Chloe tried to protect me?"

"I told you that Chloe was a deep-down good person, Eden. When Zac found out you were in the hotel suite with Nash, he went ballistic. Chloe tried to stop him from going after you, and he beat her up pretty badly. I'm just glad she called me, and Grayson was able to drive me to pick her up."

"Grayson?" Eden was now thoroughly confused, and she figured things weren't going to get any clearer until she could talk with Madison face-to-face. "So are you at the hospital? Tell me which one, and I'll meet you there."

"Nope, we're not at the hospital. In fact, you're not going to believe where we are." Madison giggled. "We're going to Fiji!"

* * *

Eden soon learned that there was a big difference between traveling when you were a normal person and traveling when you were a rich person. Normal people had to deal with grumpy airline clerks, security, and late planes. Rich people didn't have to deal with any of that. They just hopped in a car and drove to a private airfield, where they boarded a private jet and sipped champagne until the plane took off.

Not that Eden took the champagne offered by the smiling airline attendant with the purple-lip-printed scarf. She was too worried about Madison. Nash declined the champagne as well before guiding Eden into the plush cabin. As soon as she saw Madison, she realized her mistake in being worried. Madison looked no worse for wear. In fact, she looked quite content, reclining in the leather seat with a champagne glass in one hand. When she saw Eden, she quickly got up and gave her a hug, swaying a little in her high-heeled shoes.

"Isn't this great? Even Freddie didn't have his own private jet. And I can't believe that I'm going to be a French Kiss model...of course, they might change their minds when they see me in a swimsuit."

On the ride over, Nash had told Eden all he had learned about Grayson wanting Madison for the swimsuit catalog, and she couldn't be happier for her friend. "I think you'll make a perfect model."

Nash looked around. "So where is my brother?"

"He's in the back trying to get Chloe to lie down—"

"I don't need your fuckin' sympathy!" The curtain that

separated the back cabin from the forward was jerked open, and Chloe appeared. Eden sucked in her breath at the bruises on her face.

"Oh my God!" She hurried over. "Are you okay?"

Even with the swelling, Chloe was able to roll her eyes. "Do I look okay to you?"

"No, you look like you need to go to the hospital."

"That's the same thing the Woman Whisperer keeps saying." Chloe glanced back over her shoulder. "But like I told him, I'm not going to a fuck—"

"I think we get it." Grayson walked out and handed her a plastic bag filled with ice. "No hospital, but at least use this."

Chloe jerked the ice pack out of his hand. "Gee, thanks."

"It looks like you could use some ice yourself, Gray," Nash said, and Eden finally noticed Grayson's swollen eye. "You okay?"

Grayson didn't take his gaze off Chloe as he nodded. "I should've killed the bastard."

Madison giggled. "You almost did. And if anyone needed to get his ass kicked, it's Zac." She took a big gulp of champagne. "Of course, there will be a price on your head when you get back. And next time, Zac won't be alone."

Chloe looked at Grayson. "She's right. You shouldn't have forced me to come with you. If I'd stayed, I could've calmed Zac down."

"Calmed him down?" Grayson stared at her. "Sorta like you calmed him down by becoming his punching bag?"

"That's none of your business! I understand you wanting to save Madison so you can exploit her body in your catalog, but I'm not working for you, and I sure as hell don't need saving." She headed for the cabin door, but Grayson stepped in front of her and blocked her way.

"Gray," Nash said, "what has gotten into you? If she wants to go, you can't keep her here."

Grayson didn't move. "She stays."

Eden knew he was right. If Chloe went back now, there was a good chance Zac would kill her. "I agree with Grayson. She can't go back to Zac."

Chloe turned on her. "I don't need you chiming in. You playing escort was the reason I got my ass kicked in the first place."

Eden cringed and glanced at Nash, but he didn't seem to catch the slip.

"But she didn't take any money from Nash," Madison said. "So there's no reason for Zac to be mad at her."

Chloe looked at Nash. "You're the Dark Seducer?"

Before he could answer, a voice came over the speakers. "This is your captain speaking. If you'll take a seat and buckle up, I'll get this bird in the air."

Grayson and Chloe continued their stare-down, but once the plane started to move, Chloe released an exasperated grunt and flopped down in the seat next to Madison. At that point, Eden should've spoken up. She might not work at the newspaper any longer, but she did work at The Lemon Drop, and she couldn't just take off without getting someone to cover her shifts.

She glanced at Nash. He didn't say a word. He just stood there looking delectable in his jeans and Henley as if waiting for her to make a decision. It didn't take long. She chose a window seat and quickly buckled up. Nash sat down in the seat next to her and took her hand, firmly linking their fingers together. He smiled a sexy smile that took away any reservations she still had before he leaned over and whispered, "Good choice."

CHAPTER TWENTY-THREE

It was hard to stay focused on goals when you were stretched out on a cushioned lounge chair with warm, white sand beneath your feet and a cold, fruity cocktail in your hand. Eden had come out to the beach to organize her thoughts and figure out a plan for her life. Now that she wasn't going to be a reporter, she needed to decide on a new career path. Instead, her gaze kept drifting to the beautiful turquoise waters that sparkled beneath the bright tropical sun. And her mind kept drifting to a man with mesmerizing violet eyes that sparkled with the unquenchable heat of desire.

They had arrived in Fiji the day before. Since everyone was jet-lagged from the trip, they had headed straight to the hotel where the rest of the models and camera crew were staying. It was a five-star resort nestled between the ocean and a coconut plantation. Her and Nash's room had spectacular views of both. Not that they had paid much attention to the views.

Nash's aversion to touching women was over. Eden had been thoroughly touched. And not just her body. Nash touched something deeper. Something more than just flesh and bone. He had touched Eden's heart. It ached for the young boy who had lost his mother. The sensitive teenager who had lost his faith. And the jaded man who had lost his way. And at the moment, the only goal she could think about was making Nash smile. Which was hard to do when he wasn't with her. He had left early that morning to help Grayson with the photo shoot, and because Eden had gotten little sleep the night before, she had stayed in bed. Now she wished she had gone with him. After just a few hours, she felt lost.

Unable to resist, she lifted her phone and texted him.

How's photo shoot going? I bet it's hell being surrounded by all those hot models.

His reply came quickly. I'd rather be surrounded by one hot bartender.

Smiling, she answered. Okay...if you insist. When are you coming back?

Her phone pinged seconds later. If I wasn't worried about Grayson getting the models to strip, I'd be there now. Speaking of naked, are you?

She looked down at her tankini and typed. As a jaybird.

Ping. God, you're killing me.

She grinned. How is Madison doing?

Ping. Surprisingly well. She seems to take to the camera like a duck to water.

That didn't surprise Eden. Madison was a master at seduction, and now she had a venue to seduce the entire world. Eden couldn't have been happier for her. The rich and famous model lifestyle was a perfect match for her new friend.

Her phone pinged, and she glanced down at Nash's message and laughed.

I spoke too soon…she just demanded a chocolate eclair or she's quitting. Better see what I can do. Text you later.

Not knowing how to reply to that, Eden tapped over to her emoticon screen. She intended to send a cute smiley face with sunglasses as a goodbye, but instead she texted something stupid. And once the single red heart popped up on the screen, it looked extremely pathetic. She quickly tapped a variety of faces and images, in the hopes that the heart would get lost in the emoji clutter, but before she could send them, her phone pinged.

A single red heart. A single red heart that made Eden's heart want to jump right out of her chest. It probably didn't mean anything. Nash was probably just mimicking hers. But that didn't stop her from releasing a squeal of delight, followed by a lounge-chair happy dance that included wiggling her hips and lifting her hands over her head in a wild wave.

Her crazy antics drew the attention of a woman walking along the beach in a tiny, black string bikini, huge sunglasses, and a floppy hat. She stopped and stared at Eden as if she was a complete idiot. Feeling like one, Eden lowered her hands and offered the woman a weak smile and lame wave. After only a second's hesitation, the woman walked toward her. It wasn't until she stopped at the foot of the lounge that Eden noticed the nose stud and tribal tattoo on her hip. Eden mentally groaned.

Chloe.

The sunglasses covered the majority of Chloe's bruises, but not the cut on her full bottom lip. The sight made Eden feel bad for disliking the young woman so intensely. Her compassion fizzled when Chloe spoke in a belligerent tone.

"What do you want?"

Eden tried to smile. "I just wanted to say 'hi.' So you didn't go to the photo shoot?"

"No." She flopped down on the lounge next to Eden. "I have no desire to see a bunch of anorexic prom queens strut around in bathing suits for a couple of goody-goody billionaires." She tipped her chin down and looked over the rim of her sunglasses. "Although I guess Nash isn't such a goody-goody, is he? Who would've thought that one of the panty billionaires was a pervert? Of course, I should've guessed. What kind of a man runs a lingerie company?"

Eden felt her spine stiffen. "There are lots of men who work in female apparel. And Nash is not a pervert."

"Right." Chloe snorted. "He just likes to pay women so he can talk dirty to them in the dark."

Eden bristled. She had spent the last two days trying not to think about Nash talking dirty to Chloe in the dark. Now Chloe was forcing her to think about it. And Eden couldn't stop a myriad of questions from popping in her head. What dirty things had Nash said to Chloe? Had she stripped? Had he touched her? The thought made her so queasy that it was hard to keep her hotel breakfast down.

Chloe pushed her sunglasses back up on her nose. "Well, that explains that. You've fallen for the billionaire pervert, haven't you?" She tipped back her head and laughed. "Now that just made my day."

The laughter coupled with the image of Nash and Chloe in a dark hotel room caused Eden to lose all patience. She sat up and glared at her. "No. I have not fallen for the pervert—I mean Nash. But even if I have, it would be better than falling for a bad-breathed street thug who likes to punch women. Although I can certainly see why he wanted to punch you. You are the meanest person I've ever met in my life, and I don't know why Madison puts up with you!"

After she finished her tirade, Eden braced for a flying fist or at least a stinging slap. Instead, Chloe picked up Eden's mai tai from the table and took a long sip from the straw before she spoke.

"Yeah, you're right. I am a pretty big bitch. And I don't know why Madison puts up with me. She must be a glutton for punishment." She took out the umbrella and sucked on the end before pointing it at the ocean. "Do you think there are sharks in the water?"

It was hard to yell at someone when they agreed with you, especially when they had two black eyes. Eden stared at Chloe for a moment before she reclined back on the lounge. "I doubt that a shark would swim this close to shore."

"I guess you didn't watch Shark Week," Chloe said. "Most attacks happen within fifty feet of the shore."

"So I gather you didn't live close to an ocean."

"Close enough, but my parents weren't what you'd call beach people. They preferred a glass of wine by the pool."

"You had a swimming pool?"

Chloe took another sip of mai tai. "What? Did you think I grew up poor?"

Eden had thought that. "So if your family has money, why haven't they helped you?"

"Maybe I don't want the control that comes with the money."

"And you don't think an escort is controlled?"

Chloe's lips pressed together in a firm line. "I'm not a prostitute. Zac didn't let me go with guys who wanted sex. Just guys like your boyfriend who wanted a peep show."

"What a nice guy."

Chloe jerked off her hat and tossed it to the foot of the lounge chair. "So I guess we both fell for jerks. And what made you want to become an escort? I'm not buying the entire romance writer thing."

Eden could've made up another lie, but there was no reason to now. She wasn't going to be a reporter. "Until I was fired, I worked for a newspaper. My editor wanted me to write a story about prostitutes. I was trying to get the inside scoop."

"So I was right. You are using Madison."

"I was at first," Eden said, "but then I made a major journalism mistake and got too close to my story. Madison became more than just a means to an end. She became my friend."

Chloe studied her as she twirled the umbrella between her fingers. "And is that what happened with the billionaire pervert? You got too close to the story?"

"Yes." Eden sighed. "And now I can't do a story on him or Madison."

"Wow. You are a shitty reporter."

Eden tried to think of a good comeback, but it was hard to argue with the truth. "You're right. It seems I didn't get one of my dad's journalism genes." She expected to get a satisfied smirk from Chloe. Instead, Chloe surprised her with a compliment.

"Yeah, well, you might be a shitty reporter, but you're a good friend for letting Madison move in with you. I didn't do a thing to stop Zac from kicking her out of her apartment—not one damned thing. I was too chickenshit. I'm surprised she doesn't hate me."

Eden laughed. "Madison? Are you kidding? She enjoys life too much to hold a grudge."

A few moments passed before Chloe replied. "Maybe she's onto something." She glanced over and, for the first time, gave Eden a smile. It was amazing how it transformed her face. Sullen, she was beautiful. Smiling, she was breathtaking. And Eden understood why Zac was grooming her to be an escort. She would make him millions.

Correction, she would've made him millions. Because right then and there, Eden decided on a new goal. Chloe. Eden figured if she could get the Happy Hooker to quit the escort business, she could get Chloe away from Zac's clutches. But in order to do that, she would need to become her friend. Which didn't seem like such a sacrifice.

Eden returned her smile and held out a hand. "Should we let bygónes be bygones?" Behind the sunglasses, she knew Chloe rolled her eyes, which made Eden smile all the brighter.

"Fine," Chloe said, and gave her hand a side high five. "Now let's order lunch. I'm starving."

For being so thin, Chloe ate like Eden's little brothers and held her liquor like Madison. Although after their fourth mai tai, they were both pretty wasted. Which was how Eden ended up asking the question that had been swirling around in her head for hours.

"Did Nash touch you?" Once the question was out, she realized that she didn't want the truth after all. "Never mind." She flapped a hand. "I'm drunk."

Chloe sat cross-legged on the lounge chair, eating from the tray of food the waitress had brought. She finished off the fish taco before turning to Eden. She had bent the front rim of her hat up and now resembled a pirate in big sunglasses. "No, your boyfriend didn't touch me. It seems that he's a much better judge of age than our waitress. He took one look at me and requested an older woman. Not wanting Zac to be pissed, I told Nash I'd take care of getting him a new girl. That's where you came in."

"So you didn't strip for him?" When Chloe shook her head, Eden released the most girlie noise she had ever made, before she launched herself at Chloe and hugged her.

Chloe did not return the hug. "Geez, you are such a wimp."

"Says the woman who won't get in the water." Eden sat back. "So how old are you?"

"Twenty."

Eden's eyes widened. "Twenty? You're almost the same age as my little brothers." Her eyes narrowed. "Zac should be shot for preying on someone so young." She grabbed Chloe's mai tai. "And give me that. You're not old enough to drink."

Chloe laughed. "Too late, I'm already drunk." She

popped the last plantain chip in her mouth before moving the tray off the lounge and reaching for the strings of her bikini top.

"What are you doing?" Eden asked.

"What does it look like I'm doing? I'm taking off my top. Even with sunscreen, I'm starting to get tan lines." She dropped her bikini top to the sand and then stretched out in the sun. "And so are you."

"Well, I'm not taking off my top," Eden said as she glanced around. There were few people on the secluded beach, and none that were paying any attention to them. Like Chloe and Eden, they had their own little thatched-roofed cabana and were enjoying their vacation.

"We make quite a pair." Chloe laughed. "I'm afraid of going in the water, and you're afraid of showing your boobies."

"I'm not afraid," she snapped.

"Then prove it."

Dares had always been Eden's downfall. Losing a dare was like not accomplishing a goal. And since she had already failed at becoming a journalist, she wasn't about to fail at this.

She glanced around and made sure no one was watching before she reached behind her and untied her tankini top. Once it was untied, she held it to her breasts and continued to look around until Chloe snorted.

"You are the biggest wimp ever."

Eden jerked it over her head. "There! Are you happy now?"

Chloe smiled before she took off her sunglasses and flipped the brim of her hat over her face. "As a matter of fact, I am feeling pretty happy. Happier than I've felt in years. Now relax that tight ass of yours and enjoy the moment."

It wasn't easy to heed Chloe's advice. Especially when your breasts were bared for God and the world to see. But after a few moments of glancing around and discovering that no one seemed to care one way or the other if Eden was topless, she relaxed. And she soon discovered that there was something hedonistic about lying in the sunshine with the cool ocean breezes brushing against your naked breasts. She closed her eyes and smiled. Her grandparents would be so proud.

Eden woke to the feel of something cold and titillating caressing her skin. At first, she thought it was the breeze, but then she realized the touch moved in a loopy pattern, brushing beneath one breast before gliding over the top of the other. She opened her eyes to find Chloe gone and Nash sitting on the lounge next to her, his hooded gaze following the path of the piece of ice he was outlining her breasts with.

"Nash." The word came out of her mouth on a sigh as her nipples tightened.

His eyes lifted, their bluish-purple depths hot and glittery. "Do you have any idea how much I want to make love to you right now?" Heat settled in her bones and pooled between her legs, and she slowly shook her head. "You've totally captivated me, Eden. All I can think about is you . . . and being deep inside you."

His eyes grew even more intense. For a moment, she thought he was going to take her right there. And the crazy thing about it was she would've let him. But instead, he reached for her bathing suit top and helped her put it on. Once she was covered, he got up and pulled her into his arms.

He kissed her, long and deep, before he rested his forehead against hers. "I had plans to take you to dinner. But now, all I want to do is take you to bed."

Eden smiled. "And who says we can't have dinner in bed?"

CHAPTER TWENTY-FOUR

I have to hand it to you, Grayson." Deacon sat at his desk staring at the screen of his laptop. "These photographs were worth the wait. Did we sign this woman to an extended contract with French Kiss? I want her in the fashion show this fall."

Since Grayson seemed to be distracted by something outside the window, Nash answered the question. "I had Madison sign a contract while in Fiji for these pictures, but we haven't signed her for an extended contract yet."

"Why not?"

"Her best friend wouldn't let her. She wants Madison to get an agent first so we don't try and screw her." Nash couldn't keep a grin from spreading across his face at just the thought of Eden going to bat for her friend. She'd been like a protective mother tiger with her cub. Which made Nash wonder what she'd be like with her children. Probably much like his own mother. No one messed with Althea Beaumont's boys. The thought made him smile even more. It was nice to think of his mom without sadness.

Deacon stopped looking at the pictures and turned his attention to Nash. "And you find it amusing that we'll now be sucked dry by some agent."

Nash laughed. "Stop being such a tightwad, Deke. We both know that Madison has what it takes to sell whatever she puts on. She should get paid well for it."

The scowl remained for only a second longer before Deacon nodded. "Fine. Just don't let her agent skin us alive." He sat back in his chair and studied Nash. "So it looks like you enjoyed Fiji. This is the first time I've seen you smile—really smile—in a long time."

Enjoyed didn't come close to describing his feelings about the trip. The week spent in Fiji with Eden was indescribable. Once Nash had made sure the photo shoots were on track, he spent the rest of his time with Eden exploring the islands. They had lounged on the sandy white beaches and trekked through the vibrant green jungles. They had snorkeled through a school of neon-colored fish and paddleboarded on the crystal-smooth waters of a turquoise cove. They had eaten dinner surrounded by flickering, golden-flamed tiki torches and danced beneath a canopy of brilliant white stars. But the times Nash enjoyed the most were the times spent in the hotel's mosquito-netted teakwood bed.

It wasn't just about the sex. He loved the hot rush of desire and mind-blowing release he found with Eden, but he loved just lying with her even more. Talking to her. Touching her. Just listening to her breath. He had always thought it would be hell to be so controlled by a woman, but now he realized that control was overrated.

"Yes," he said. "I enjoyed Fiji very much."

Deacon studied him for a moment more before he nodded. "Good. Everyone needs to get away occasionally." He glanced at Grayson. "Did you enjoy Fiji, Gray?" When Grayson didn't turn around, he looked at Nash. "What's going on with him? He's usually only distracted when he's sketching. Where is his sketchpad, anyway?"

It was a good question. Now that Nash thought about it, he hadn't seen Grayson drawing since they returned from Fiji. And his little brother rarely went anywhere without his sketchpad.

"I don't know," Nash said. "Maybe he turned in his sketchpad for his camera. He took as many pictures as the photographer did."

Deacon looked back at his laptop. "Miles certainly did a good job. I think we should use this one of Madison in the blue bikini for the cover."

Nash got up and walked around the desk to look over Deacon's shoulder. "That's a good one, but I think the pink suit at sunset would be more eye-catching." Before they could argue over their choices, Grayson finally spoke.

"We're not using Madison for the cover."

"What?" Nash and Deacon said in unison.

Grayson turned. "We're not using Madison for the cover. We're using one of the photos I took. Last series of pictures, fifth in the second-to-last row."

Deacon exchanged glances with Nash before he clicked over to the last page of photos. He scrolled down and then clicked on the fifth photo. When it popped up on the screen, Nash knew that Grayson was right. The bright orange bikini fit the tanned, lithe body of the model to a tee and popped against the background of navy-striped lounge cushion, turquoise waters, and azure sky. Nash knew all the models, but he couldn't place this woman. Especially when her face was half-covered by a floppy beach hat.

"Who is she?" Nash asked Grayson.

"Chloe."

Nash was surprised. Chloe made no bones about her dislike of Grayson and had spent the majority of the trip avoiding him. Obviously, she had gotten over her anger, and Nash would've asked his brother what had happened to change her feelings if Deacon hadn't been sitting there.

Deacon didn't know anything about the events preceding the trip to Fiji, and on the flight home, Nash and Grayson decided that their big brother didn't need to know. Deacon wouldn't be happy that they had hired a former escort to model bathing suits, or that Grayson had beat up a thug who would no doubt want revenge, or that Nash had gotten his baby brother involved because he'd hired the escorts to begin with. Of course, they would have to tell Deacon eventually. But for now, that can of worms would remain closed.

Deacon's phone rang, and while he answered it, Nash wandered to the window and stood next to Grayson. "It's a perfect picture, Gray. I'm assuming you got Chloe to sign a release."

There was a long pause before his little brother spoke. "She doesn't know I took it." Nash glanced at him, but he continued to stare out the window. "But I'll get her to sign the release. I'll make it worth her while."

"I'm not sure money will sway her. I tried to offer her some before she got off the plane, but she refused to take it."

Grayson nodded. "So do you think she went back to him?"

"Probably. But she's over eighteen, Gray. Old enough to make her own decisions."

"Even bad ones?"

"Sometimes people need to learn the hard way," Nash said. He was a perfect example of that. Rather than take help from other people, he had thought he could handle things on his own. It had taken a person like Eden—a person who refused to give up on him—to make him see that. Hopefully, Chloe would find someone like that as well.

Not wanting his little brother upset, Nash hooked an arm around Grayson's neck and gave him a shake. "So be truthful, little brother. What has you so distracted? Are you crushing on Madison?"

Grayson frogged him in the ribs and twisted out of the hold. "Not likely."

Nash play punched him in the arm. "Oh, come on, I saw you two talking during the photo shoots. I've never seen you talk so much."

"Madison is just a friend." Grayson blocked the next punch and threw one of his own that was not quite as playful as Nash's had been. It caught him on the chin and stung like hell. It looked like Grayson was getting better at boxing. Which made Nash more than a little proud.

"Come on, you two," Deacon called, "quit horsing

around. We need to finish picking the photos for the catalog."

They spent the rest of the morning arguing over the pictures that would go in the catalog and then broke for lunch. Over deli sandwiches, Nash brought up the new line of functional bras to go with their collection. Deacon balked at first, but after listening to Nash's points, he agreed that they needed to have a design meeting as soon as possible to discuss the idea with Samuel and Olivia.

But before he could make a call to the design studio, Olivia walked in the door. She looked like she had been crying, which had Deacon dropping his sub and coming out of his chair.

"What happened, Livy? Is it the baby?"

Tears welled in her eyes. "Samuel's taken the first day off in his entire career, and it's all my fault."

Deacon moved around the desk and pulled his wife into his arms. "Now, honey, I'm sure you had nothing to do with it. After all these years, he probably just needed a day off."

Olivia shook her head. "No, it has nothing to do with that and everything to do with me meddling in things I had no business meddling in." She pulled back and looked at Deacon. "If I hadn't forced Samuel to go to the ball, he would've never eaten the Huckabees' magic brownies and had sex with my mother."

"Your mother and Samuel had sex?" Deacon asked. "But I thought Samuel was gay."

She sighed. "He is. Which is why he's so devastated, and why my mother has gotten a new lover."

That wasn't what Nash expected to hear. Last time he'd

talked with Deirdre, she was on her way to explain things to Samuel. Obviously, something had gone awry. "Your mother has a new lover?" he asked.

She nodded. "I called her this morning, and I definitely heard a man's voice in the background, calling her Dee Dee and asking her to come join him in the shower."

Nash grinned. He probably should've informed Olivia who Deirdre's new lover was, but he figured that Olivia would hear it soon enough from her mother. Although he couldn't help trying to make her feel better.

"I wouldn't worry too much about it, Livy. These things have a way of working out." He got up and pulled out a chair. "Now sit down. I want to talk to you about bras."

Olivia loved the idea for a new line of comfort bras, and as soon as the meeting was over, she headed back to the design studio to work on some mock-ups. Grayson went with her, although he didn't seem too excited about helping with the designs. Since Nash had been gone for a week, he headed to his office to take care of e-mails. But when he got there, he didn't boot up his laptop. Instead, he called Eden. She answered on the first ring, which for some reason made him smile.

"I thought you had to work all day," she said.

"I do. I just thought I would check in and see what you were doing."

"Actually, I was job hunting."

"So did you get fired from The Lemon Drop for taking the week off?"

"No, Jen covered for me. But I need another job if I want to pay my landlord." There was a smile in her voice.

Nash leaned back. "I'm sure you could work something out with him."

"Really? And just what would he expect in return for his rent money?"

"Not much. Just your body every second of every day."

"Hmm, my landlord sounds like a greedy fellow."

Nash smiled. "Very greedy. And if I'm going to want to see you every second of every day, maybe we should think about changing our living arrangements."

There was a long pause. "Are you talking about moving in together, Nash?"

Was he? He hadn't planned on talking about it, but now that he was, it felt right. "It only makes sense," he said. "Your place is too small for one person, let alone two. And I'm getting pretty sick of everything in my house being covered in Grayson's paint smudges." There was another long pause that had him fidgeting in his chair. "Look, it's not a big deal. If you don't want to—"

She cut him off. "I want to be with you, Nash. It's just that…well, my parents live together, but they're not married. And while they love each other and gave me a wonderful life, I'm a little more old-fashioned."

Nash sat up. "Are you proposing to me, Eden?"

"No! I'm just saying that I don't want to live with a man unless we're married—not that you and I are going to get married." Nash could almost see her hands waggling as she talked. "I would never presume such a thing. I just wanted you to know that it's not because I don't want to be with you. It's just because I don't want our children feeling bad because we're not—oh God, I'm really screwing this up."

How the conversation had moved from living with each other to marriage and children, Nash didn't know. Nor did he understand the feeling of overwhelming happiness that seemed to fill every cell in his body. "Okay then," he said, "absolutely no children or living together until after we're married."

Her breath released through the receiver. "Until after?"

"Until after." He couldn't stop grinning. "Now where are you? I want to see you."

"I thought you were working."

He got up from the chair. "What's the use in being the boss if you can't take off when you want to? Besides, if you're going to finish the half marathon, we need to run today. I have to swing by my house and change, and then I'll be over. We can run and then go back to my house for dinner. What do you want me to make?"

"You are actually asking me, Mr. Bossy Pants? And what if I don't want to run?"

"That's even better."

She laughed. "We'll run. And I like anything but couscous."

* * *

The little corner market that Nash stopped by on the way home was run by a German couple who were always friendly and helpful. Although today seemed to be the exception. As soon as Nash stepped in the door, the woman turned hostile. She didn't return his greeting, and when he grabbed one of the hand baskets and started shopping, she watched his every move as if he intended to shoplift something from her store. After he had picked out some potatoes and a loaf of French bread, he headed to the butcher counter, where he found the woman speaking to her husband in a voice loud enough for Nash to hear.

"I don't care how good of a customer he is," she hissed. "I don't want his kind in my store." When her husband glanced up and saw Nash listening, there was nothing for him to do except address the situation.

"Is there a problem?" Nash asked.

"You know what the problem is," the woman said before she stomped back to the front register. The man seemed to be less hostile and more embarrassed. He just stood there with a red face until Nash placed his order.

"Two rib eyes, please. Bone in."

The man pulled the steaks from the case and quickly wrapped them in white butcher paper. Once they were wrapped, he glanced back at his wife, who was now busy with a customer, and quickly motioned for Nash to step behind the counter.

"I remember what it's like to be a foolish young man," he said as he took the basket from Nash. He placed the items in a plastic bag along with the steaks before handing them back. "But women, they don't understand these things. So it might be better for both of us if you go out the back door."

"I'm sorry," Nash said, "but I don't know what you're talking about."

The man looked as confused as Nash felt. "You haven't seen the article in the newspaper?"

"What article?"

After glancing at his wife, the man waved at Nash to

follow him. Behind the swinging door was the butcher shop, where a guy in a blood-splattered white apron was carving a side of beef. The storeowner led Nash to a trash can. He dug through the trash and pulled out a crumpled newspaper. He thumbed to the second page before handing it to Nash.

"At least you didn't make the front page."

A bad feeling settled in Nash's stomach. It grew when he saw the picture of him with Melissa at prom. Above the picture was the headline: SECRETS OF A PANTY BILLIONAIRE. Nash should've felt shocked. He didn't. With his high profile, the truth about the rape charges was bound to get out. In fact, he was surprised that it hadn't gotten out sooner.

"May I keep this?" he asked. When the man nodded, he folded the newspaper and placed it in the bag with his groceries. "What do I owe you?"

"You can pay me next time you come in. By that time, the missus will have gotten over it." The man followed him to the back door. "I don't think she's mad about the charges—sounds to me like they were trumped up. But the prostitute thing always wigs women out."

It took a real effort for Nash to keep his shock from showing. "Well, thank you," he said as he stepped out the door. He walked down the alley, then around the side of the building before he stopped and pulled out the paper.

The grocer had been right. The story only briefly mentioned the rape charges and the trial. The main focus of the article was about him hiring escorts. Or not escorts as much as one escort. The article was written in the first person as if the writer of the article was the escort he'd hired.

*Why did he refuse to turn on a light? Was he ugly?
Disfigured? A pitiful Elephant Man shunned by
society? Or was he just an arrogant billionaire who
was bored with his rich lifestyle?*

"Why do you hire women?" I asked.

*There was a pause, and I thought he wasn't
going to answer me. And then his voice came out
of the darkness, low, deep, and tinged with Southern smoothness. "Why else? Because I'm sexually
deviant."*

Stunned, Nash lowered the newspaper. There was only
one escort who had ever asked him that question. Only
one escort he'd answered with that exact reply. He stumbled through his mind for an explanation. There had to be
one. Maybe there had been a hidden camera in the room.
If that was the case, then the hotel and the newspaper were
about to get hit with a major lawsuit. Not to mention the
writer who had produced the poorly written piece of crap.

Wanting to know who he was going to sue the hell out
of, Nash glanced at the byline. For a second, he thought
his eyes were playing a trick on him. But after several
blinks, the two words remained the same. Two words that
shattered his entire world.

Eden Huckabee.

CHAPTER TWENTY-FIVE

If that dopey look on your face isn't love, I don't know what is."

The words snapped Eden out of the second thoughts she'd been having about not moving in with Nash, and she glanced over at Chloe, who was stretched out on the couch, leafing through one of Madison's celebrity magazines. Her bruises were almost healed, and the ones that weren't were well concealed by the deep tan she'd gotten in Fiji. For whatever reason, she'd removed her nose ring and had cut her long hair. With the short-cropped style, she looked even more like Audrey Hepburn. A delusional Audrey Hepburn.

"I'm not in love," Eden said. "I'm in lust."

"What's the difference?" Madison came out of the kitchen with a bag of Chips Ahoy! cookies and flopped down on the bed next to Eden.

Eden promptly took the bag from her. "Oh no, you don't. You complained about your weight the entire trip and begged me to help you diet. And chocolate chip cookies are not part of the program I pulled up for you on the Internet." She tossed the bag to Chloe, who could use a few extra pounds.

"No fair," Madison grouched. "I'm starving."

"Eat a carrot." She walked into the closet to get her running shoes so she would be ready when Nash arrived. When she came back out, she continued the previous conversation. "And there is a big difference between love and lust. One is about emotions and the other about physical attraction. I am extremely attracted to Nash—both his body and his brain."

Madison fell back on the bed and kicked her feet in the air like a child throwing a tantrum. "But I don't want a carrot. I want CHOCOLATE!" She stopped kicking and rolled to her stomach. "Which only proves my point. Once you lust after something long enough, you start to love it so much that you can't live without it."

"That's a bunch of phooey," Eden said. "You can live without chocolate, Madison. You just don't want to. And I can live without Nash, but I just don't want to. I wouldn't call that love."

"Whatever, Queen of Denial." Chloe tossed a cookie to Madison, who dove in front of Eden before she could intercept it.

Eden sent Chloe a hard look. "Speaking of the Queen of Denial…"

"I'm not in denial. I know that Zac's a loser."

"Then why did you go back with him when you could've moved in here with me and Maddie?"

"It would've been like a slumber party every night."

Madison stared at the cookie for a moment before she sighed. "I love you, cookie, but I must let you go if I want to become the next top model." She tossed it in the trash can as Chloe spoke.

"I'm not much of a slumber party girl. And I'm tired of you two trying to butt your noses in my business. I let you shanghai me to Fiji, but I'm not letting you talk me into leaving Zac. I know you don't understand it, but it's just the way it is." She got to her feet. "And if that means we can't be friends, then I guess we can't be friends."

After getting back from Fiji, Eden had done research on abusive relationships, and one of the things the articles stressed was not pushing the victim into a corner. "Now wait," Eden said, "no one said we weren't going to be your friends if you stayed with Zac."

"She's right." Madison pulled her gaze from the cookie in the trash can. "I've never gone with the 'hoes before bros' thing. If you love Zac"—she sent her a weak smile—"you love Zac. We just don't want him to hurt you anymore."

Chloe glanced between them before she sat back down. "He's not going to hurt me again. He only got mean when I tried to stick up for Eden. He was in a much better mood when I got back."

"Maybe Grayson knocked some sense into him." Madison's eyes turned dreamy. "For an artist, that man has a mean right hook."

"It wasn't the Woman Whisperer," Chloe said. "I think it had more to do with finding out that Eden was a reporter and not some freelance prostitute trying to horn in on his business."

Eden stopped tying her shoes and glanced up. "So you told him I was a reporter?"

"I didn't tell him." Chloe took a bite of the cookie. "He found out while I was gone. He read your article in the newspaper about Nash."

There was a moment when Eden thought she might black out. All the air left her lungs, and her heart seemed to seize in her chest. Like a zombie, she walked to the breakfast bar, where her laptop was still open from her job hunting. It took only a few clicks to bring up the newspaper's website. She entered her password and then placed her name in the search engine. Numerous articles came up, but it was the most recent that had her eyes widening.

"Oh my God," she breathed as she covered her mouth with her hand. Chloe and Madison hurried over to stand behind her. There was a moment of silence as they read the article before Madison spoke.

"I don't understand. I thought you were writing a fictional story. Why didn't you tell me you were a reporter, Eden?"

"You didn't tell her?" Chloe asked.

Eden was so broadsided to see her story in print that she couldn't speak. All she could do was stare at the screen. Which left Madison to draw her own conclusions. The right conclusions.

"So you were just using me to get information," she said. "Which means that you really aren't my friend." Before Eden could find the words to explain, Madison grabbed her purse and walked out, slamming the door behind her.

"Holy shit," Chloe said. "You have really crapped in

your nest. I thought you weren't going to publish the story about Nash."

"I didn't," Eden whispered as she continued to stare at the words on the screen. "But I think I know who did."

* * *

The drive to the newspaper office took Eden less than five minutes in the Porsche. When she got there, she didn't park in the employee parking. She parked in the fire zone. At this point, she didn't care about a ticket. She cared about only one thing…killing Mike. She found him at his desk typing away. He glanced up when she stepped into his cubicle.

"Where have you been? I thought you would show up as soon as the story broke." Completely unaware of her anger, he leaned back in his chair and crossed his arms, giving her a smug smile. "Stella has agreed to give you another chance. So you want to thank me now? Or over the dinner you owe me?"

Eden gritted her teeth as she stepped closer. "Thank you for stealing my article and having it published without my permission? Is that what I should thank you for?"

Mike sat up. "Whoa. Are you pissed?"

"Yes! I'm pissed! How could you do it, Mike? Why would you do it?"

His face lost all color. "I thought that's what you wanted. And when you ran off after I told you about Nash's trial and left your laptop, I decided to help you out. And it's a great story, Huckabee—a little dramatic, but a great story. Everyone is talking about it and Nash Beaumont."

Eden cringed. "But I didn't want everyone talking about Nash."

"But isn't that the entire point of being a reporter—to get people talking about your articles?"

Her shoulders slumped. "Not that article."

"Then why did you pitch it to Stella? Why did you spend all the time researching it? And why did you want me to edit it?" Mike held up his hands. "Look, I'm sorry if I screwed up. But it's that article that made Stella want to rehire you."

"What is going on in here?" Stella came around the corner. When she saw Eden, her ChapSticked lips tipped in the closest thing Eden had ever seen to a smile. "Well, I have to hand it to you, Miss Huckabee, you are the walking definition of the saying 'if at first you don't succeed, try, try again.'" She held out a hand. "Congratulations on a great story—"

Eden cut her off before she could finish. "There's been a mistake, Stella. The story shouldn't have gone out. We're going to have to recall all the newspapers and write a retraction immediately."

At this point, Eden could've very easily thrown Mike under the bus. But as angry as she was with him for editing her article and then sending it to Stella, he didn't deserve to get fired over it. Not when he thought he'd been doing her a favor. So she took the blame. It wasn't like she had to worry about getting fired.

"There was a mix-up," she said. "I wanted to send you the story on the marathon to publish, and instead I sent you..." She scrambled for a good lie: "a page out of my journal."

Stella's face puckered. "Are you telling me I just published one of your fantasies as real news?"

Eden nodded. "That's exactly what I'm telling you." She held up her hands. "I know I'm really and truly fired this time. I'll go and clear out my things from the janitor's closet, but first you have to get those newspapers back."

Stella stared at her like she'd lost her mind. "You really don't know crap about the newspaper business, do you?" She looked at Mike. "I don't suppose you have anything to add to this crazy conversation?" When Mike didn't say anything, she issued an order. "Go get me some coffee and don't skimp on the sugar." Then she motioned for Eden to follow her.

Once they were in her office, Stella sat down behind her desk. "I don't believe the pile of crap you just told me about your journal. And since you seem so angry at Mike, I'm going to make a guess that he's somehow involved." When Eden remained silent, she nodded. "Okay, don't tell me. It's probably best if I don't know. But what I do need to know is how much of the story is true."

Realizing that she would need Stella's help if she wanted to fix this, Eden came clean. "Most of it."

Stella's shoulders relaxed. "As long as you will testify that Mr. Beaumont hired you as an escort and talked dirty to you, we shouldn't have to worry about losing a lawsuit."

Eden shook her head. "I won't testify to that, Stella."

"Excuse me?"

"I'm sorry, but I can't. I didn't take money from Nash, and everything that I did I did because I wanted to."

"For the story?"

It had started out that way. But somewhere the line

between career and personal life had become blurred. Eden wanted to call it lust—to believe that she could live just fine without Nash. But the fear that gripped her stomach made her realize the truth. She loved Nash. With that realization came another one. This wasn't fixable. They couldn't recall all the newspapers. When the story reached Nash, he would never forgive her. He had trusted her, and she had broken that trust.

"No," she whispered. "I did it because I love him."

Suddenly too overwhelmed to remain standing, she sat down in the chair and gave up. She gave up on her dream of becoming a reporter. She gave up on her dream of finishing the marathon. And she gave up on her dream of marrying the man she loved and living happily ever after. Unable to stop them, tears flooded her eyes and dripped down her cheeks in a steady stream.

Seeing them, Stella released a long sigh. "I'm getting too old for this crap." She grabbed a tissue and held it out to Eden. "Stop sniveling. We'll figure some way out of this mess. We'll get a retraction out in the morning issue. And until then, you better pray that the panty billionaires have better things to do than read our little newspaper." That hope died when the door opened and Mike walked into the office.

"Where the hell is my coffee?" Stella asked.

Instead of answering, he looked at Eden. "Nash Beaumont is here. He stopped Suz in the hallway and asked where your office was, and she directed him to the janitor's closet."

"Well, that's great," Stella said, "now he'll think we torture our employees by tossing them in a closet." She got up. "Show Mr. Beaumont in here—"

Eden cut her off. "No. I need to talk to him alone." She owed him that. And much, much more. Wiping at her eyes, she got to her feet. "Thanks, Stella. After I talk to Nash, I'll clear out the closet."

Stella shook her head. "Somehow I don't think I've seen the last of you, Eden Huckabee."

Trying to keep her chin up, Eden walked out of the office and down the hallway. The door of the janitor's closet stood open, and before she even reached it, she could see Nash standing at her makeshift desk, studying the pictures that remained on her corkboard. He was dressed for work but without the suit jacket. His lavender shirt emphasized his broad shoulders and was slightly wrinkled in the back, and his gray pants hugged his hips and tapered down his long legs.

Obviously, he had gotten the news before he'd changed into his running clothes. It hurt to know that they would never run together again. Ignoring the pain, she walked into the closet and closed the door behind her. He didn't turn around. Nor did he say anything for several heart-wrenching seconds. When he finally did speak, his voice sounded distant and strained.

"Nice office."

She swallowed the lump in her throat, but it raised right back up. "I'm sorry I lied to you, Nash. At the time, I was trying to get a story."

His shoulders tightened. "And you got one, didn't you?"

She moved closer, but still kept a good distance. "I swear I didn't want the story published."

"But you wrote it."

It wasn't a question, and still she answered. "Yes."

"To publish."

"Yes."

Eden wanted to say more. She wanted to explain and justify her actions. But there was no justification for her lies. So she just stood there and watched as he slowly turned around. Eden didn't know what she expected to see, but it wasn't a face as blank as a sheet of copy paper. No fake smile. No real one. No passion. Or compassion. No tenderness. No forgiveness. Just nothing. But when he spoke, his voice held all the emotions his face wasn't showing. Disbelief. Pain. But mostly anger.

"I should've known you weren't an escort. You were a lousy lay." He brushed past her and walked out the door.

CHAPTER TWENTY-SIX

There was comfort in the fact that, while everything else in Nash's life had changed, Grandpa's fishing shack had remained the same. The bottom porch step was still missing a slat. The screen door hinges still squeaked. And the inside still smelled like fish and gym socks. Having arrived the night before, Nash probably could've fixed those things—replaced the slat, oiled the hinges, cleaned the house—but instead he sat on the front porch staring out at the woods. At least, that's what his body did. His mind did something else entirely. Like an iTunes song on repeat, it kept going over and over every second he'd spent with Eden.

Every word.
Every touch.
Every lie.

Nash couldn't seem to stop it. Or maybe he didn't want to. Deep down, he was hoping that his brain would find something. Some shred of truth that would make the ache in his chest go away. But no revelation arrived. And when hunger finally broke the cycle, he got up from the rocker and drove into town for groceries.

DuPont was a midsize town—not so small that he knew everyone, but not so big that he wouldn't run into a few people who would recognize him.

"Well, if it isn't Nash Beaumont!" The bearded guy in the blue vest grinned broadly as Nash stepped through the sliding doors of the Walmart. "I didn't think I'd see you back in this Podunk town. How's Deacon doing? Tell him that I sure miss our high school days together."

Just the mention of his brother had guilt tightening Nash's stomach. He should've called Deacon and explained things. Of course, the newspaper article would explain it all. And maybe that was why he hadn't called Deacon or charged his cell phone when it died. He couldn't stand to hear the disbelief and hurt in his brother's voice.

"He's good, Jimmy," Nash said. "How are you doing?"

"Good, but not as good as the Beaumonts." He thumped him on the arm. "You boys were always lucky sonofabitches. And how much luckier can you get than owning a lingerie company?" He leaned closer and spoke in a not-so-soft whisper. "I hear those supermodels trot around buck-naked backstage of that fashion show. Is that true?"

"Not quite buck-naked, but close enough."

Jimmy's eyes glazed over. "Holy shit. Like I said, you're lucky sonofabitches." He paused and lifted one shoulder in a half shrug. "Well, besides what happened with Melissa. That was about as unlucky as you can get."

Not having the energy or inclination to talk about Melissa, Nash grabbed a shopping cart. "Well, it was good seeing you, Jimmy." He hoped Jimmy would get the hint. Unfortunately, he left his station by the door and followed him.

"I hate to say it, man, but even though you were my good friend's little brother, I had my doubts that you were innocent. Especially after Melissa ended up taking all of her mom's sleeping pills. But then I started dating Jolene Montel, who works as an accountant for the mental health-care facility. She's a couple years older than me, but a sweet little thing who has the nicest ass—"

"Look, Jimmy," Nash cut him off, "I'm kind of in a hurry."

"Oh, sure, sure. I just wanted to tell you that I was sorry for blaming you, because Jolene said that Melissa was nuttier than a can of Planters peanuts long before you had sex with her."

Nash stopped the cart by a tower of cereal boxes and turned to Jimmy. "What do you mean?"

"I guess Melissa was a patient of one of the psychiatrists at the clinic for years and had tried to kill herself twice before—a fact that her parents were able to keep hush-hush at the trial due to that doc-patient privacy thing. And Jolene really couldn't say anything because that's her job and all. But she said she would've spoken up if they had found you guilty." He glanced back at the door. "Well, I better get back to work. My boss can be a real pain in the ass." He walked off, leaving Nash more than a little stunned.

Nash should've felt some kind of redemption in

knowing that Melissa had mental issues long before the night in the hotel. But he didn't feel better. He just felt sad. Sad for Melissa. And sad for her family. And sad for all the years he'd blamed himself for her death.

No longer hungry, he grabbed only the bare essentials—milk, bread, eggs, sugar, and tea—before heading to the liquor department. Once he got back to the fishing shack, he had every intention of doing some serious damage to the bottle of Johnnie Walker. But after only one shot, he felt sick to his stomach, so he screwed the cap back on and made a jug of sweet tea. He had just poured himself a mason jar full when he heard the crunch of tires on gravel. He carried his drink out to the porch and watched as a Mercedes pulled next to the house. He didn't recognize the car, but he recognized his father behind the wheel.

The Mercedes was brand new and pimped out with flashy gold trim and hubcaps. And when Donny John stepped out of the car, he wore almost as much gold as his vehicle. Several chains hung in the open collar of his white shirt, a watch and bracelet cuffed his wrists, and a ring that could easy be awarded to a Super Bowl victor graced one pinkie finger. And the hoop he normally wore in his ear had been replaced with a huge diamond. Leave it to Donny John to thoroughly enjoy his new status as father to billionaire sons.

The sight would've normally annoyed Nash. He and his father had never been what you would call close. Some said it had to do with the fact that they were too much alike. Of all the boys, Nash looked most like his father and had a way with people and with women. But

Nash knew it had more to do with what happened after his mother had died. Donny John had given up on life and his sons. Nash had a hard time forgiving him for that. Yet today, Nash didn't feel annoyed. He just felt relief. He didn't know where the emotion came from, but it was there, settling around him like a warm blanket on a cold autumn day. It seemed that even bad dads were still dads, and seeing them made you think that everything was going to be okay—even if it wasn't.

"How did you know where to find me?" he asked.

Donny John flashed a smile. "Deacon called and said that you'd gone missing, so I took a chance." He held open the door, and a hound dog jumped out. Blue had been Nash's dog before the move to San Francisco. So it wasn't surprising that the dog let out an earsplitting howl when he saw Nash and raced around the corner of the porch and up the steps to greet him. The big paws on Nash's chest and the wet tongue on his face released a swell of emotion that had been sitting in his chest like a bag of wet cement.

"How ya doin', boy?" His voice cracked as he set down his tea and pulled the dog closer to scratch his ears.

"He's missed you." Donny climbed the steps. "He spent the entire night howling at the moon the day you and Grayson left to join Deacon in San Fran."

"I'm sorry, boy," Nash said and continued to scratch Blue's ears, "but you wouldn't have been happy in a city without any coons and ducks to chase."

"That dog does love to chase things. He treed my new neighbor's cat just when I was about to get a dinner invitation, and the woman has ignored me ever since."

Nash sat down in one of the rockers. "You moved?"

"I had a house built in that new subdivision just outside of town. Four bedrooms and three bathrooms, just in case my sons want to come visit." He glanced around. "And I can tell you that it's a darn sight better than this old shack."

"I like this old shack. In fact, I'm thinking about living here."

Donny John studied him for a long moment before he nodded at the glass sitting on the railing. "You got any more of that tea?" Without waiting for a reply, he opened the squeaky screen door and went inside. When he came out, he took the chair next to Nash. Nash expected him to start talking. Donny John had always been a talker. But instead, he just rocked and sipped his tea that was no doubt laced with some of the whiskey. After a while, Blue pulled away from Nash and flopped down between the chairs, lowering his head to his paws.

Nash picked up his tea and joined the rocking, the creak of the chairs keeping time with the chirps and buzz of the evening insects. When the last of the sun spilled across the porch like warm honey from a spoon, Donny John finally spoke.

"Can't say as I blame you for wanting to move back. Too many people and not enough land in San Fran. And here, you've got good trout fishing. The best hound dog in the state. And plenty of Southern girls to keep you company." He paused. "Although you didn't really care for Southern girls after Melissa, did you?"

Nash took another sip of tea. "I don't want to talk about Melissa."

Donny John nodded. "You've always kept your thoughts and feelings close to your vest. Did you realize that you've never talked about your mother after she died? Not once. Grayson and Deacon bring her up all the time in our conversations, but you don't bring her up at all." He continued to rock. "I get it. Sometimes it's hard to talk about painful things. Unfortunately, sometimes you have to go through the pain in order to get to the healing."

Nash stopped rocking and looked at his dad. "And you don't think I've gone through pain?"

"No. I don't think you've gone through anything. I think you're stuck smack-dab in the middle of pain and refuse to swim to shore or ask for help."

Nash got up so quickly that Blue thought he wanted to play and jumped up to dance around his feet. But Nash was too upset to pay him much attention. "Ask for help from who, Dad? You? Because after Mom died, you were nowhere around. You were off chasing women and ignoring the fact that you had kids. And how could I ask Deacon for help when he was burdened with all the jobs that you were supposed to be doing? So yes, I ignored the fact that my heart felt like it was ripped in two." He held up his hands. "Instead, I became Easygoing Nash Beaumont who has the world by its tail. But it's all a lie. I have nothing by its tail but bad luck."

Donny John didn't seem fazed by his son's burst of anger. He continued to rock and reached out to scratch Blue's ears. "There's no doubt that I was a crappy father after your mother died. I wish I could go back and change it, but the only thing I can change is the here and now." He looked up. "If you want to talk about what's brought you home looking like Blue on bath day, then I'm here, Nash, and I'm listening."

It would've been so easy to tell Donny John to go to hell. It wasn't like the man didn't deserve it. But something stopped Nash. Maybe it was because he had no right to cast stones. Or maybe he was just tired of being smack-dab in the middle of pain. Whatever it was, he sat back down in the rocker and told his father everything. His pain after Melissa died and hiring the escorts to make sure he had complete control. And he talked about Eden. He talked about the first time she walked into the hotel suite until the day he walked out of the newspaper office. When he was finished, night had fallen, their tea was nothing but melted ice, and Blue had left the porch to chase raccoons. He expected Donny John to have something to say about how stupid it was to hire escorts or how wrong Eden was to betray him. Instead he keyed in on something else entirely.

"You say she dressed up like a hooker just to get a story?" He chuckled. "Now that's quite a woman. Sounds like she has no trouble going after what she wants."

Nash sent his father an annoyed look. "And she doesn't care who she uses in the process."

Donny John nodded. "But sounds to me like you were both doing a little using. She was using you to get a story. And you were using her to get over Melissa."

"I wasn't using her!" When his father lifted an eyebrow at him, he backpedaled. "Okay, so maybe I was using her at first. But not after we started seeing each other. I was completely truthful with her. While she told me nothing but lies."

Donny John's other eyebrow hiked up. "Completely? Sorry if I don't believe you, Son, but I've never known a man in my life that was completely truthful with a woman. If we want to stay in a relationship, we can't be. Because if women truly knew what went on in a man's mind, they'd go screaming back to their mamas in a New York second."

"So you're saying you lied to Mom?"

"I'm saying I stretched the truth a little. Like telling her that I liked that ugly haircut she got after Grayson was born and the puke-green dress that made her look like a puffed-up frog. I lied and told her I hadn't looked when Norma Willis lost her top at the lake—but what man in his right mind wouldn't look at those huge hooters?" He rested his head on the back of the rocker. "And I lied when I promised her that I'd find another wife for me and a mom for you boys. I tried. Hell—I guess I'm still trying. But there is no replacement for your mother. She was one in a million." He turned his head and looked at Nash. "But what I never lied about was how much I loved her. Did you tell this Eden that you love her?"

Nash could've denied that he ever loved Eden, but the hole in his chest said otherwise. "No. And I'm glad I didn't. If I had, I would really look like a fool."

"Ahh." Donny John went back to rocking. "There's nothing worse than looking like a fool." He paused. "Of course, she looked like even more of a fool when she published that retraction in the newspaper."

Nash sat up so quickly that the rocker cracked him in the back of the head. "What retraction?"

Donny John tossed the melted ice out of his mason jar. "According to Deacon, Eden wrote an article retracting the first article—or not retracting it as much as explaining it. It seems there was a big mistake made at the newspaper and someone sent in pages from her journal. Pages where she was fantasizing about being with the panty billionaire in a hotel room."

Nash stared at him. "But that's ridiculous. No one is going to believe that."

Donny John shrugged. "Maybe not, but you've got to give her credit for trying."

"I don't have to give her credit for anything. Especially when she shouldn't have written the article in the first place."

"Maybe she just wanted to get her job back. According to Deacon, she'd been fired from the newspaper weeks earlier."

Eden's office being in the janitor's closet suddenly made sense. Obviously, she had refused to leave the newspaper until she'd written the story about him. "But then why would she write a retraction?" He spoke more to himself than his father. "If she'd let the story stand, she might've gotten her job back. Now her creditability as a serious reporter is completely ruined."

Donny John started rocking again. "Maybe she doesn't care about her creditability. Maybe she just cares about you."

CHAPTER TWENTY-SEVEN

$\mathcal{E}$den's room at her parents' house had been turned into a yoga studio the day after Eden had left for San Francisco. Her mother had never believed in dwelling on the past. She was a firm believer in living in the present. Which explained why she hadn't asked Eden any questions about why she'd returned to Grover Beach. She had just hugged Eden close, then moved the yoga balls so they could pull down the Murphy bed from the wall.

Now, Eden was tucked into that bed, staring up at the glow-in-the-dark stars on the ceiling. They were the only things that remained of her childhood and were a vivid reminder that the little girl who had dreamed of reaching them had returned home a failure.

She didn't care about failing at being a reporter or a marathon runner. Those goals were meaningless now. But she was devastated at breaking Nash and Madison's trust. She had tried to call Madison before she left, but Madison hadn't answered. So Eden had left a lengthy apology.

No excuses, just a plea for forgiveness. She had tried to do the same with Nash. But all she got out was his name before she'd started sobbing and hung up. It didn't matter. He would never forgive her. Not after everything she'd done. Besides lying and betraying him, she had publicly humiliated him. And not even her retraction letter would change that.

The retraction letter was getting as much attention as the original article had. Before Eden left San Francisco, Mike had called to ask forgiveness for publishing her article and to tell her that the newspaper had been flooded with e-mails about her retraction. It seemed that men didn't believe it while women did and wanted Eden to share more of her journal pages and fantasies about the Beaumont brothers. Mike thought she should pitch the idea to Stella. But the newspaper business had lost its sparkle for Eden.

Which left the question . . . where did she go from here?

Before she could even begin to answer the question, the door flew open and her brothers Trace and Bronson came charging in and dove on the bed with a bone-crushing jar.

"Whassup, Sis!" Trace hooked an arm around her neck and gave her a rough rub on the head with his knuckles while Bronson took her pillow and stuffed it under his head.

"Hey, there are still stars on your ceiling," he said.

She elbowed Trace in the stomach to gain her release, then jerked the pillow back from Bronson and hit him in the face with it. "It's after midnight, you hooligans."

"So? Did you expect us to wait until morning to see

our big sister? We haven't seen you since Christmas."
Trace gave her a sloppy kiss on the forehead before flopping onto his back.

As much as the twins had made her life miserable growing up, their presence on either side of her eased the tightness around her heart. "Where have you two been?" she asked. "Don't tell me you had dates."

Trace gave her a nudge with his elbow. "What? You don't think your brothers are cute enough to get girls?"

They were definitely cute enough. They both had gotten Dad's blond hair and Mom's hazel eyes. They were suntanned and muscled from hours spent on their skateboards or surfing. And they had contagious smiles. Of course, as their sister, it was up to her to make sure that their heads didn't get any bigger than they were.

"If they like scrawny surfer dudes that smell like seaweed," she said. "And if you get sand in my sheets, I'm going to kill you."

Bronson laughed. "I've missed you, Ed. Not the lists you used to make me of things you thought I should be accomplishing, but your badass attitude."

"Speaking of accomplishments..." Trace moved the pillow over so Eden could share it. "How's the newspaper reporting going? Won the Pulitzer yet?"

If Eden had ever wanted to lie, it was that moment. Her brothers had always looked up to her, and she couldn't stand the thought of disappointing them. But lying had cost her Madison and Nash, and she had learned her lesson. Or at least she had learned it after she'd stretched the truth about the article being nothing but her journal pages.

"Actually, I got fired." She could feel both of her brothers shift toward her.

"Fired?" Bronson said. "As in canned? Man, Dad is not going to be happy. You were the one who was going to live his dream."

Bronson's wording was like a wake-up slap to the face. All the hours she'd spent trying to achieve her goal, and it hadn't even been hers. It had been her father's. The realization should've made her even more depressed. Instead, it made her laugh. And once she started laughing, she couldn't seem to stop.

"What?" Trace sat up. "What's so funny?"

"Me," she gasped between laughter. "They weren't even my own stars I was reaching for. And yet I convinced Stella to hire me and wrote all those horrible stories—not to mention what I did to poor Nash." Just the thought of Nash turned her hysterical laughter into heart-wrenching sobs. Which had her brothers panicking.

"Holy shit." Trace jumped off the bed as if she had cooties. "Why is she crying?"

"How would I know?" Bronson said. "But you better go get Mom."

Only a few minutes later, her mother came into the room and turned on the light. She took one look at the sobbing mess Eden had become and pointed to the door. "Time for bed, boys." Her brothers never minded so quickly. Once they were gone, her mother turned off the light and crawled in bed next to Eden. She didn't say anything. She just pulled her against the soft material of her Soma pajamas and stroked Eden's hair.

"I crushed him," Eden sobbed. "He trusted me, and

I crushed him like a bug. And there's no way to take it back. There's no way to fix it. I should've told him the truth from the beginning, and instead I was too caught up in Dad's dream that I couldn't see that my dream was right in front of me."

Her mother smoothed her hair back. "I'm going to assume that you're talking about the Dark Seducer."

Eden pulled away and tried to see her mother's face in the dark. "You read the article?"

"Of course I read the article. I've read all your articles, Eden."

"Why didn't you ever say anything? You've always acted like you were more interested in my chakras than my career."

"I'm interested in every part of you—mental, physical, and spiritual." She kissed Eden's forehead. "You, on the other hand, are only concerned with the mental and physical. Which is exactly how you ended up trying to do something you were never meant to do. You listened to your brain, not your heart."

Eden sniffed. "Gee, thanks, Mom. You could've saved me a lot of time and tears if you had told me that in the first place."

"I did tell you, Eden. I told you all the time, but you have always been too stubborn to listen."

Eden thought about her stubborn refusal to leave the newspaper. "You're right." She sniffed. "Once I get something in my head, it's hard to get it out. I guess I just wanted to make Dad happy."

"How many times do I have to tell you, Eden, that you're only responsible for your own happiness?"

Eden sighed. "And I've even screwed that up."

"So tell me, love." Her mother hugged her close. "What will make you happy?"

It only took a second to answer. "Nash Beaumont," she said. "I want to marry him and have his children. And I want to live in a house close to a park where Nash and I can run in the mornings and take our kids to play in the afternoons. And I want to have friends like I never had in high school. The kind of friends who will come over if I'm in trouble or just need to talk. And I want a dog. Yes, I really want a dog—" Her mother chuckled, and Eden pulled back and stared at her. "What's so funny?"

Her mother smiled. "I just never thought that my goal-setting daughter's top goal would be to become a wife and a mother. But I guess I should've expected it. You didn't like the fact that your father and I never married."

Tears filled Eden's eyes. "I don't care that much if he marries me, Mom. All I care about is if he loves me as long as Dad has loved you. But that isn't going to happen. He hates me."

"Even after you wrote the retraction?"

She swallowed. "It wasn't pages from my journal. I really did pose as an escort to get a story."

"I see." A few moments passed before her mother got up and tucked the sheet around her. "Good night, sweetheart." She placed a kiss on her forehead. "I'm making multigrain pancakes in the morning."

"Wait," Eden stopped her before she could get to the door. "Is that it? You don't have any advice for me?"

Her mother walked back to the bed. "I don't need to give you any advice, Eden. You just told me what it's going to take to make you happy. Now the choice is yours. And somehow I think that the young woman who had enough guts to go to San Francisco by herself and then pose as an escort to achieve someone else's dream will have enough guts to go back and achieve her own."

For a moment, Eden just sat there as the truth of her mother's words washed over her. She did have a choice. She could stay here with her parents and feel sorry for herself or she could go after her dream. Suddenly her heartache and depression were eclipsed by strength and determination.

"I'm going back to San Francisco," she stated as she started to get out of bed.

Her mother stopped her. "Not tonight, young lady. I won't have you driving on the highways this late at night. You'll get a good night's sleep and leave first thing in the morning."

"But I'm really not tired, Mom."

"That's because your chakras need to be cleaned out." She rubbed her palms together. "Now lie down on your stomach. Once your spirit channels are clear and open, you'll have a much better chance of making good decisions."

Eden sighed and lay down on the bed. Once her mother had massaged her back, cleared all chakras, and kissed her good night, Eden had to admit that she felt better. Or maybe she just felt better because she now had some goals. Her own goals.

Grabbing a pen and paper from the nightstand, she made a list. *Get Nash to love me. Get Madison to forgive me. Find a new career.* When written down on paper, they seemed a little daunting. But she ignored the sinking feeling in the pit of her stomach and listed the things she'd have to do to achieve her goals.

First and foremost, she would have to move back to San Francisco. Then she would need to get a job. Thinking that she was leaving for good, she had quit her job at The Lemon Drop. Hopefully Joe hadn't found a replacement yet. Since she had left her apartment to Madison and Madison now hated her, she would need a place to live. Mimi and Pops's was the best choice. Not only because she could live there rent-free but also because her main goal lived right next door. Which meant she would run into Nash on a regular basis.

Eden had just written down *buy sexy running clothes* when her cell phone rang. The first thought that popped into her head was *NASH!* Diving for the phone, she answered. It wasn't Nash, but the voice that came through the receiver was just as welcome.

"Thank God you answered," Madison said.

"Maddie, I'm so glad you returned my call. I wanted to tell you how sorry I am for lying to—"

Madison cut her off. "Okay, I forgive you. Now we have other problems. Chloe's life is in danger."

Eden sat up on the edge of the bed. "What happened? Is it Zac? Has he hurt her again?"

"Yes, but this time, he only got in a few punches before she sprayed him in the face with the mace I gave her and got out of there."

Relieved, Eden laughed. "Good for her! I hope it stung like hell."

"Me too." Madison had a smile in her voice. "Except

now we have another problem. Once Zac gets his eyes flushed out, he's going to be hopping mad and gunning for Chloe."

"Please don't tell me that she still refuses to call the police."

"Yes, but it doesn't matter. Someone called the police and told them about Zac's escort business, and the cops set up a sting operation and now have one of his escorts in custody. Which is why Zac got so mad at Chloe. He thought she had turned him in. Did you, Eden?"

"No. After the article came out, the police came and questioned me, but I didn't tell them anything. And it doesn't matter how they found out. What matters is keeping Chloe safe until Zac is behind bars. Where are you right now?"

"We're at your apartment."

Eden smiled. "You mean, our apartment? It's yours as much as it is mine. And there's something else I need to say . . . I love you, Maddie. You're my best friend."

There was a long pause before Madison sniffed. "You're my best friend too, Eden. Which is why I was so upset when you didn't confide in me."

"From this point on, I promise I'll always be truthful—"

"Yeah, yeah, you two are the best buddies ever." Chloe's voice came through the receiver. Obviously, Madison had the phone on speaker. "But right now I need you two BFFs to focus before Zac shows up here and our bodies are found floating facedown in the bay."

It was hard for Eden to keep the smile off her face. Not because she wanted Chloe and Madison to be found floating facedown in the bay, but because she suddenly realized that she had two BFFs. One that needed her help ASAP.

"You're right," she said as she got out of bed. "First things first, you two need to get out of that apartment. That's the first place Zac will come looking. Then we need to come up with a safe house—a place where Zac can't find you."

"Good luck with that," Chloe said. "Zac has spies at almost every hotel in San Francisco."

"Then we need to get you out of town," Eden said as she paced. "At least until the police have him in custody." About then the door opened, and her mother peeked her head in.

"I heard you talking. Is everything okay, Eden? Is that Nash?"

Eden stared at her mom for only a second before she smiled. "Mom, how would you like a houseguest? I have a friend who could really use her chakras cleansed."

CHAPTER TWENTY-EIGHT

*N*ash tried to pretend that Eden's retraction meant nothing. After his father and Blue left, he made himself an egg sandwich, then turned off all the lights and went to bed. But he had been in bed for no more than a few minutes when the questions started. Why had she done it? Why had she lied and said that the article was false? Especially if she wanted to be a reporter? The breaking story of a Beaumont brother being a pervert would've been more than enough to get her out of the tiny closet she used as an office. It made no sense at all.

He mulled the question over for hours. And by the time the sky brightened with dawn, Nash could come up with only one answer. Eden really did care for him. The thought should've brought some satisfaction, but instead it just made the hole in his heart bigger. It didn't matter if she cared for him. Or even loved him. He could never be with a woman he didn't trust.

With the realization, he finally fell into an exhausted

sleep. He slept for only a few hours before the heat of the sun woke him up. The hole was still in his chest, but for the first time in days, his head felt clear. Rolling out of bed, he packed and headed to the airport.

He wasn't able to get a seat until the last flight of the day so he arrived in San Francisco well past midnight. From the window of the plane, he looked down at the city lights that sparkled like jewels cast between the bays of black velvet. He had first come here in hopes of regaining control over his life. But in the last year, he'd learned that control was only an illusion. No one had control. Life took you where it would. You could only hope that it would take you to a place where you could find happiness.

When the plane touched down on the runway, Nash didn't feel happy. But he did feel a sense of coming home. This was where his family lived. Where he lived. And where he worked.

After thinking he would never work at French Kiss again, he now realized how much he had grown to love the company. He loved selling clothing that made women feel sexy and beautiful, and he loved working with his brothers. He just hoped that they hadn't kicked him to the curb for leaving them to clean up his mess.

But he would have to wait to find out. When he arrived home, Grayson's black Range Rover was gone from the garage. It was just as well. Nash was too tired to have his butt chewed out. Not that Grayson would yell at him. That was more Deacon's style.

He woke the next morning content to be back in his own bed and on his own routine. After hooking his cell phone up to the charger and getting on his running clothes, he headed to Grayson's room. But Gray wasn't in his room. Not that it was easy to tell. As always, his little brother's room was a mess of rumpled sheets, dirty clothes, easels, canvases, paints, and paintbrushes.

Closing the door, Nash climbed the stairs to the kitchen and living area, but Grayson wasn't there either. Nash could've called him, but decided it would be better to confront both his brothers' anger at French Kiss, where the chances of them thoroughly kicking his ass were slimmer.

Since he hadn't eaten much the day before, he made himself a power shake before his run. He had just poured it in a glass when Jonathan Livingston Seagull pecked at the balcony door for his breakfast. Once Nash opened the can of sardines, he took it and his shake out to the balcony. The audacious gull jumped up on the table and waited for Nash to set down the can of sardines.

"Hey, Johnny," Nash said. "Did you miss me?"

"I certainly did."

It wasn't the words as much as the voice that had Nash freezing. He slowly turned his head and found Eden standing on her grandparents' balcony holding a watering can. She had on running clothes that he hadn't seen before, although she didn't look like she was going running. Her hair wasn't in a ponytail but rather fell around her face in soft curls, and she wore makeup and pink lipstick that made her lips look shiny and tempting. While he tried to catch his breath, she smiled brightly as if it were any other day—as if she hadn't been the breaker of his heart.

"Good morning," she said. "How was Louisiana?"

"What are you doing?"

She held up the watering can. "I'm watering my grandmother's geraniums. Although since it rained yesterday, they don't really need it."

"I wasn't talking about the flowers."

"Oh!" She lowered the can. "You mean why am I at my grandparents' this early in the morning. Well...because I moved in with them." Her smile got even bigger. "So it looks like we're going to be neighbors."

Just the thought of having to see her every day made his stomach tighten. "You moved out of your apartment?"

She nodded. "I thought this would work out better because now you won't have to run all the way to my apartment every morning."

His hand tightened around his glass as he wondered what kind of game she was playing. "We're not running together anymore, Eden."

"Of course we are." She tried to keep smiling, even though it looked like it was a struggle, and her hands waggled as she continued. "How else are we going to be ready for the marathon? Not that you won't be ready. I'm the one who needs all the conditioning. Is that a protein shake? Maybe you should make one for me before we go. Mimi's steel oats were good, but if I want to get some extra miles out of these wimpy legs, I could probably use some protein—"

"Stop, Eden," he said. "We're not running in the marathon together. I don't know what game you're playing, but it's not going to work. Whatever we had is over. You made sure of that." Without another word, he walked back inside, sliding the door closed behind him. For extra measure, he locked it. Although the lock wasn't enough to keep his heart from pounding with fear.

He knew that he would eventually run into her, but not this soon. He hadn't been ready. Figuring that, if he ran now, he'd have a heart attack, he went downstairs and got ready for work. When he stepped out of the bathroom, his phone was pinging. He walked over to where it was charging and glanced at the screen. There had to be at least twenty texts...all from Eden.

Without reading a one, he erased them, then got dressed and headed to work, not once glancing up at the Huckabees' balcony as he backed out of the driveway. His phone pinged all the way to French Kiss until he finally had to shut it off. When he arrived, he walked straight to Deacon's office only to find Jason leaning over Kelly's desk giving her a kiss.

Nash cleared his throat, and they sprang apart.

Jason looked embarrassed as he tried to explain. "Umm...we were just—"

"Kissing," Kelly said with a big smile. "All the naughty stuff we save for after work."

"I'm glad to hear it," Nash said. "So how are the wedding plans going?"

"Expensive," Jason said at the same time that Kelly said, "Amazing." They exchanged looks and laughed.

"I guess they are expensively amazing," Kelly said as she got up from her chair. "Which is why you need to drink plenty of coffee, Nash. Your cups should go for a pretty penny on eBay after that sexy article." She came around her desk and spoke to Jason. "Did you know the reporter who wrote it is related to those two old hippies with the magic brownies? Which probably explains why she has such a vivid imagination. Growing up with mind-altering drugs will do that for you." She straightened Jason's tie before she headed down the hallway.

When she was gone, Jason looked at Nash. "The article wasn't just a fantasy, was it?"

Before Nash could answer, Deacon peeked his head out. "Well, it's about time you got back. Now get your butt in here and get to work."

Once inside the office, Nash expected a butt chewing. Instead, Deacon was calmly sitting behind his desk going over sales reports. "Look, Deke," he said as he took a chair, "I'm sorry. I shouldn't have run off and left you to deal with my mess. I wish I had a good excuse for what I did, but there's no excuse. Anyway, I'm back now. And whatever you want me to do to try and fix things, I'm willing to do."

Deacon glanced up, his eyes not angry as much as concerned. "The only thing I want you to fix is keeping secrets from me. You're my brother, Nash. Your problems are my problems."

"They shouldn't be. Especially when I keep screwing things up."

His brother shook his head. "I'm to blame as much as you are. I should've gotten you professional help after what happened with Melissa. You just seemed like you had things under control."

Nash ran a hand through his hair. "That's what I kept telling myself. But it turns out that I don't have control over anything."

"Who does, little brother?" Deacon asked as he tossed Nash the newspaper that sat on his desk. "I assume that since you raced off like a scalded cat, you read the first article. You might want to take a look at this one."

It didn't take long for Nash to find and read Eden's retraction. It was as ridiculous as he thought it would be. He crumpled the paper and tossed it at the trash. "Obviously, no one is going to believe that shit. So what do I need to do for damage control?"

Deacon studied him for a moment before he grinned. "Actually, it's fifty-fifty. Most men believe you hired an escort, and most women believe Eden's fantasy story. And since women are who buy our lingerie…" He slid a sales report across the desk.

Nash took one look, and his eyes widened. "You're kidding. Sales are up?"

"By fifteen percent. Even the new bra line." Deacon laughed. "It would seem that even when you land in shit, baby brother, you end up smelling like a rose. Of course, I think we have Miss Eden Huckabee to thank for her fantasy." He arched an eyebrow. "Or more like a flowery way of telling the truth."

Nash released his breath. "It was the truth. I hired her."

Deacon nodded. "And did you also make her fall in love with you?"

Just hearing the words caused Nash's heart to ache. "She doesn't love me."

"Hmm?" Deacon sat back in his chair. "Then I guess she's just a stalker. She calls here numerous times a day looking for you, and Olivia told me that she moved in with her grandparents."

"She's not a stalker." Nash didn't know why he defended her. Especially when she had become a bit of a stalker. "She's just stubborn." Not wanting to talk about Eden anymore, Nash changed the subject. "So where's Grayson?"

Deacon looked surprised by the question. "I thought he was with you. He called and said he was going out of town for a few days. It was after Dad called and said you were at the fishing cabin so I just assumed. You haven't talked to him?"

Now concerned, Nash pulled out his phone and checked his messages. There were ten from Eden, which he ignored, and one from Grayson, which he listened to.

"I have to get Chloe out of town. Same problem as before. I'll call you later."

"Did Grayson call?" Deacon asked.

Since Deacon still knew nothing about Madison and Chloe being escorts, Nash stretched the truth a little as he slipped his phone back in his pocket. "He's fine. He just took some model on a little trip. No doubt he's sketching her on the beach somewhere."

"Well, when you talk to him, tell him to get his ass back to work. I want that catalog out by the end of next month."

"Roger that." Nash got to his feet. Once out of Deacon's office, he tried calling Grayson. When he didn't answer, he turned to Kelly. "Do you have Madison's number?"

"I can look it up for you. But if you want to talk to her, she's doing fittings in the design studio."

Madison wasn't in the design studio, but Samuel and Deirdre were. And it appeared that all employees had decided to take the name of the lingerie company literally. Except Samuel was kissing Deirdre much more intensely than Jason had been kissing Kelly. And when Nash cleared his throat, they didn't spring apart. Samuel kept his hands on Deirdre's waist, and she kept her fingers entwined in his mussed hair. Which, for some reason, had Nash apologizing.

"I'm sorry. I was looking for Madison."

Since Deirdre looked a little dazed, Samuel was the one who spoke. "She just finished trying on the mock-ups for the new line of comfort bras and I sent her to lunch. So you might want to try the break room. Someone mentioned that there were chocolate-covered doughnuts, and we all know that chocolate is Madison's weakness."

Nash did find Madison in the break room, but she wasn't indulging in the doughnuts as much as watching one of the designers eat one.

"Describe it," she said in a hushed voice. "Is the chocolate rich with plenty of cocoa or light with just a touch?" She licked her lips as the designer took a big bite. "And the pastry? Is it yeasty and airy? Or more dense?"

"Madison," Nash said, "could I speak with you for a minute?"

It took a while for her to pull her gaze away from the doughnut. When she saw Nash, she looked relieved. "You're here!" She got up and hurried over to hug him. "I've been worried sick that you weren't going to come back. You guys have made up, right?"

He glanced at the designers who were listening intently to the exchange before he guided Madison out of the break room and into the deserted hallway. Rather than talk about Eden, he got straight to the point.

"Where's Grayson? And what happened to Chloe?"

Madison looked disappointed. "So you haven't talked with Eden."

"I talked with her, but she didn't mention Grayson. Now where is he?"

Madison looked around before speaking in a whisper.

"He's taking Chloe to Eden's parents' house. But you can't tell anyone because Zac thinks Chloe turned him in."

"She didn't turn him in. I did. The bastard needed to be behind bars."

"I agree, but now we have to hope that the cops find him before he finds Chloe. Although I doubt he'll tangle with Grayson." She smiled. "It's hard to believe that someone so quiet and creative as your brother can be such a badass. And such a sweetheart. When I called Grayson to say I would be late for the fitting today because I was taking Chloe to the bus station, he didn't hesitate to volunteer to take her to Eden's parents'. And since I was worried about Zac following us, I thought it was a better plan."

"But why didn't Eden go with them to her parents?"

"Because she wasn't here. She had moved back to Grover Beach. According to Chloe, she was devastated that we both thought the worst of her."

Nash snorted. "She didn't look devastated this morning." And maybe that was what had pissed Nash off the most. There had been no tears, and no begging for forgiveness. Eden had just acted like nothing had happened, while his heart had felt like it went eighteen rounds with a world champion.

Madison studied him before she shook her head. "You don't understand Eden at all, do you? She's not the type of person who is going to let anything keep her down for long. She's the type of person who, when she gets knocked on her butt, is going to get up and continue to fight for what she wants."

"And just who knocked her on her butt, Madison? If

anyone was throwing the punches, it was Eden when she wrote the article and published it."

Her eyes widened. "But she didn't want the article published, Nash. After she got to know you, she planned to leave the newspaper. It was some other writer at the paper who sent it to her editor."

It took a few moments for Nash to process the information. "So Eden didn't want the article published?"

"Of course not. Why would she want to humiliate the man she loves? Which is exactly why she wrote the retraction letter. And came back here. And moved in with her grandparents. Eden is willing to do whatever it takes to achieve her new goal."

"Her new goal? What's her new goal?"

"You. You're Eden's new goal."

CHAPTER TWENTY-NINE

After two weeks of making a complete fool of herself, Eden was starting to wonder if Nash was ever going to forgive her. He had ignored all her phone calls and texts, the "Please forgive me, sugar" sugar cookie bouquet and "I'm sorry, so sorry" singing telegram, and was doing a good job of avoiding her at home. She hadn't seen him coming or going once from his house. When she'd called Grayson and asked, all he'd said was that Nash was busy at work. Which was just a nice way of saying that Nash was hiding from her. And there was only so much pleading a girl could do before she started to look pathetic. Of course, according to Chloe, she had passed pathetic long ago.

"You do realize that you've become a stalker, right?" Chloe asked as she executed a perfect downward dog yoga move. One that she had no doubt learned from Eden's mother during her two-week stay.

Chloe had arrived back in town the day before, looking

happy and chakra-cleansed. The police had finally apprehended Zac, and after the scuffle that had injured two officers, a judge denied him bail. Although Eden figured that the denied bail had more to do with her mother's phone call than Zac fighting with the cops. Her mother had decided to take Chloe under her wing. Not only had she called the judge to fill him in on Zac's violent history, but she'd also helped Chloe get enrolled in classes to get her high school diploma. She was convinced that Chloe had great potential that she had yet to tap. What Chloe had tapped was a lot of anger at Eden for waking her up so early and forcing her to come to the marathon.

"And besides a stalker, you've become an even bigger pain in my ass. Who runs this early in the morning?"

"Runners." Eden stretched her hands over her head. "And I'm not a stalker. I had planned to run in the marathon long before Nash did."

Chloe straightened and rolled her eyes. "But if Nash showed up right now and said he was headed to the bakery across the street, you'd forgo the running for a cup of coffee, wouldn't you?"

"They have delicious hot chocolate too." Madison took a sip from the paper cup she held. The diet Eden had put her on was long forgotten when the French Kiss swimsuit catalog came out. Madison's voluptuous body was a hit with both women and men. Her new fame had landed her a big-bucks contract and close to a million likes on Facebook. Not to mention all the hits on her website, where she blogged about the joys of chocolate, modeling, shoes, and how to seduce a man. It seemed ironic that Madison would become a more popular writer than Eden.

Although Eden was hoping that would change. After returning to San Francisco, an editor from a big publishing house had contacted her. The editor had read the retraction letter and thought Eden had talent. Not nonfiction talent, but fiction talent. And if Eden ever wrote a romance novel based on the premise of a dark seducer, the editor wanted to be the first one to read it and make an offer. That was over a week ago, and as of now, Eden had sixty pages. Her goal was to have it finished in two months.

In the meantime, she had another goal to accomplish.

"I don't want coffee," Eden said. "I want to finish this race with my friends. I couldn't care less whether Nash is here or not."

Chloe shrugged and went back to stretching. "Then I guess I won't mention that he's standing right over there."

Eden whirled around so fast that she bumped into Madison and knocked her cup out of her hand. It hit the ground and splattered everywhere. But Eden didn't pay any attention. Her gaze was locked with a pair of violet-colored eyes. Eyes that gave her hope that all the weeks of e-mails, texts, and singing telegrams had paid off. That he'd finally forgiven her and they would cross the finish line of the half marathon together.

But then the air horn blasted, and without one word— not an *I forgive you*, an *I love you*, or even an *I strongly like you*—he took off running. Leaving Eden far behind.

As she watched his amazing butt disappear in the crowd of runners, the truth finally hit her like a wrecking ball right between the eyes. Nash wasn't going to forgive her. They weren't going to get married. Or even live together. She had failed. She had failed at the one goal she'd wanted to achieve more than anything else. And there was nothing left to do but accept defeat.

"I'm not sure," Madison said, "but I think that blaring noise means the race started. So shouldn't we be running? Or at least, lightly jogging."

Eden fought back the tears. "I'm not running."

"What's going on?" Chloe pushed closer as runners swarmed around. "If you want to catch Nash, Eden, then you better hurry. He looks like he's running to win."

"I don't want to catch him," she said. "You were right. I'm just a pathetic stalker. A pathetic stalker who needs to realize that it's over." Feeling like a snail surrounded by a swarm of ants that all had a purpose, Eden walked over to the curb and sat down.

Madison and Chloe followed, Madison sitting down next to her. "You're not a pathetic stalker. Tell her, Chloe. Tell her that she's not a stalker."

"I'm not going to tell her that. Especially when she has been acting like a stalker." Chloe reached down and grabbed Eden's hand before yanking her to her feet. "But that's what makes you Eden. You're one of those annoying people who flat out refuse to give up. No matter what the odds are or what anyone else thinks, you keep your chin up and keep on going. It was you who got Madison to believe she could do something besides being a hooker—"

"I was not a hooker," Madison cut in.

Chloe rolled her eyes. "Right. And I wasn't Zac's punching bag." She looked at Eden. "You made me realize that, Eden. And you also made me realize that whatever dream I can dream, I can achieve if I only work hard,

And now after I just started to believe it, you're going to tell me that you're quitting?" She threw up her hands. "Fine. Then I'm quitting my GED classes. They're too hard, and the one teacher makes me feel like a stupid idiot every time I ask a question."

"She's right." Madison got up. "And I'm just going back to being an escort. It's much easier than modeling. And keeping up with all the social networking is much more than I can take—"

"Absolutely not!" Eden yelled. "You can't quit modeling, Maddie. Not when you have become such an inspiration for full-figured women." She looked at Chloe and shook a finger. "And you, young lady, will not drop out of high school the second time."

Chloe sent her a sardonic look and crossed her arms. "Then you can't give up either. You need to go catch the man you love."

Madison nodded. "Nash knew you would be here. If he didn't want to make up, he wouldn't have come."

Hope bloomed. "You really think so?" Eden asked.

"It makes sense," Chloe said before she slapped Eden on the butt none too gently. "Now run, Eden, run!"

That was all the urging Eden needed. Without another word to Chloe and Madison, she joined the other runners. It was hard at first. Her pace was off, and her breathing erratic. At the one-mile mark, she felt like her lungs were going to burst from her chest. At the two-mile, she wanted to throw up. She had no illusions that she would catch Nash. Being a much better runner, he was no doubt far ahead of her. But she didn't run for Nash. She ran for herself. And for Madison. And Chloe. And for every woman who had ever dreamed big but thought that they couldn't achieve those dreams.

The thought empowered her, and somewhere around the four-mile marker, she hit The Zone that she'd read about on the Internet. Her muscles stopped hurting and begging for mercy, and every breath didn't feel like it would be her last. In fact, she felt better than she had felt since Mike had published her story. She might not ever get Nash back. She might not find her ideal career. She might not be able to live in San Francisco. But she was going to finish the marathon.

Or her name wasn't Eden Huckabee.

Funny thing about a runner's high. It didn't last forever. Her mind might be convinced that she would finish the race, but around the tenth mile, her body started having second thoughts. With every step, her feet hurt and her legs cramped and her knees felt more and more like rubber. Like a donkey in a horserace, she fell back in the pack, her run becoming more of a sluggish jog. Sweat trickled into places she didn't even want to talk about, and the paper cups of water the volunteers handed out seemed to seep from her pores as quickly as she downed them.

Eden was just about to call it quits when she looked up and saw Nash.

He wasn't running. He stood on the sidelines searching the runners. When he saw her, he jogged out to join her, his strides matching her much slower ones. Eden wanted to say something, but it was hard to talk when you were a ball of sweating, aching muscles. Besides, after all the e-mails and texts she'd sent him, she figured that she had said everything she could possibly say. So they just kept running—or slowly jogging. A good mile later, Nash finally spoke.

"So what took you so long?"

She glanced over. He wasn't smiling, but there was definitely humor sparkling in his eyes. Which made her more than a little snappy. "I could ask you the same question," she panted.

A dozen or more steps and he replied. "Beaumonts have been known to be a little stubborn. Lucky for me, my girlfriend is just as stubborn." Eden stumbled. But rather than reach out and steady her, Nash only slowed until she'd regained her balance. Once they were running again, he continued. "The cookies were delicious, by the way. And the singing telegram gal was so good that my brother's assistant hired her for her wedding—which happens to be next weekend. So you might want to mark your calendar."

Tears welled up in her eyes and joined the sweat on her cheeks. But Nash didn't notice until she released a tiny little squeak of a sob. She expected some kind of sympathy. Instead, he gave her the exact opposite.

"Damn it, Eden," he said, "don't you dare start crying now."

Her temper flared. "I'll cry if I want to! Especially after the hell you've put me through the last few weeks."

"And you don't think that you've put me through hell, woman? Why didn't you tell me that you weren't the one who published your story?"

"I tried, but a certain pigheaded Beaumont didn't give me a chance. You just completely ignored me and made me feel like a pathetic stalker." She patted her chest.

"Well, I'm not pathetic. I'm just a stupid woman in love with a jerk of a guy!"

Nash looked over at her and smiled, but didn't stop running. In fact, he picked up the pace. Suddenly, her aching muscles were energized with anger, and she quickly caught up with him.

"That's it? You're not going to say a word after I told you that I love you?"

His smile got even bigger, but still he didn't say anything. He just ran faster.

"Oh no, you don't." She ran after him. "If you think you're going to get away from me, you've got another think coming." People cheered and cameras flashed, but she ignored them as she continued. "Because I'm not letting you get away, Nash Lothario Beaumont. Not now and not ever."

Nash reached out and took her hand, slowing them to a walk. He walked until she stopped panting like an overheated dog, then he stopped, pulled her into his arms, and kissed her—completely unconcerned by her sweaty condition. After a few minutes of hot kisses, Eden wasn't that concerned either.

When they finally parted, his eyes were filled with something more than just heat. "That's good. Because I'm never letting you go either, Eden Tulip Huckabee. You and I are going to get married and finish life just like you finished this race—with a whole lot of guts and plenty of determination."

Joy like Eden had never known welled inside her, and she flung her arms around his neck and kissed him again until his words finally registered. She stopped kissing him and blinked. "I finished?" She glanced over her shoulder at the red-and-white banner draped over the street that marked the finish line of the half marathon, before she released a squeal. "I ran a half marathon, Nash! I ran a half marathon!"

He picked her up off her feet and hugged her close. "I know, baby. But there was a moment when I thought it wasn't going to happen. Your tears almost did me in."

She drew back. "So that's why you yelled at me? You wanted me to finish?"

He nodded. "If you had stopped, your muscles would've tightened up. And I wasn't about to keep you from achieving your dream."

"My dream?" Eden shook her head. "Finishing the marathon was a goal, not a dream."

"So what's your dream, Eden?"

She stared into his pretty violet eyes and smiled. "To marry a panty billionaire. What else?"

The most mysterious of the billionaire brothers, Grayson Beaumont is an artist in search of a muse. When beautiful Chloe McAlister agrees to pose for him, she inspires his art— and so much more...

Please see the next page for a preview of

Waking Up With a Billionaire.

$\mathcal{G}$rayson Beaumont had lost it. He knew this and had known it for the past six months. But he just didn't know how much he had lost it until Chloe McAlister had walked into his studio wanting to pose for him. Until that moment, he'd thought there was a chance that he could pull himself back from the deep dark abyss that threatened to consume him. After all, he was the level-headed Beaumont, the one who could stay calm in any given situation. But he didn't feel calm now. He felt as if he'd toppled right over the edge of insanity and was flailing around trying to grab on to anything that would save him from hitting rock bottom.

Needing to get out of the building as quickly as possible, he headed for the elevators. He had just bought a brand-new Bugatti sports car, and he planned to drive until the desperate panic that clawed at his guts subsided. But on the way down to the parking garage, the elevator stopped at the lobby. And when one of French Kiss's top models stepped in, he changed his plans.

"Gar-a-a-son?" Natalia said in her thick Russian accent. "Is that you? I had heard that Paris made you a little more...how do you say in English...hungry? Just look at you. You look like my Uncle Bo-o-oris." She stroked a hand over the stubble on his jaw. "But much younger and much sexier, of course."

Grayson ignored the elevator doors opening at the parking garage and pulled her into his arms and kissed her. She didn't protest. The times he had painted her, she made it perfectly clear that any advance would be more than welcome.

"Oooh, you are hungry," she whispered against his lips as she curled her arms around his neck and her leg around his waist. Grayson guided her back against the wall of the elevator.

He wanted to feel desire, or passion, anything that would stop the panic. But all he felt was disappointment. Not in Natalia. She was a beautiful woman and kissed like she modeled, with enthusiasm and heat. No, his disappointment was in himself for using her. He didn't use women. At least, he didn't used to.

He started to pull away and apologize when the elevator doors opened, and he found himself looking into the big brown eyes that had started his downward spiral. Eyes that rolled up in disgust. At one time, he had found the habit endearing. Not anymore. A road trip had cured him from any endearing thoughts toward the woman. Paint her naked? Not in this lifetime. He'd rather be locked in a closet with a rabid wolverine than spend hours in a studio with Chloe.

With his eyes still locked on hers, he deepened the

kiss, causing Natalia to moan and Chloe to release an exasperated grunt as she stepped into the elevator with a disgusted look.

Natalia finally noticed that they were no longer alone and stepped away. "Gar-a-a-son"—she swatted his chest— "you make me forget myself." She turned her full model-smile on Chloe. "What is it with American men and elevators?"

Chloe sent him a smug look. "I think it has to do with having a woman cornered with no means of escape."

Natalia laughed as she pressed the button for the tenth floor. "Perhaps you are right." She glanced at Grayson. "Although I have no desire to escape." Only seconds later, the elevator stopped, and she gave him a quick kiss on both cheeks before she got out. "I have to meet with Samuel in the design studio, but I should be done by five. Call me."

Grayson should've gotten out with Natalia—not just to explain that he wouldn't be calling her later but also to get away from Chloe. Instead, he watched the doors close and realized that now he had no means of escape.

"New pretty girlfriend?"

He turned to find Chloe studying him. She had cut her hair, something he had noticed during their road trip. The deep brown mop was short and choppy, with uneven bangs...and still she was the most breathtakingly beautiful woman he'd ever seen. The unwanted thought had him snapping a reply. "New bad haircut?"

She fidgeted with her bangs. "I know. I really butchered it. Maybe it's a good thing that I can't afford beauty school tuition. I probably would've flunked out on the first day."

Was that why she wanted to pose for him? She needed money for beauty school? It seemed unlikely. Not only because he couldn't picture her as a hair stylist but because all she had to do was ask Eden or Madison if she needed money. They would be happy to help their friend out. Of course, Chloe had never been the type to take handouts. Something she had proven time and time again.

"So what happened in Paris to screw up your painting mojo?" she asked.

It was his worst fear put into words, and he felt like she had kicked him with her pointy-toed boots right in the balls. "You think I can't paint?" He poked himself in the chest. "Well, I can paint anything I want to paint." He hated the way he sounded like a spoiled five-year-old.

Chloe's eyebrows lifted beneath the fringe of uneven bangs. "Like an apple?"

"You looked at my painting?"

She shrugged. "I was curious."

While he struggled to get his anger under control, the elevator arrived at the lobby. Chloe lifted a hand as she stepped off. "I guess this is goodbye." But Grayson couldn't let her go. Not now. Not when his pride was on the line. He got out with the intentions of telling her that a lot of talented artists painted fruit when the security guard took her arm.

"Ma'am, what did you do with the ducky floral arrangement?"

Hearing the guard, some muscled guy in a white polo with a flower on the breast pocket came hurrying over. "Is she the one who took my ducky?" He pointed a finger at her. "Give me back my ducky!"

Grayson wasn't sure why he did it—maybe because he had never liked bullies—but he stepped in front of Chloe. "What's going on?"

The flower guy gave him the once-over. "I don't need some street bum butting into my business."

The security guard spoke up. "That's not a street bum. That's Mr. Beaumont." He turned to Grayson. "I'm sorry for the disruption, Mr. Beaumont, but this man says he had his flower bouquet stolen." He looked at Chloe. "And I did see this young woman with a big ducky of daisies."

"But I didn't steal it," Chloe looked at Grayson. "Tell them."

For the first time since she had strolled into his studio, Grayson felt in control, and he wasn't about to give up that feeling. He squinted his eyes. "I'm sorry, Miss, but do I know you?"

She rolled her eyes. "Very funny. Now tell them that I brought the floral arrangement for the birth of Deacon's son to your office."

Thoroughly enjoying himself, he smiled. "What exactly would I do with a ducky filled with daisies?"

Just that quickly, the belligerent young woman Grayson remembered so well made an appearance. And for some strange reason, he was happy to see her. "How about you shove it up your ass?" Chloe snapped.

"Don't you dare talk to Mr. Beaumont like that." A blonde hurried up. Grayson didn't recognize her face, but he did recognize the standard purple dress and heels that all the receptionists wore. The woman pointed an orange nail that clashed with her dress at Chloe. "This is the same woman that was trying to sneak into French Kiss earlier. She thought she could see a Beaumont without an appointment." The woman looked at him and batted her eyelashes. "As if you would want to talk to someone with a bad haircut and faux leather boots. Which is exactly why I told her to take a hike and come back when she had a clue."

As much as he was enjoying toying with Chloe, this woman's arrogance didn't sit well. Especially when he had grown up poor and knew what it was like to have bad haircuts and cheap clothing pointed out by the wealthier kids. He was about to put her in her place when the door opened and two police officers walked in. Upon seeing them, Chloe raced toward the opposite doors.

The policemen gave chase, and Grayson figured that his fun was over. It was one thing to let Chloe get hassled by a security guard and another to let her get arrested and thrown in jail. Unfortunately, by the time Grayson got out to the street, the police officers had Chloe on the ground, handcuffing her. Or trying to handcuff her. As expected, she was putting up one hell of a fight.

"Get your hands off me! I did nothing wrong."

"If you did nothing wrong, ma'am, then why did you run away from us?" The officer who had her on the ground finally got ahold of her wrist and pulled it behind her back.

"Let her go," Grayson ordered as he walked up.

The other police officer stepped in front of him. "Back off. This is none of your business."

"It's exactly my business. I'm Grayson Beaumont, and I own French Kiss."

The officer looked him over and then laughed. "Sure you

are. And I'm Donald Trump. Now go about your business before I haul you in for interfering with an arrest…or for loitering."

Grayson glanced down at his tattered, paint-splattered jeans and couldn't blame the officer. He did look like a vagrant. "Look, I can prove it." He went to pull out his wallet, but then remembered that he'd left it in his studio. Unfortunately, the officer didn't take kindly to Grayson reaching for something behind his back and grabbed Grayson and shoved him against a parked car. The arm Grayson brought up was more reflex than anything. When you grew up with two older brothers who loved to box, you had to have good reflexes. He didn't intend for his elbow to clip the officer's jaw and send him stumbling back.

Before Grayson could ask if the guy was all right, the other officer joined the fray and Grayson found himself lying facedown on the sidewalk next to Chloe.

Grayson grunted as the cop's knee dug into his back and cuffs were slapped on his wrists. "You want to tell them who I am?"

Chloe squinted. "Do I know you?"

Grayson didn't know why he laughed. He should've been pissed that she had turned the tables on him. And he was pissed, but he could also see the humor in the situation. He continued to laugh as the police officer got him to his feet and escorted him to the cruiser.

"Wait!" Chloe yelled. "He is Grayson Beaumont, and if you just go inside and get the receptionist, she'll identify him and this entire misunderstanding will be cleared up."

The officer that Grayson had elbowed in the chin

pushed him in the backseat of the cruiser. "I don't care who he is. He hit an officer. He's going to jail. And since you resisted arrest, you're going with him."

As soon as Chloe joined him in the backseat, she glared at him with murder in her eyes. "This is all your fault."

He tried to adjust his handcuffed arms so he could sit back. "How do you figure? I wasn't the one who stole the ducky."

"No, you were just the one who wanted to be an ass and not tell the security guard that you knew me. What happened to you? I thought you were the nice Beaumont brother—the one who always does the right thing."

He had always done the right thing. Whether it was getting good grades in math or eating all his peas, he did what was expected of him and never complained. With two headstrong older brothers, compliance had been the easiest route. So he had kept his mouth shut and gone along. If something had bothered him and he needed an outlet, he would go to his room and sketch or paint. Through his art, he learned to express all the emotions that he couldn't express with his brothers...not without getting called a wimp or his lights punched out. His paintings were his release. Or at least they had been. Now he couldn't even paint an apple. Chloe was right. He had lost his painting mojo.

"Maybe I got tired of being the perfect Beaumont," he said.

"I didn't say you were perfect. I said you were nice. Now you're just as grumpy and mean as I am. And let me tell you, it's not very becoming."

They rode in silence the rest of the way to the police station. When they arrived, Chloe finally spoke. "Do you think they'll fingerprint us?"

He glanced over. She didn't look as cocky anymore. In fact, if he didn't know better he would think she was scared.

"Probably," he said, "but it's not a big deal."

"How do you know?"

"I watched a lot of *Law and Order* when I was a kid."

She didn't get the humor. In fact, her face lost all color. "I don't want to be fingerprinted."

Grayson knew she'd had a hard life, and he couldn't help wondering if she'd been in jail before and had a record. "Look, it's going to be okay. I'll call my lawyer, and he'll have us out within the hour." Fortunately, he didn't need to call Jason, French Kiss's lawyer. While he was getting fingerprinted, a female sergeant recognized him.

"You're one of the panty billionaires, aren't you?"

"What?" The female officer who was fingerprinting him stopped and stared. "Holy crap!" She released his hand and scrambled to pull her cell phone out of her pants pocket, leaving ink prints all over the case as she took a picture.

Grayson cringed. He had little doubt that it would be all over the Internet within hours. Deacon would not be happy with the bad press. It was one thing to get thrown in jail and another to have the information released to the general public. And once the female officer took a picture, everyone seemed to have a cell phone in hand, snapping pictures.

The officer who had arrested him looked appalled. "He

is Grayson Beaumont? You've got to be kidding? Why would women want to wear panties made by this guy?"

The sergeant sent him an annoyed look. "I'm going to assume that you have a good reason for arresting Mr. Beaumont, Officer Spencer?"

It took only a few minutes to get the facts straight. Grayson apologized for the large bump on Officer Spencer's chin, and Officer Spencer apologized for jumping to conclusions. Once they were released, Grayson posed with every policewoman and female office worker at the precinct before he asked about Chloe. She had been taken to another area to be processed, and by the time he explained what happened and got her released, she didn't look happy. Not happy at all.

"You're just as big of a jerk as every other guy," she said before she walked out the door. He had to squelch the desire to go after her. He was still staring at the door when the sergeant walked up.

"She's sure a pretty little thing. She reminds me of that actress in *My Fair Lady*. What was her name?"

"I don't know. I've never seen the movie."

"Well, it's a good one. I loved the scene where the drunk dad is getting married." She used a thick English accent as she sang in an off-key voice about getting married in the morning. When Grayson glanced at her, she cleared her throat. "Anyway, it was a good movie, and your friend sure looks like her. Which I guess is why you hired her to model for you."

"She's not modeling for me." Grayson didn't know if he was reminding himself or the sergeant. "And we're not friends."

The sergeant looked confused. "But she told me she'd changed her name. That was why a different one popped up when we scanned her prints."

Grayson turned to her. "Chloe changed her name? From what?"

The sergeant shook her head. "I can't release that information, but I can tell you that she hasn't always been Chloe McAlister."

Fall in Love with Forever Romance

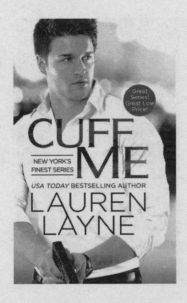

CUFF ME
by Lauren Layne

USA Today bestselling author Lauren Layne brings us NYPD's Finest—where three Moretti brothers fulfill their family's cop legacy. Seeing his longtime partner Jill with someone else triggers feelings in Vincent he never knew he had. Now he'll have to stop playing good cop/bad cop, and find a way to convince her to be his partner for life...

Fall in Love with Forever Romance

A BILLIONAIRE AFTER DARK
by Katie Lane

Nash Beaumont is the hottest of the billionaire Beaumont brothers. But beneath his raw charisma is a dark side that he struggles to control, until he falls in love with Eden—the reporter determined to expose his secret. Fans of Jessica Clare will love the newest novel from *USA Today* bestselling author Katie Lane.

Fall in Love with Forever Romance

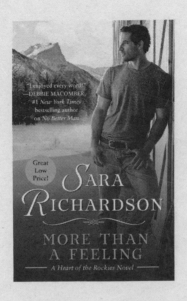

MORE THAN A FEELING
by Sara Richardson

"Charming, witty, and fun. There's no better read. I enjoyed every word!"

—DEBBIE MACOMBER, #1 *New York Times*
bestselling author on *No Better Man*

Fall in Love with Forever Romance

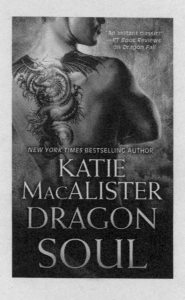

DRAGON SOUL
by Katie MacAlister

In *New York Times* bestselling author Katie MacAlister's DRAGON SOUL, Rowan Dakar can't afford to be distracted by the funniest, most desirable woman he's ever set eyes on. But no prophecy in the world can ever stop true love...